Twice stolen

Susanne Timpani

Published by Armour Books
PO Box 492
Corinda QLD 4075

Cover photography by Konradbak.
Design and layout by Book Whispers.
Border Art by Lyn Lovegrove Niemz, Ngarrindjeri Nation, SA (Coorong River People) Mi-mini

ISBN: 978-1925380033

National Library of Australia Cataloguing-in-Publication entry :
Creator: Timpani, Susanne, author.
Title: Twice stolen / Susanne Timpani.
ISBN: 9781925380033 (paperback)
Subjects: Love stories.
                  Medical fiction.

Dewey Number: A823.4

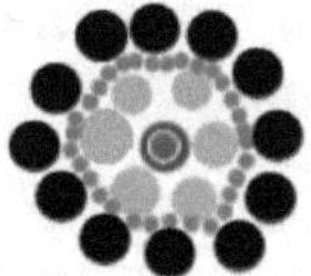

Author's note:

I am not an indigenous Australian, and I have created this story from that perspective. In my work as a community nurse with Aboriginal families and colleagues, I have become aware of my lack of knowledge and understanding of the history and cultural impact of the Stolen Generations upon their community. As the characters in my book read and listen to stories, their journey of growth reflects my own. All characters, cultural communities and places are fictional.

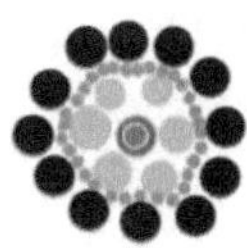

Introduction: Dimitri

Dimitri clicked on the map of Australia in Google Earth and stared at the vast expanse of desert. *My parents are out there; buried somewhere beneath that red ochre.*

The printer churned out the final page of his application. He retrieved it and laid it on top of the pile. *If only I can land this position, I could kickstart my search for Dad and Mum.*

The door between the family restaurant and the living space burst open. Greek music floated up to his attic. He groaned. *Not Zorba again.* The worst mistake he'd ever made was showing his uncle the repeat function on the CD player.

'Dimitri!' Aunt Elpida called out. 'Come down. No good you stay up there on your own.'

'I'll be down in a minute.'

His aunt muttered something in Greek and closed the door.

On the lower toolbar of the computer another minute flipped over. *Three hours before submissions close.*

He rested his hand on top of the printout. The words peeked between his fingers. *'Outback Photography Inc. Traineeship Application.'*

Dimitri leaned back in his chair. He had plenty of time to scan and email it. But he didn't have the signature of a parent or legal guardian. The blessing of his family. And family was everything.

He inhaled and blew air from his cheeks, releasing his frustration. He would be eighteen next birthday. If he was old enough to commence a traineeship, surely he was old enough to go it alone?

Dimitri had always known his yaya wouldn't be happy with his plan and he'd been right. He shook his head, remembering her explosive response.

'What you wanna do that for?' she had screamed. 'You just like your dad. Look what happened to him, eh? He go and work someplace out there.'

'It's not like …' Dimitri had been surprised by the attack. He'd had to duck to avoid her flapping hands and poking fingers.

'An' he get himself killed. I not losing my grandson too.' Sitting down with a wail, she had wiped her face with her apron. 'He belonged here with us, not …'

He stretched his fingers across the page. Yaya had never finished that sentence. He knew she really wanted to add: '… out there with your mother.'

She had sealed the conversation with 'the look.' The one designed to make him feel guilty. And it had worked. He'd wound up making a promise to stay and help in the restaurant until he was twenty-one.

But that doesn't mean that I can't have hobbies, does it? Or holidays?

Though he wondered how he'd manage those with pocket money but no pay.

He clenched his hand and looked down at the form again. How amazing was it that the studio had liked his photographic portfolio? He'd never expected it, even with his teacher's praise. Especially since he'd just been using Papou's old camera.

Despite the odds, he'd been shortlisted. Now he had to win the studio over with his answers. That was the easy part.

'Why is this Traineeship important to you?'

The monitor had darkened and he tapped on the keyboard.

The map of Australia filled the screen again. He had very few clues where his parents had lived. The Traineeship would give him an opportunity to begin his search.

The door down below opened again. This time the smell of roasted coffee wafted up in a cascade of music.

'Dimitri!'

'Coming, Aunt Elpida.'

She left the door ajar as she retreated.

Dimitri glanced down at the time.

Two hours and fifty-five minutes.

He pushed back his chair and stood up.

May as well face it: it's just a dream. His yaya had refused to agree. It didn't matter how many arguments he marshalled to try to get her blessing. He'd turned his charm up to full strength, tried explaining how momentous the opportunity was. He'd enthused about Papou's camera being part of it.

Even pulling the Papou card, he hadn't been able to get her consent.

'We have agreement. You say twenty-one. Your word no mean anything? What kind grandson go back on his word?'

'It's a six-week Traineeship,' he'd explained. But nothing had budged her.

He could hear his aunt and uncle pushing tables and chairs around as they cleaned up. He knew he needed to get down there to help.

Two hours and fifty minutes.

He made his way to the restaurant. Unlike this afternoon, it stood empty.

Dimitri couldn't remember the last time he had seen it so packed with relatives. Possibly for Papou's funeral, but that was so long ago.

He swallowed back the lump in his throat. Today had been Yaya's turn.

She was barely dead—and he was already wanting to go against her will. Was she right? A dishonourable grandson?

'Ah, Dimitri! You been up there too long! No good you cry too much for your Yaya. She was ninety-two and she's gone home now.'

Dimitri turned away before Aunty caught his guilty look. He mourned the loss of his grandmother, no question. But he hadn't been upstairs crying for her.

Today had been more of a celebration than a wake. His extended family ate and drank and cried and caught up on family gossip. He reached across the counter and switched the CD player off.

Silence! Sweet!

'How ya doin', son?' Uncle Spiros threw a tea towel over his shoulder and lowered his hefty bulk onto a chair. 'Coffee, Elpida.'

Dimitri joined his uncle at the table for two.

'Ah! Yaya. We gonna miss her, no?' His uncle took out a handkerchief from his back pocket and wiped his eyes.

'Yes, we all loved our Yaya.' *Even if she did run our lives.* His friends at school were always on about how strict their parents were, but they knew nothing about living under the rule of an iron queen. Yet he'd never felt any real resentment. Yaya had been a good and generous woman who loved him; even if it had been to the point of suffocation.

Aware of a tightening knot in his throat, he wondered if he was being totally honest with himself. He brushed the thought aside.

Aunt Elpida brought over two cups of thick black coffee in china cups. 'I'm off to sleep. Don't stay up much longer.'

It was a bit late to be drinking coffee, especially this kind. He glanced up at the clock behind the counter.

Two hours and forty-one minutes.

If he could stall going to bed, maybe—just maybe—he had a chance with Uncle. He shoved another pang of guilt aside. Buried only a few hours and here he was, plotting to go against Yaya's wishes. His uncle and aunt knew full well what they were. And they had never gone against them. Not once.

'Whatcha think?'

'Sorry, Uncle Spiros, what was that?'

'All that incense and chants. Do you think she was happy?'

'You know she loved going to that church. It's what she wanted.' He wondered why Uncle needed reassurance. 'And we always give her what she wanted.' *Two hours and thirty-eight minutes.*

Uncle sipped his coffee. Dimitri knew he had to launch in before the reminiscing continued. 'Uncle Spiros, you know that Traineeship I'm applying for?'

Uncle frowned and Dimitri doubted if Uncle remembered anything at all. If it were Aunty, now—that would be a different story. Dimitri raced on. 'It's to be a professional photographer.'

Uncle put down his cup and stared.

Not good. He remembers the screaming match. 'Well, it's due in at

The most beautiful of songs — SS ¹³

midnight and …' Dimitri's heart thumped against his chest. '… I didn't want to submit it, going behind your back.'

'Is that the one that upset your Yaya?'

'Yaya was scared to let me go into the Outback.' Dimitri knew he had to choose his words with care. 'Uncle, I know my parents were killed in a plane crash out there. But it doesn't mean it's going to happen to me.'

Uncle shook his head. 'Your Yaya, she never got over that. It's no use, son; she would never have wanted it.'

Dimitri clamped his jaw, trapping the words that raced to his mouth. *Yaya is gone now. Why does she still have to rule everything?* He looked down, allowing his frustration to ebb away.

Closing his eyes, an image of his father slumped over the pilot's dashboard leapt into his mind's eye. He straightened with a jerk, and when he turned back to his uncle, his heart felt like it wanted to break. 'But would my dad have wanted it for me?'

He hadn't meant to say the words aloud.

Uncle sat back and stared. Dimitri could see shock and confusion radiate across his face. No one ever spoke about the accident.

The clock echoed in the empty room. His heart thumped hard against his chest. He had just broken the rule of absolute silence.

He expected an angry slapdown but Uncle's voice was a hoarse whisper. 'Whatcha talkin' about? None of us could know what they wanted. They're gone.' He slammed his cup on the table. 'Your Yaya would have preferred it to be me, you know.' He clapped his hand across his mouth in obvious horror. 'I have spoken ill of the dead. You forget what I said, son?'

Dimitri stared. *How come I never realised that? That Yaya was spreading her pain across the whole family, not just me.*

Was this the chance to speak about what he carried in his heart every day? He'd been three years old, and no one thought he remembered anything. He did. Whether they were memories or just dreams didn't matter. Those last few moments were crystal clear.

He saw his mother kicking the door open from inside the plane. He smelt the smoke as it robbed his father of his breath. He saw the flames race along the seats. His tiny arms felt pathetic as he failed to free her legs from crushed metal. He felt her pushing him in the back and heard her screaming for him to run. He thought about the scars on his feet.

Another silent subject.

He heard his screams as he landed on the burning grass. Most importantly of all he remembered his mother's words as he turned around for his one last look.

'Run Mitri, don't forget …' He had to concentrate hard on her last words. Sometimes the words were broken up, sometimes he heard a phrase. Either way he had no idea what they meant. '… don't forget the wombat.'

Dimitri's fist clenched. No one wanted to hear about his nightmares. 'It's just a dream,' Yaya had told him. 'Don't you go thinking about it all the time.'

With that, the subject was closed.

His uncle rested his hand over Dimitri's.

'I don't know what my brother would have wanted, son. But everyone has a right to be with family.' He blew his nose with his handkerchief. 'Go on, submit your application. I'll sign whatever you need.'

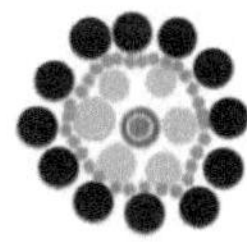

Introduction: Leah

'You'll be the best nurse.' The words came out in a rasp as Leah's mother struggled to speak.

Oh Mum, how many times do I have to explain? I'm a student midwife, not a nurse. Leah squeezed her mum's emaciated hand and said nothing. Her throat was swollen with the pain of holding back her tears.

It was all wrong. A mother should comfort her child, not the other way around. That had been her mum's refrain all this year.

Leah had to hold herself together. *There'll be time for me later … after …*

She looked over again at the open wardrobe. Her father's side was empty. *He could have waited.*

'Call Jenny, darling.'

I don't need to call anyone. 'You don't need to be worrying about me, Mum.' They had done without her dad, since …

Leah couldn't think of a time when her father had been there for them. He would binge drink and disappear for weeks. Mum would put up with him, even knowing there were other women.

Leah tensed her jaw as she remembered the vicious comment Abbey had posted on her page last night. 'If Leah's mum wasn't so ugly that creep wouldn't have to hang around here with mine all the time.'

Her eyes ached with the pain of holding in her tears. It shouldn't matter. They weren't in high school anymore. Her real friends would ignore it. She looked at her mother's shrunken body. Brave threads of grey barely covered

By King Solomon. — SS 1:1

her scalp. Without the colourful crown of her bandana, her mother's head appeared cold and sallow.

Her mum wasn't ugly. She was dying.

'Call Jenny.'

'Okay, Mum.' She traced her fingers over her mum's paper-thin skin but didn't move.

Jenny couldn't help—not this time.

She liked Jenny. At first she didn't trust her. Jenny was a church volunteer whereas her family rarely went there. The usual; Christmas and Easter occasionally, weddings, funerals …

Apparently the church never saw it like that. When word got around about their situation, Jenny went right to work. She never preached. She brought over meals just at the right time. She even took her mum's bedding home to wash. Leah didn't know how she would have managed on her own.

She had to get her father back.

Leah stood up and grabbed her mum's empty water bottle. An old bible lay next to it. Her mum had made her climb a step ladder and retrieve it from the top of the wardrobe. She would read poetry from there to her mum. Beautiful, but sometimes heartbreaking, poems. She loved poetry and the bible was the last place she had expected to find them.

She swallowed hard and her words came out in a mumble. 'I'll get you some fresh water.'

Leah headed downstairs to the kitchen. She placed the bottle under the tap.

Water splashed over the sink as she lost concentration. She shut off the tap and tipped out the water. She shook the bottle again and again, emptying it of every drop. Even when there was no water left, she kept shaking. Her tears welled up and she kept shaking and shaking.

She was terrified of death. It would steal her mother away. Sitting down at the kitchen table, she buried her head in her arms and, in the darkness of her little cocoon, tried to slow her thoughts down. The fridge hummed. This was the kitchen where she had grown up. It no longer smelt of the pot roasts and sweet curries her mother had cooked. There was no

By King Solomon. — SS [1:1]

smell at all. Her mother had lived on Jenny's soups for the past few weeks while Leah subsisted on packet food.

Outside in the back garden a flock of parrots screeched as they fought over the apples on the tree. *They can have them all.* Mum used to tell her to hang old CDs from the branches to scare them away. But there was no point.

Leah slowed her breathing. It was no good getting upset. When her mum passed away, Dad would probably want the house back. She would move far away. She'd leave all the bad memories behind.

Eve Barrett, her midwifery tutor, had promised to help her. When Leah had asked for an extension on her Aboriginal Health assignment, Eve had learnt the truth. After that, she had gone out of her way to advocate for Leah in all her subjects. She would ask for updates about her mum and interpret medical jargon. The worst day was when the doctor told her that the breast cancer had not responded to treatment.

'They must be able to do something,' Leah had pleaded with her tutor. 'Can't you get them to try something else?'

But she knew the answer in her heart before Eve had spoken. Eve promised to be available anytime she needed to be. She also said she would organise on campus accommodation…*for after…*

Leah grabbed a tissue and wiped away her sudden tears. Eve had done so much—even offering her a final year placement with her cousin in a rural Aboriginal community. This was all she had to look forward to. She pushed back the kitchen chair and picked up her phone. For now she had to call Jenny.

By King Solomon. — SS 1:1

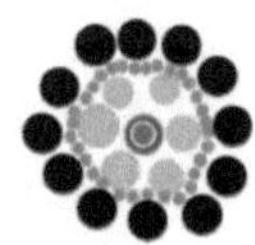

1: Dimitri

Dimitri woke up, drenched in sweat and fighting his way out of a tangle of sheets. The dream had been more vivid than ever. It had faded over the last six months as he'd plunged into a round of interviews, each more gruelling than the last. Just when he was sure Rick had finally chosen the private school kid with the stunning photography blog as his apprentice, he'd emerged triumphant instead.

He could hardly believe his dream had come true. But the last two nights the nightmare had returned. *With a vengeance.* It was almost as if, having arrived in the Outback, a deeper, more intense memory had been triggered. He'd spent all his dreamtime running. Just running. Away from something. *Or was it towards something?*

When he was inside the nightmare, it was all clear but, as soon as he woke, he could never capture the sense again. He only knew his mother was crying out to him. 'Run, Mitri! Don't forget the wombat. Don't stop.'

His promise was always the same. *I am running, Mum. Can't you see me? All these years and I promise you I haven't stopped. But I don't know where to find the wombat.*

Dimitri shook his head. He'd never been able to look properly at a wombat, even in a textbook. Every time someone mentioned one, a fragment of the dream would rush into his mind: he would see his mother's hand gripping his dad's.

Her knuckles were white.

His were bleeding.

The two of them were in the biplane. It exploded in front of him.

He wrenched the sheets aside and picked up his water bottle. The moisture cleared away the dryness in his mouth and brought refreshment to the back of his throat.

Strips of daylight peeked between the wooden louvres of the hotel window as he got up. The Bilyja region was a photographer's dream. Rick would give him a lecture on having already wasted the best part of the morning. He smiled to himself. He wasn't quite a photographer yet.

But he was determined to make this short-term apprenticeship with award-winning landscape photographer, Rick Martin, a stepping stone to big things. He'd already arranged to complete his last few months of school externally so he could focus on what he *really* wanted to do.

And now here he was in Bilyja. Outback. On the edge of the desert.

Almost home.

He knew it was a romantic thought: *Dad and Mum could have lived anywhere in the thousands of kilometres north of here.*

Opening the lever to the blinds, he took in the vast expanse of red desert dotted with saltbush. Adelaide was where he grew up, but somewhere in that lonely wilderness was where he was born. *And became orphaned.*

Dimitri thought about the nightmare. As distressing as it was, at least it kept him connected to his parents. Especially to his mother.

He looked across the flat plain. By squinting, he could just see where the red earth merged with dry, yellow pastures. Somewhere, in a place not unlike that plain, his parents' light aircraft had plunged to the ground. He may have only been three years old but he remembered every searing detail. But perhaps it was all imagination.

He also remembered his mum and dad blowing out candles on his birthday cake. Four candles.

Everyone knew that was impossible. They'd died before he turned four. He shook his head. Like Yaya and Papou had said, his mind made things up.

He shrugged. He probably would never learn the difference between fantasy and truth. He should just be thankful that he had survived. If it weren't for his mother pushing him out of the plane, he too would have died.

Lover: How beautiful you are, my darling! — SS 1:15

Dimitri turned away from the window. The night was well over and no doubt Rick was up and waiting for him. He grinned. A certain dark-haired girl might be as well. He rummaged through his travel bag until he found his favourite Roxy t-shirt. He may as well dress to impress.

Initially he had felt ambivalent when Rick explained the subject of the contract. 'We're heading up to the traditional Aboriginal lands to cover the launch of a bible.'

'The *bible?*' Dimitri winced as he remembered his reaction. It wasn't as if he had anything against the bible. It just wasn't something he expected.

Rick had laughed, clearly not fazed by his response. 'It's not actually the whole bible. Parts of it have been translated into the local Aboriginal language. It is a massive achievement. There's a whole week of celebrations to cover.'

Dimitri sat himself down at the table, booted up his laptop and inserted the SD card. Hundreds of photos downloaded from the card at lightning speed. He pushed the chair back. He may as well have a shower while the transfer was underway.

Whoa! He sat back down, clicking the mouse to pause the transfer. There was that girl; and again. How did she get into so many shots of the crowd? He whistled. *Gorgeous.* There was a close-up of her chatting to an elderly Aboriginal woman. It was a great shot of them both. He remembered Rick had pointed out the older woman as a community elder.

But who was the girl? *Definitely classy. Well, maybe not classy*, he reconsidered, *so much as natural.*

Dimitri had never really gone in for the fake tan and bleached hair look that would send his cousin Konstantinos into raves. This girl's beauty was wild. *Wild, and all natural.* He grinned. *And, best of all, Kossie the chick-hunter, isn't anywhere near here.*

Her thick, black hair sat on her shoulders, framing a lightly freckled face. He couldn't be too sure about her eyes, definitely dark, but possibly with flecks of green. She seemed to be of Celtic origin. *Yaya wouldn't approve.* His grin became wider as he kissed a silent apology to heaven. *What's she doing in Bilyja? Is she a local? Or maybe up on a student project like me?*

No, she definitely looked older. Probably around twenty, maybe twenty-one.

Lover: How beautiful you are, my darling! — SS 1:15

Dimitri ran his fingers through his unruly black curls. *Totally out of my league.* He clicked the mouse to continue the import. He'd better hurry.

'Good afternoon to you!' Rick called out, knocking on the door.

A bit sheepish, Dimitri mumbled, 'Come in, Rick. Sorry! I guess I'm not a dawn person.'

'We'll have to fix that.' Rick's grin was infectious. Nothing ever seemed to put him out and Dimitri knew he was forgiven. He also knew he was about to get a lecture that dawn shots were often the most priceless ones. But it didn't happen.

'Here's something I think you can handle on your own.' Rick passed him a notice. 'And it's in the evening, so it should be right up your alley.'

He cast his eyes over the flier. 'Isn't this the Aboriginal elder we interviewed yesterday?' Dimitri's heart skipped a beat. Maybe her gorgeous young friend would be there as well.

'That's right. Apparently, she's also a community midwife. I want you to cover the talk she's giving at the town hall tonight.'

Dimitri frowned. 'Midwife?' That's not what the flier said. *Isn't that babies?*

'You should see your expression!' Rick threw back his head, releasing one of his belly laughs. 'No, it's about the bible launch. Aunty Paula is apparently a bible scholar, as well as everything else. Smart lady. Her talk tonight is about bible translation.'

Dimitri scanned the paper again. *'The Biblical Song of Songs is the greatest love song of all time. Come and experience its connection to Aboriginal spirituality.'* He beamed at Rick. 'Sure thing.'

Rick gave him a curious look but said nothing. He just shrugged.

Dimitri couldn't believe his luck. That woman had seemed very friendly with the girl in his photos. Surely she would be there tonight. *And what better place to meet than in a lecture about a love song?*

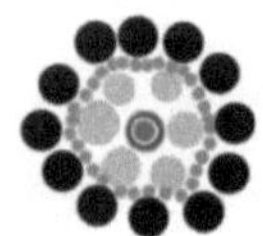

2: Leah

'Excuse me …' A low, husky whisper interrupted Leah's concentration. 'Is anyone sitting there?'

Not bothering to look up, she removed her bag and jacket from the seat next to her. *What's with this guy? There are plenty of spare seats in other rows.*

'Thanks.' He blocked her line of sight momentarily as he sidled in front of her. And brushed a little too close to her legs.

Leah shook her head, glancing at him as he sat down. Blood rushed to her face as he flashed her a stunning smile.

I don't believe it. It's that photographer.

Captivated by his fine facial features, sleek hair and athletic physique, she had virtually stalked him as he worked. Had he noticed her turning up in all his crowd photos?

That would be so embarrassing.

He propped his camera and tripod on the back of the empty seat in front. When he looked at her, she returned his smile. No way was she going to reveal her discomfort. Leah had spent half the day acting like a besotted teenager. Better to show this charmer how mature and disinterested she could be.

With a deep breath, she turned back and stared at the stage. She had missed out on some of the Mayor's introduction of Aunty Paula.

I wonder if he's got a girlfriend.

Forcing aside her distraction, she joined the rest of the audience in her applause. Already in admiration of Aunty, Leah had looked forward to this evening's talk.

Beloved: 1 am a rose of Sharon — SS [2:1]

Held in high regard as an Aboriginal elder and leader in the church, Aunty Paula was also her midwifery supervisor.

Of course he has a girlfriend. He's probably got a whole string of them.

'Thanks for coming this evening. As Mayor Nancy says, my people call me Aunty Paula. When you get as old as me, this shows respect.'

Forcing herself to focus on the speech, Leah tried to block the intensity of the guy's presence next to her.

A generous smile stretched wrinkles across Aunty's face as she touched her white hair. 'I'm kind of like the community nanna.'

Leah grinned. She enjoyed her supervisor's light humour.

'Before we start, I want to give you all a traditional welcome to what we call Country.' Aunty smiled again and scanned the audience. 'That describes the country, or region of Australia where our particular Aboriginal people belong. Some of you might have already seen this kind of welcome, or heard the acknowledgement, maybe at school or work.'

Leah nodded. *When Mum was* … She winced at the familiar stab of pain. As usual, she forced herself past the memory and refocussed.

After her mum's funeral—there, she could do it. After her mum's funeral, she had kept going to the church. Their service always began by acknowledging the Kaurna people as the traditional owners of the greater Adelaide region.

'This evenin' I'm goin' to sing you a welcome song in our local language. The words are much the same as the acknowledgement. It tells you how the local Aboriginal people are the custodians of this area. It explains that we have the same relationship with the land as in our previous generations. It asks you to respect our customs carried out in this region. They are as important today as they were in those times.'

Leah leant forward. *Breathtaking.* She had seen a traditional welcome on TV but never in real life. A teenage boy came up on stage, handed Aunty two clap sticks and pushed the podium to the side.

She stepped forward and a wave of anticipation over the audience stilled the room. Her voice throbbed with a wild, untamed pulse, both raw and throaty. Leah shivered as goose bumps prickled her skin. She imagined Aunty Paula's great, great grandmother chanting the same song. Tears sprung to her eyes.

Beloved: I am a rose of Sharon — SS ^{2:1}

Did my great-great-grandparents get it? Ever? Why hadn't the white settlers understood that songs like these were ones of welcome?

Leah sighed. She thought of her ancestors who had come and staked out a claim, pushing out the families who had always lived on the land.

Relaxing back on the seat, Leah drank in the welcome as Aunty sang and moved about in time with her clap sticks. *Click-clack, click-clack, click-clack. How elegant and graceful is that rhythm?*

I'll have to ask her the meaning of the movements.

Too soon, Aunty finished and handed the clap sticks back to the young boy—and he pushed the podium back. Applause filled the auditorium.

That was magnificent.

'I performed that brief ceremony as a genuine welcome. But I also wanted to create an Aboriginal context for tonight's talk.'

She leant forward on the podium. 'Does it surprise you that the beautiful Hebrew *Song of Songs* shares all the elements of our Aboriginal identity? The song draws on delightful images from nature, as well as descriptions of culturally significant places, feasts and ceremonies.'

Leah had read the song last night for the first time. She had to admit she didn't really understand it. Would Aunty read some of the verses out loud? She hoped not. Not with that guy sitting right next to her. Some of the verses were pretty… umm… *explicit.*

'Aboriginal people value nature. The land is not only precious to us, we are part of it, we belong to it. From this, we can survive. It gives us our food.' Aunty paused at each point. 'Our shelter. Our clothin'. The rhythm of seasons brings life to the land. Elements of nature weave it all together.' She raised her hand. 'But nature isn't only about survival. It's about beauty. There is much in nature we can do without; they are like an added bonus. There are minerals, jewellery, perfume, body paint, makeup.' She touched her hair and smiled. 'And for some, hair dye.'

A ripple of laughter emerged from the audience.

Leah shifted slightly in her seat. *Mm, nice aftershave. Vanilla and cinnamon.*

She gasped at her own thoughts. And then froze as he turned his gaze to her. *Awkward.* Detecting perfume on a guy was all very well in the *Song of Songs*, but a bit tricky in the real world.

Beloved: I am a rose of Sharon — SS ^{2:1}

Aunty's face took on a more serious expression. 'You and I have an important relationship with the land. With relationship comes responsibility; caretaking, preserving and ultimately passing on the knowledge. The *Song of Songs* uses all these images to pass on knowledge.'

Next to Leah, the photographer stretched out his legs.

He's distracting me from the talk. *A waterfall of dark hair… mm, good try, but I'm definitely not a poet.*

'Before we have a look at a few verses, I'd like a show of hands if you know anything at all about the *Song of Songs*.'

Leah glanced sideways and the guy smiled and shrugged. *Oh well, I probably know more than he does.* She raised her hand a couple of centimetres.

'Okay, thanks. That's great. Probably around half of you have at least heard of it.'

Aunty lowered her voice, luring the audience to attend to her presentation. 'This is a love song. Some of the verses are written by the woman, using the character name, Beloved, and some by the man, with the character name, Lover.' She frowned as a snigger came from one of the front rows. 'It's a passionate song. We think that King Solomon may have written it. It's possible that it's his description of his romance with a village girl, whom he wants to marry. I've even heard people say that the *Song of Songs* is considered erotica.'

Leah fixed her eyes straight ahead and hoped the flush in her neck wasn't noticeable. *Aunty Paula certainly says it as it is.*

'But it's not,' Aunty went on. 'The descriptions are definitely impressive; and when we don't understand the Hebrew context, they're easy to misinterpret. Why don't we have a look for ourselves? If you've brought along your bible, I'll give you a minute to flick through and find the right section.'

Leah shifted in her seat to get more comfortable and settled back. *A bible reading; time to zone out.*

'Here, would you like to share mine?'

Whoa! That came from left field. *He had a bible?*

She turned to find the guy glowing at her. His teeth sparkled. Like a toothpaste commercial.

Beloved: I am a rose of Sharon — SS [2:1]

He said share, not stare!

'I'd l … l … lov … e … ew …' she stammered.

'Love you?' he asked.

'To … to … love you to …' The heat in her face was like a furnace. '… to share, I mean.'

She looked down at the tiny, red bible in his hands. She was sure her face was the same bright shade. And then she realised. It was a Gideon's. 'You stole it.' The bubble of embarrassment broke.

His smile was enchanting.

'I borrowed it from the motel.'

She giggled.

'Is that funny?'

His eyes—soft, and adorable—searched hers.

'It's only the New Testament.'

He looked blank.

'*Song of Songs* is in the Old Testament.'

He closed the book. 'Oh.' He didn't look in the least embarrassed.

Cool as a cucumber, that's what he is. Stop it, Leah! Keep away from the nature imagery in a talk like this. She turned away, pretending to focus on Aunty Paula.

The rustling of pages settled as Aunty began again. 'In the song, the village girl can't believe the king could fall in love with her. She has similar feelings for him, but when he gets too serious she avoids him.'

A jangle of sound echoed through the hall and Leah jumped. *Who's left their phone on? After Aunty especially asked everyone to make sure they were off? And what kind of ringtone is that? Zorba the Greek!*

It took her a moment to realise the sound was right next to her. She turned to the photographer with a frown.

Beloved: I am a rose of Sharon — SS [2:1]

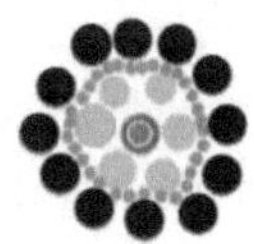

3: Dimitri

Dimitri's absorption with the girl next to him broke. *Hey, Zorba the Greek! Someone's got a ringtone just like mine.*

Aunty Paula's gaze moved over the crowd as *Zorba*'s dance got more exuberant.

How rude. Answer your phone, vlakas. Or switch it off.

Aunty Paula's stare settled straight on him. It was *his* phone. Half the audience turned and glared. Along with the girl next to him.

He jumped up, pulled the phone out of his camera bag and pressed *End*.

'Have a look at the first chapter.' Aunty seemed unperturbed by the interruption. 'In verse six the Beloved tells the Lover, "Do not stare at me because I am darkened by the sun." The king could choose any princess from his palace …'

Zorba started up again. Dimitri's eyes scanned the room. He had to get out of there. *Quick.* There goes any chance of impressing the girl next door. He spun around, clambered over the back of his seat and stumbled across the rows to the back.

'… any princess with skin softened by lotions and protected from the weather. The village girl's was rough from working outdoors, looking after her family's vineyard.' Aunty Paula's voice receded as Dimitri escaped through the back door. The phone remained lit up. He must have pressed *Answer*.

He leaned over the railing. 'Yeah?'

'Hey, cuz, it's Kossie. What's the story?'

Beloved: a lily of the valleys — SS ²⁷

'Kossie?' He hadn't heard from his cousin Konstantinos for months. 'You interrupted any chance I had with this gorgeous girl.'

'Sorry, mate, that's not like me.'

Dimitri pressed his teeth together. *Not like him?* It was exactly like him. Kossie wouldn't think twice about cutting him out with a girl. How about that time with Sarah? And Molly? Then there was Chiara. She was the first girl he had ever really dated and he'd even managed to take her to the movies—twice—before he caught her two-timing with Kossie.

He shrugged. Family was family. And this girl was out the back of nowhere with him. *Kossie get in my way this time? No chance.* So long as he kept his Greek god of a cousin out of sight he was safe. That's if he stood a chance, anyway.

'What was that?'

Kossie had been yapping the whole time.

'You need to get back here. Can you leave right away?'

No way. 'You kidding? This girl's gorgeous, Kossie. I've got to at least try to say *hi*.'

'You don't get it. You gotta get back. What about tomorrow?'

Dimitri's stomach tightened. He moved along the railing and slouched against the post. 'What's wrong? Is it Aunt Elpida?'

'Yes ... I mean, no.'

Why did Kossie sound so agitated? 'What's wrong? Is it Uncle ... I mean, your dad?'

'Nah, he's cool about ...' Kossie broke off. 'You gotta get back here, Dimitri.'

Since when did Kossie call him 'Dimitri'? *Something's up.* 'I can't. My boss is out in the desert somewhere. Waiting for the perfect sunset. Or, if that doesn't work out, sunrise. He's my wheels.'

'Catch a bus.'

A bus? Dimitri took a deep breath and looked out across the gathering shadows. He was kilometres away from everything.

'This is the Outback, Kossie. Back-of-nowhere Bilyja.'

'Yeah, I know where you are.'

What? He hadn't heard from Kossie for ages. How did he know

Beloved: a lily of the valleys — SS [2:1]

where he was? Dimitri had been away on location several times so far during this Photography apprenticeship. But Kossie hadn't asked him once where he had been.

'Who told you that?'

'That's the problem. Mum found your itinerary and, well, she went on and on about it when I went over for dinner …' His cousin's voice trailed off.

Dimitri thought Aunt Elpida was over that. She had gone ballistic when she found out his assignment wasn't on Kangaroo Island, after all. She'd simmered down when he told her they were going to photograph the state's biggest impact crater at Lake Acraman and he'd made it vague after that.

He'd been disturbed by her reaction. He'd never heard her raise her voice before. Not like Yaya used to. 'What do you want to go up Outback for?' she'd shouted. 'That place has nothing for you anymore.'

So, clearly she wasn't over it. Or had something else happened?

'Kossie?'

Nothing.

Dimitri looked at the phone. Had the battery died?

His cousin's voice returned, hesitant and uneasy. Unsteady but clear. 'You know the birth certificate you applied for?'

Dimitri's heart beat picked up. Had it been delayed? He had thought there might be a long wait. Back when he wanted to apply for a learner's permit so he could do the defensive driving course at school, Yaya said they had problems finding it. She wouldn't let him apply for one, so he'd got a statutory declaration from one of his teachers and used a whole heap of other ID instead. He'd felt vaguely guilty about going behind Yaya's back but he found her fears for his safety suffocating.

But this time a birth certificate was essential. He needed a passport as soon as possible. Rick was talking about New Zealand later in the year. Nothing was definite but …

'Well, there was an official letter with it.'

'*Megas!* It's arrived. Thanks for letting me know. If Rick gets the nod from the guys in New Zealand, he says he might just take me.'

'Stay cool, Dimitri. Mum went mad that you went and did that without telling her.'

Beloved: a lily of the valleys — SS [2:1]

'Applying for my birth certificate? How did she know?'

'She opened it.'

'What's Aunt Elpida doing in my private mail?'

He looked around, wondering if anyone had heard him yelling into the phone. Aunty Paula's voice continued uninterrupted in the background. Still, he lowered it a tone. 'All right, tell me what's going on. What's the big deal about getting my own birth certificate?'

'Cuz, I swear the red horseman of the apocalypse has been stampeding through our restaurant. It's been open war. Mum wants to destroy the letter and the certificate but Dad says there's no point. It had to come out sooner or later.' Kossie sighed. 'I've saved your mail from the pizza oven. I'm on the run with it. And I wanna go home to mamma's cooking. You know what I mean? Just come back.'

'No, I don't know what you mean.' Dimitri's body tensed and his voice became terse. 'I'm eighteen now and it's no one else's business. She had no right to open it in the first place.'

'Well, that's the thing. You're not eighteen.'

'What do you mean? Not eighteen?'

This was impossible. He *had* to be eighteen. He was tall for his age. Always had been. And the smartest kid in the class. Teachers had always told his grandparents that he seemed more mature than the other kids. He'd even hit puberty long before anyone else in his year. One of the teachers had tried to convince Yaya to let him skip a class. But she had been adamant that he stick with kids his own age.

And he'd agreed with her. He hadn't wanted to lose any of his friends. But he had wondered if his own parents would have let him. He shoved aside the intrusive thought and the twist of pain it caused him.

Younger than eighteen? No way.

Kossie coughed. 'This next birthday, it's your twenty-first.'

'What?'

The phone went dead.

Dimitri stared at the phone and tapped the screen. Battery power down to one bar, and no signal. He leapt over the railing and strode out onto the footpath into the pale moonlight, desperate for reception.

'Stupid place.' After storming up and down the road in a fruitless attempt to find a signal, he went back into the hall. He intended to simply grab his cameras and find a way out of town. Kossie was right. He had to get back home. Hitchhike, if need be.

He made his way back to his row and sidled past the girl. He caught her glance sideways at him.

Aunty Paula's voice settled over him like soothing ointment. 'The Lover and Beloved try to outdo each other using these amazing images from nature to describe the other person.' Aunty's smile could be felt in her voice. 'This is what you call a love song.'

Dimitri smiled and felt himself calming. He liked that. The girl shifted slightly in her seat. Imagine if he called her his Beloved. *Right. Get real!*

He loved images from nature. That's why he was up there, in the middle of nowhere. *Kossie!* He had to get back.

His cousin's words hit him. *Almost twenty-one? How could he almost be twenty-one?* All those times Yaya had fought with ticket sellers! She had insisted on a child's ticket, saying he was big for his age. Those spitfire performances had embarrassed him more than once. It had been different when he'd got to high school. The basketball coach had almost salivated that first day on seeing him stand head and shoulders above his weedy classmates.

Weedy classmates? Were they just who they should have been? Had he been even more out of place than he felt? *Apparently.* Come to think of it, he'd not only hit puberty earlier than the others, he stopped growing sooner too. He'd never thought to question Yaya's off-hand statement that all the Kostos men developed early.

He felt his face burning: he wasn't sure if it was with anger at Yaya's deception or his own gullibility.

'Despite the Beloved's rejection, the Lover never stops lovin' her.' Aunty's voice was like liquid honey. He sat down to gather his wits, allowing his heart rate to slow. 'He respects her decision and leaves her to think about it,' Aunty went on. 'It doesn't take long before she realises what a dumb mistake she has made, and she goes in search of him. Eventually

Beloved: a lily of the valleys — SS [27]

they find each other. In the next part of the song, the couple try to outdo each other with compliments about how they look. To do this they use metaphors from nature.'

Nature images were something Dimitri understood. After all, this is why he had taken up photography.

'Let's have a look at a verse.'

Time to go. I need to recharge my phone. Dimitri reached over to the seat in front and picked up his camera bags. The girl cleared her throat and he looked up only to find her with her eyes firmly fixed on Aunty Paula. He turned to the front to find the older woman staring straight at him. He knew that look. It was the same as Yaya's.

'Here.' The girl held out her phone in her palm. 'I've just downloaded it.'

Between Aunty Paula's look and the girl's smile, he was lost. He let go of the bags.

'Have a look at verse one.' Aunty was in command again. 'The Lover says, "Your hair is like a flock of goats descendin' from Mt. Gilead."'

Dimitri stifled a smile. *A flock of goats?* No, that's definitely not something he would say to a girl. On the other hand, he could imagine Yaya really liking it. All those stories about the beloved goats she had when she was a kid ... He grinned to himself. He'd share that line with Kossie: goats she had when she was a kid. *Get it? Goats? Kid?*

The girl glanced up at him, her smile fixed.

I hope I didn't say that aloud. That was so lame.

His thoughts circled back to Kossie. *Twenty-one?* How could he be twenty-one? Why would Yaya lie about his age? It didn't make sense.

Aunty's voice drew his attention back to the front. 'The girl makes her reply in the next chapter, in verse ten: "His head is purest gold; his hair is wavy and black as raven."'

Dimitri loosened the muscles in his neck. He needed to calm down. Think about something else. Looking around the community hall, he wondered about the audience. A real mixture of backgrounds. Some were Aboriginal; others not. Some had probably travelled in from a long way and others would have been townspeople. Not everyone had a bible. There were probably people there because it was a bit religious, but others may have

Beloved: a lily of the valleys — SS [2:1]

come because of the cultural significance.

Dimitri had enough of culture for one night. He tensed his jaw. *What made Aunt Elpida think she had the right to open his mail?* It was bad enough to be raised by overprotective Greek grandparents. A pang of guilt for his lack of appreciation stopped his thoughts. Only for a moment. He clenched his fist. They had been hiding something from him. Something big.

Aunty's white teeth appeared in a huge smile. 'One last verse for tonight. Look at how the Lover expresses his delight in the Beloved's hair, "Your hair is like royal tapestry, the king is held captive by its tresses."' She snapped the bible shut. 'I just have a little bit of homework for you to do before tomorrow's talk.'

The crowd gave a mock groan and she lifted her hand. 'It's pretty easy. Read through the song. It's only about five pages. Make a list of all the animals, plants and precious stones you can find. Also make a note of the seasons and the weather. We'll compare these images with the ones in our own country.'

Her gaze held the audience. 'I also want you to consider this point. Solomon either collected or wrote over a thousand songs. Why did he name this one the *Song of Songs*? What was it that made it number one? And, why did it end up in the bible?'

Dimitri picked up the cameras again. *Won't be here to discuss any homework. Don't have a proper bible anyway.*

'If you don't have a bible, there are plenty of free apps you can use to download one.'

Is this woman a mind reader or something?

She lifted her hand to quieten the audience. 'Thanks for coming tonight. You've been a wonderful audience. Please feel free to join us in the back kitchen for supper.'

Everyone stood and applauded before they broke into chatter. Dimitri started to move. It was pointless trying to strike up a conversation with the girl. For one, he would be on the road soon, and for two, he'd made himself look like a loser. *As usual.*

'Hi, I'm Leah.' The girl's smile lit up her face.

Wow! Better than one of Rick's sunrise shots. He grinned. 'I'm Dimitri.'

Beloved: a lily of the valleys — SS [2:1]

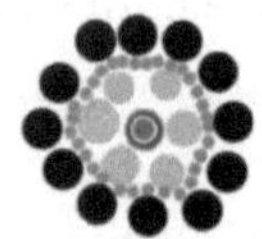

4: Leah

'Leah.' Dimitri sounded out her name. 'I like it. It suits you.'

'Thank you.' Her face flushed. He was direct. She could be too. 'Are you going to stay back for coffee?'

'No. That call I took; I have to follow it up; quick time.'

Well, that worked really well!

He picked up his equipment. 'Are you in town for long?'

Does he want to catch up with me? 'I'll be here until next weekend.'

He flashed her the same smile he had greeted her with. 'Might see you around the place then. Gotta go.'

Leah moved along the aisle, allowing him room to pass. Clearly her company was of no interest to him. Determined not to let her disappointment show, she gave what she hoped was a casual smile. 'Okay, see you around then.'

He waved and disappeared through the exit.

Well, that was just great. She had worked up enough courage to introduce herself and he couldn't shoot through quick enough.

'Leah!' Aunty Paula beckoned her towards the stage. 'Come and have a hot drink with us.'

Leah looked up. 'I'd love to.' She moved towards the stage. 'Great talk, Aunty. I'm looking forward to tomorrow night.'

'Who was that young man who was so interested in you?' Aunty laughed. 'The one *"with hair as wavy and black as a raven?"*'

Leah felt that annoying flush creep over her face. 'Interested in me? He

Lover: Like a lily among thorns — SS [2:2]

couldn't get out of here quick enough!'

Aunty chuckled and took her by the arm. 'Let's remedy our disappointments in love right now. The restorative power of hot chocolate is not to be underestimated.'

Leah smiled at her own seriousness. *Disappointment? More like delusional.* Someone as sophisticated as him, interested in *her?* She didn't think so.

Lover: Like a lily among thorns — SS [2:2]

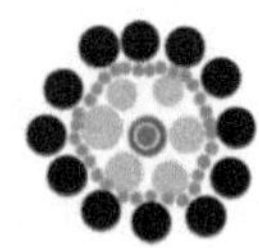

5: Dimitri

What's wrong with me?

The girl of his dreams had invited him for coffee and he'd snubbed her!

I'm not thinking straight. How could I be almost twenty-one?

Dimitri made his way down the main street of Bilyja towards his hotel. He needed to find a way to get to Adelaide, like Kossie said, and sort it out. That didn't leave any room for getting to know someone new. But if Rick wasn't back in the morning and he couldn't get away soon, maybe …

Ah, what's the use? He had just blown it with Leah.

He slammed the motel door behind him, frantic to find the phone-charger. Dumping the cameras onto the spare bed, he noticed the landline on the bedside table. That's easier. He flopped on top of the quilt and dialled the number.

'Hello?'

Dimitri groaned inwardly. It would have been much simpler if Uncle had picked up the phone. It sounded like Aunty had been more than a bit cagey with Kossie. 'Yassou, Aunt Elpida.'

'Dimitri? Oh, so good to hear you. Everything okay?'

You tell me! 'All good with me. What about you? Anything new?'

'New? What ya mean?'

Kossie was right. Dimitri knew that strain in her voice. Aunt Elpida was trying to hold herself together. Well, he wasn't going to help her out. She was the one who had hidden information from him.

'Well, Dimitri, it's not good you know.'

'Mmm?'

Lover: is my darling among the young maidens. — SS [22]

28

'To be honest, I wish you could be home with us, Dimitri. I am worried about Konstantinos. He is acting so strangely. Last night he flew into a rage and we haven't seen him.' A deep sigh echoed down the phone line. 'Have you heard from him?'

She's fishing! He said nothing.

After a moment she went on, 'You know how much I worry about my boys—and you have been like a son to me. Tell me, has Konstantinos got in with a bad crowd? Please, tell me the truth. Is he doing drugs?'

'*Drugs?* No way.'

'You know any reason he fly off handle?'

Dimitri's heart beat picked up. Aunt Elpida was asking him to tell her the *truth*. He had just found out he had three years missing from his life. How many other lies and secrets were there to uncover?

He was still framing a reply when she sniffed and said, 'Well, thank you, Dimitri.' The phone clicked, followed by the whine of disconnection.

Dimitri stared at the receiver. *She hung up on me!* Not even a 'yassas.' He rolled over and replaced the handset. If Aunty could pretend nothing had happened then he would bide his time. He hated confrontation, and he wasn't about to do it over the phone.

The numeral on the bedside clock flipped over. Nine fifteen. Too late for travel; that was a crazy idea anyhow. Too early for bed. His heart rate picked up and he grinned. There was something he could do to distract himself. That cuppa had been an open invitation from Aunty Paula. Just maybe Leah had stayed on.

Dimitri retrieved his charger. He cast his eyes around the room looking for a power point and spotted the cameras. Memory clicked in. He was supposed to get some shots of Aunty Paula. *Rick will be furious!* He'd been so distracted by Leah, and then the phone call, he had completely forgotten why he had gone there in the first place. If he messed up something as simple as this, there was no way Rick would include him in the New Zealand trip.

He pulled the clock from its socket and set up his phone. He would do the unthinkable and leave it behind. Besides being almost flat, it meant his family couldn't spoil the rest of the evening.

Almost twenty-one!

Lover: is my darling among the young maidens. — SS ^{2:2}

29

How could they have lied to him? And how could he have swallowed it for so long? *Stupid, stupid, stupid. Loser, loser, loser.*

He scooped up his gear, grabbed his keys and headed back. The lights in the hall pierced the darkness of the sleepy main street. A few people must still be around. He pictured women Aunt Elpida's age sitting around sipping tea. His instinct was to flee at such a prospect. He steeled himself. He had a job to do.

Dimitri made his way inside but the auditorium was empty. The buzz of conversation came from the back. There must be a kitchen area out there.

Slowing his breathing, he sauntered up the centre aisle and tried to look as casual as possible as he entered the room. *Phew! Leah's still here, talking to Aunty.*

Dimitri checked his thoughts. It was Aunty he had come back to see, not Leah.

He put on his most charming smile—the one that had almost always melted even stern, unyielding Yaya—or at least, until tonight, he'd always thought it had. 'A great talk tonight, Aunty Paula.'

'How would you know?'

Ooh, she's sharp. 'Sorry I missed most of it. And apologies for the interruption. Urgent phone call from home.' He flashed his best smile again. 'Would you mind if I took a couple of shots of you?'

Aunty Paula arched one eyebrow. 'And you are?'

He cringed. *Ouch!* He hadn't even introduced himself. 'I thought everyone in town knew who I was.'

Ouch! Another blunder. *How self-important that sounds.* He glanced over at Leah, who appeared to be enjoying the whole exchange.

Aunty Paula grinned and came to his rescue. 'You're Rick Martin's apprentice, eh?'

'Yes, I'm Dimitri.' He extended his hand to Aunty. 'Dimitri Kostos.'

Aunty Paula's grip was warm and friendly. 'That's right. Rick told me he'd send you to take my photo for the article. He's gone into the desert for sunset takes, and thought this would be a pretty easy task for you.' She winked at Leah. 'We can help this young man out, can't we, hon?'

Leah's face flushed pink.

So, maybe she doesn't think I'm a total loser. Gaining confidence, he opened up his cameras and went to work.

Lover: is my darling among the young maidens. — SS [2:2]

'That's great.' He nodded to Aunty as he clicked away. He moved back, trying different angles and distances. The lighting wasn't the best but she had a radiance that might just surmount that problem.

'Now let's include Leah here,' Aunty said. 'She'll add a bit of richness to your collection.'

'Aunty!' Leah drew back. 'There's nothing about me in the article.'

'Why not? It's not every day we get a young midwife up here on placement from the city.'

'Really? You're a midwife? That's awesome.'

Leah shook her head. 'I'm not a registered midwife yet; I still have a few more babies to deliver.'

Dimitri's curiosity had been captured. He had no doubt Rick would be impressed with the shots. He just needed a bit more information. 'This is a long way to come for a placement. Does Bilyja have a maternity hospital?'

Leah laughed. 'Not really. There's a ward in the general hospital but I'm mainly based out in the community health centre with Aunty.'

'Uh uh.' He clicked his camera in quick succession, capturing Leah and Aunty Paula's expressions as they chatted about their work.

'Okay, that's enough.' Aunty smiled. 'These old bones need rest for the night.' Her eyes sparkled as she turned to Leah. 'It's a bit dark out there. You might need someone to walk you back to the nurses' home.'

There was that pink flush again.

'I'd be happy to take you.' Dimitri tried to short circuit Leah's embarrassment, but her colour only deepened.

She pushed back her chair, turning her head away. Fussing around for her jacket and bag, Dimitri felt sure her mumble had meant, 'Okay.'

'Well, that does it then.' Aunty smiled. 'You're welcome to leave your tripod here; it will be safe overnight.' She stretched out her hand. 'Nice to meet you, young man. Make sure that Rick has made it back safely for the night before you turn in, won't you?'

Dimitri was sure Rick could take care of himself. 'Will do, Aunty.'

She pushed back her chair and looked from Leah to Dimitri. 'So, we'll see you both back here tomorrow night, eh?'

Dimitri grinned. He liked her. A lot. How could he not like anyone who'd set up an opportunity for him to be with Leah?

Lover: is my darling among the young maidens. — SS ^{2:2}

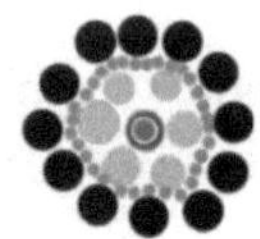

6: Dimitri

Dimitri welcomed the cool evening air when they stepped outside the hall.

'That's better,' Leah said. 'I didn't realise just how stuffy it was in there.'

'A few rickety ceiling fans weren't quite enough,' he agreed. 'Being in the Outback is great, but the facilities are pretty basic.'

'Are you sure this isn't out of your way? I've managed to walk home plenty of times since I've been up here.'

Dimitri looked down the quiet main street. A strip of street lights ran parallel to the median strip, illuminating both sides of the road. Fluorescent signs outside local businesses dispersed shadows from the footpath. He shrugged. It looked safe enough. But there wasn't a chance he would rescind his offer. 'I'm happy to do it. I don't think we're too far from each other anyway. I've seen the hospital sign at the entrance to the town. Is that where the nurses' home is?'

'That's right. It's that ancient stone building right at the back of the hospital.'

Her voice is soft; it echoes in the quiet.

'So you do need a guard. It's dark back there.'

'You win. I'd love some company to walk home.'

Company. Me too. Especially after tonight's news.

They walked side by side along the footpath.

'What about yourself? Where are you staying?'

'At the Red Ochre Inn; hardly any distance from you. Mind you, that

Lover: Your eyes are doves. — SS ^{1:15}

applies to just about any place in town.' With a cheeky grin he added, 'But I'm sure not all of them have a Gideon's bible to borrow.'

Her laughter rose above the night crickets and cicadas.

'Sorry about that.'

'About the Gideon bible thing?' They made their way down the main street. 'Didn't bother me at all,' he reassured her. 'So, you seem to be pretty comfortable finding things in the bible?'

'Only a little. What about yourself?'

'Not really; my yaya would take me to church with her sometimes. It was all a bit confusing with the incense and priest's gowns and stuff.'

'Greek Orthodox?'

He nodded. 'But you know, it probably sounds a bit funny, but I actually liked the chants. They carry a similar sort of beauty that I find through photography.' He ignored the warning voice in his head. 'Plus I happen to like poetry.'

He looked at her from the corner of his eye, waiting to be teased.

'Me too.' She looked away.

Was that a flicker of pain in her eyes?

'The Psalms were my mum's favourite.' Her voice cracked and she looked down.

Were her mum's favourite? He fought back the desire to reach out for her hand. He knew grief when he saw it.

He had lived with it for long enough. Probably different, but piercing all the same. He couldn't even identify what his mother's favourite things were. His family never mentioned her. Ever.

They continued in silence for a few moments before Leah continued, 'Mum passed away not long ago.'

'I'm so sorry to hear that. It must have been a tough year for you.'

A tough year? What gave him the right to say that? He didn't have a clue what kind of year she had. Yet he did know that grieving hurt.

Leah nodded. 'Breast cancer.'

Dimitri clamped his fists. What he wouldn't give to offer her a warm hug. He searched around for the right words but everything felt flat, and fake. In the end he mumbled a barely audible, 'I'm sorry to hear that.'

Lover: Your eyes are doves. — SS ^{1:15}

'I have my moments, but it's a touch easier now.'

'My parents passed away too. In a plane crash when I was three.' *At least I think I was three. Or was I six?* The irritation with his family flared up, but he ignored it.

'That's awful! I'm sorry to hear that as well. Were you raised by your grandparents?'

He nodded. 'Yes, my yaya was a tough, old world grandmother, who loved me to bits. She ruled the house—all of us, Papou, Aunt, Uncle and cousin Kossie. Who, by the way, was the person who called me during that talk.'

'If you had arrived at the start you would have heard the reminder to switch phones to silent.'

That's better. A bit of ribbing to sooth the sadness they both shared.

'Are you always late?'

'Always.'

Her gentle laughter trickled into the night air.

'The Psalms by the way…' He grinned at her. '…are in the Old Testament, but can be found in a Gideon. Surely I wasn't a total ignoramus to think the *Song of Songs* might have been in there too?'

'Touché!'

They turned into an avenue lined with pines and walked in comfortable silence. In the darkness created by their long shadows he once again resisted reaching out for her hand.

Why would someone as gorgeous as her be remotely interested in him? Yet she had allowed him to take a peek at her grief. She didn't have to tell him that. Nor did he have to share his own sadness. Yet they had. Did Leah feel the same connection that he did?

There was an air of mystery about her. He couldn't imagine too many girls his age wanting to do a placement out here.

His age? What was his age? He shoved aside that thought.

His mind turned to the endless plain surrounding the town, the stark, harshly beautiful desert.

'I like being away from the city. It's very peaceful.' She interrupted his musing and he was surprised that her thoughts matched his.

'Me too. I liked what Aunty Paula said about the relationship people

Lover: Your eyes are doves. — SS [1:15]

have with the land. Somehow I can relate to that. I feel like I have a strong bond to all this.' He gestured towards the surrounding land. 'It's probably why I love landscape photography the most.'

'I'd love to see some of your work.'

You would? 'I'd love to show you, but most of my work is back home, in Adelaide. We could always catch up for coffee once we both get back? I mean, that's if you're from there. And going back.' His invite was out there before he could change his mind. The words felt like they hung in the air between them.

'I finish up this week. And I do live in Adelaide. And, I think having coffee with you would be … nice.'

Was she looking around for a better word? It didn't matter. She had just agreed to catch up with him.

He exhaled, only then realising he had been holding his breath. Would he be pushing his luck if he asked to see her sooner?

'Why leave it until Adelaide? I mean we could do lunch tomorrow?'

'I'm working all day tomorrow, from nine.'

He tried not to sound too deflated. 'And dinner's out for me. I can't be late for Aunty Paula's speech again. I need to get there in time to set the cameras up.'

'And somewhere in all that, we have to find time to do our homework.'

'Oh, yes, homework.'

They both laughed.

'We could always have breakfast,' Leah suggested.

'Great! Breakfast it is. Red Ochre has an all-you-can-eat buffet and they put on a pretty good spread this morning.'

'Okay, let's do it then.'

At the gate of the driveway to the nurses' home, a giant pine tree towered over them as if standing guard. Dimitri wondered how many nurses had stood beneath it with that special guy in their life. The moon peeked between the leaves, crowning Leah's head. He felt too self-conscious to whip out his camera. Yet he didn't need it to preserve this image. Even if he never stood here with Leah again, he would remember this picture always.

He reached out to hold the tiniest wisp of her hair. 'Your hair is like royal tapestry, the king is held captive by its tresses.' *I've lost my mind. What on earth caused that? She'll never turn up for breakfast now.*

Without a word Leah turned and made her way up the path and disappeared through an ancient wooden door.

Dimitri berated himself for the quote all the way back to the motel. He thumped his fist against his forehead. As he did, the phone call from Kossie flashed across his mind.

In one day he'd met and probably lost the girl of his dreams and a mystery had exploded, shattering everything he thought he knew about himself. He had no doubt his life was about to go down unmarked territory.

He reached the motel's car park. Rick's vehicle wasn't there. Dimitri recalled Aunty Paula's warning to make sure his boss had returned for the night. He unlocked his door and put the camera bag away. The last thing Rick would want was someone checking up on him. He was, after all, a veteran of the Outback.

Just like Dimitri's dad had been.

Lover: Your eyes are doves. — SS [1:15]

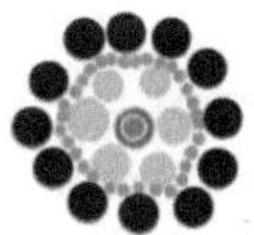

7: Leah

'Leah McEwen.'

Leah cringed. Nurse Phillips was in sergeant major mode, as usual. No one made staff call them 'Nurse' these days. It was Leah's last day at the hospital and she was out to assert her authority one last time.

'Today I'd like to see you manage Room Six.'

Leah felt the blood drain from her face. 'But that's not Maternity, it's Palliative Care.'

'That's right.' Nurse Phillips' voice floated above Leah's head. 'Student midwives have to perform a number of general nursing tasks as well as midwifery. Mrs Reeve is an Oncology patient and I want you to check the progress of her morphine infusion.'

Leah tightened her grip on the chair. 'I …' She hesitated.

'That will be all. Off you go.'

Leah's knees barely held her as she made the short trek up the corridor. Her hand on the door of Room Six, she settled her breathing. This wasn't meant to happen. She had signed up for midwifery. To bring life into the world, not to …

A tear squeezed out through her lashes and she desperately blinked it back. She was stronger than this!

Her thoughts had been jumbled since early that morning. Dimitri had stood her up. After sitting in the dining room for half an hour—conspicuously alone—she decided to leave for work. Heading out through the car park, she'd noticed the four wheel drive blazoned with *Outback Photography Inc*

Beloved: I looked for the one my heart loves: — SS ^{3:1}

wasn't there. Rick had obviously begun his day's work already.

For a moment she was tempted to excuse Dimitri. *Maybe he was out taking dawn shots.* But was leaving a message such a big ask? They hadn't swapped mobile numbers, but he knew where she was staying.

The day had started out badly and deteriorated. Nurse Phillips had been snappish since the shift began. Leah strapped on a smile she didn't feel as she approached Mrs Reeve's bed. The paper white hand resting on the sheets reminded her of her mother. She took a deep breath.

The scream of an ambulance siren pierced the quietness of the room. Leah's heart pumped faster. 'I'll be back as soon as I can, Mrs Reeve. I'm on call in the ambulance bay …'

Leah hurried back to the nurses' station.

'Good, Leah McEwen, I'm glad you know how to respond to an emergency.' Nurse Phillips was still in a belittling mood. 'When you get into the Emergency Room, don't forget you are a student and you are not to get in the way. Do you understand?'

'Yes, Nurse Phillips, I understand.'

'And don't forget to clean your hands *before* you leave the ward and *before* you enter ER. Emergency or not, there's no excuse to forget good infection control.'

'Yes, Nurse Phillips,' Leah muttered, her hand already on the hand sanitiser.

Leah rushed down to the Emergency Room, a burst of adrenaline pumping through her veins. The ambulance could have brought anything in, and she was going to be there to see it all.

She pumped another squirt of alcohol into her hands and pushed open the *Staff Only* door. The bay buzzed with activity. Two ambulance officers wheeled a barouche into a cubicle and two orderlies transferred a male patient onto the bed. A nurse in the cubicle grabbed an oxygen mask and placed it over the patient's face. A doctor threw questions at one of the ambulance officers as the nurse took down the details.

Leah stood taking it all in, wondering at what point she should help. The nurse looked up, catching Leah's eye. 'Ah, there you are. You're the student, aren't you? Leah?' She took a deep breath. 'This is a Motor Vehicle

Accident. It's too soon to know anything just yet but you could do me a favour.'

'Of course. What would you like me to do?'

'This man had someone with him. He may also have been in the crash but we don't know. He's wandered off. Would you mind finding him and getting some details?'

'Sure.' Leah turned away. She hurried out to the waiting room and scanned the faces of the few people sitting there. Two parents with a baby and a toddler sat in one corner. An elderly woman sat nearby, leaning forward, supported by her walking frame. A middle-aged man lay, eyes closed, with his head resting against the wall. *Him?*

Leah started towards him and almost walked into a man exiting the male toilet.

'Sorry.' The man sounded apologetic. 'I just couldn't wait to get that blood washed off me.'

Leah gaped. 'Dimitri?'

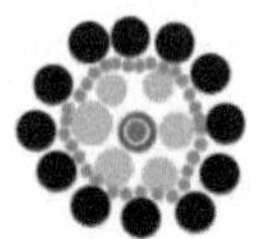

8: Leah

'Leah! You don't know how good it is to see you.'

'What happened? Are you okay?' In an instant, she guessed who the patient was. 'Was that Rick in the ambulance?'

Dimitri nodded. 'Rick rolled his car. When we found him he was unconscious. He had dragged himself away from it and it looks like he might have broken his leg. Not to mention a nasty wound to his head.' He rested his hand on her shoulder. 'I'm so glad it's you that's rostered on. At least you'll be able to tell me what's going on.'

Leah tightened her lips. Dimitri was pleased to see that she was on *duty*, not to see *her*. 'I'm afraid I don't know anything just yet. In fact, I think the staff were hoping you could help us … are you okay?'

Dimitri swayed and reached out for the wall. 'I'm fine. It was a long night.'

Leah gripped his elbow. 'You were outside all night! It gets freezing up here. Come on, let's find an empty cubicle.' She steered him through the double doors into the patient bay. 'You could be going into a bit of shock. I think you need to see the doctor, too.'

She settled him onto a bed. 'You stay put and I'll go and speak with one of the nurses.'

'I knew you'd look after me.'

Leah's face grew hot. She wondered if he may have been putting it on. *No, he definitely looks grey.* 'Of course I'll look after you, but please remember I'm just a student. Dimitri, I have to go and find someone.'

Beloved: …I found the one my heart loves. — SS 3:4

40

'Not *just* a student ... and not *just a pretty face ...*' His voice trailed off and he closed his eyes.

Leah turned away. If her face appeared as hot as it felt, it was very embarrassing.

'There you are.' The nurse who had sent Leah out looked up. 'Looks like you located the man. What did you find out?'

Leah realised Sergeant-Major Phillips would be furious at her actions. Instead of taking details from the man and coming back with some helpful information, she'd moved him from the waiting room to the bay. *Queue-hopping. Without permission.* What was she thinking? She threw a backward glance at Dimitri on the bed. He definitely didn't look well.

'I'm really sorry, but I've brought the man through to Cubicle Three. Dimitri looked like he was about to faint.'

'Well done, you've shown good initiative. Why don't we go and take a History together?' She looked back over her shoulder. 'That's Rick Martin, the driver of the vehicle. He was very lucky Dimitri thought to speak to the motel owner and they both went looking for him. He's covered in glass wounds, has probably fractured both his right tibia and fibula, and has sustained a head wound; not to mention concussion.'

Leah looked over the room. 'Where's the motel owner? Is he okay?'

'I assume so. The ambos said he drove back into town to raise the alert.'

'Leaving Dimitri out there? *All night?*' Leah's voice increased in pitch and her own pulse raced. She pulled herself up. Dimitri was her patient. She was supposed to care, but ... to care *this* much?

'Rick was found three hours from here; he'd gone bush-bashing off the track.' The nurse sighed as she shook her head. 'No mobile coverage at all. He was lucky Dimitri called on Joey; no one else would have seen the signs in the dark where he'd left the main road.' The nurse grinned. 'Come on, let's have a look at your patient and take some vital signs.'

Was that a sparkle in the nurse's eye? Leah could have kicked herself. Was she always so transparent? *Was* he more than a patient to her?

'Well, Dimitri, you should be commended for both bravery and initiative by the sounds of things.'

Dimitri opened his eyes, looked from the nurse to Leah and closed them again. Leah watched his chest rise and fall. *Is he struggling to catch his breath?*

'I'm Jill, the nursing team leader here. Leah and I are going to check you over, okay?'

Dimitri nodded.

He looks so weak.

'So, what can you tell me just by looking at Dimitri?'

Leah's fists were clenched and a tight ball of pain knotted against her abdomen. He didn't look good at all. 'He looks pale, and very tired. Maybe even a bit breathless.'

'Good observations. How about you grab an oxygen mask and we'll see if we can improve his breathing?'

Leah moved to the back of the bed, retrieved a new mask and attached the tubing to the oxygen pipe. 'I'm just going to cover your face with a mask.' She moved his head very gently and stretched the strap over his hair.

'Great.' Jill smiled at her. 'Now go ahead with the rest of your Obs and I'll begin the paper work.'

Leah busied herself gathering the appropriate equipment and charts. She rested her fingers over Dimitri's wrist. *Rapid and thready.* 'I'm just going to insert the thermometer into your ear.'

Dimitri's eyelids flickered but he didn't open them.

Temperature is a bit on the low side. 'Okay, now I need to put this clip on your finger to check your oxygen level.'

Also a bit low.

Leah took a deep breath. *He's definitely showing signs of shock.* She wrapped the blood pressure cuff around Dimitri's arm and pumped it up. After a couple of attempts at listening for the heart beat, she removed the stethoscope from her ears. 'Jill, would you mind rechecking the blood pressure? I haven't used these manual ones very much."

'What did you get?'

'Eighty over fifty.'

'Ouch. That's low. What about the rest of the results?'

Leah passed her the chart. Jill pursed her lips. 'I trust your reading; it fits in with the rest of his vital signs. Go and find Dr Campbell, and

Beloved: ...I found the one my heart loves. — SS ³ˑ⁴

then bring back a digital blood pressure machine, and a blanket from the warmer. Meanwhile I'll set up for an IV.'

Was that a hint of concern in Jill's tone? As she hurried away, she heard Jill mutter, 'We need to get some fluids into him. Fast.'

Her mind was a blank as she located the blanket warmer and grabbed the BP machine. Somehow she managed to give Dr Campbell the run down as she led him back to the bedside. A fog just descended and stayed there. Her brain seemed to be operating on auto-pilot as she fetched and passed equipment for the doctor and Jill.

This was Dimitri lying on the bed. A hypotensive crisis they called it. Dimitri; who had sat next to her and walked her home last night. Young, strong and fit. And likeable. *So likeable.*

'Leah.'

'Sorry Jill; I … was in a daze.'

'He's going to be fine now. I'd say he's naturally got low blood pressure anyway. This combined with hypothermia, dehydration and sheer exhaustion put him into shock. With the IV, oxygen and warm blankets we've managed to get that blood pressure back up without drugs. Good work.'

Dr Campbell nodded in agreement. 'He really put himself out there for Rick. Without Dimitri's help, that man would have lost a lot more blood and suffered from cold exposure. Dimitri used all the coverings he could find for his friend, and had to apply pressure to that head wound every time the bleeding started up again.'

He looked back at Dimitri. 'The police found his cousin's number in his mobile. Konstantinos will be up this evening to take him back to Adelaide tomorrow.' He picked up the patient file. 'I'll go and write up a letter for him to give to his local doctor as soon as he arrives.'

Tomorrow? Dimitri was leaving tomorrow? They had only just met.

Jill rested a hand on Leah's shoulder. 'It's almost three o'clock. You've worked hard today. Why don't you finish up?'

Three o'clock? Where did the day go? 'You mean go home?'

Jill laughed. 'Of course I meant go home.'

Leah held her breath. She didn't *want* to go home. She looked at

Dimitri. He still looked so vulnerable. How could she leave him on his own? He had no family here …

Dimitri opened his eyes and focussed on hers. 'Stay.' It was a whisper.

Leah looked from Jill to Dimitri. He was a patient and she was a nurse. It was totally unethical for her to stay in her off duty time.

'Your student placement is almost finished?' Jill enquired.

'This is my last hospital shift. I have tomorrow rostered off then I'm back at the community health clinic. I finish my time in Bilyja on Friday.'

'And you would like to stay with Dimitri?' Jill raised her eyebrows. 'I gather the two of you have met previously?'

Leah nodded, a glimmer of hope igniting. Perhaps Jill might waive the rule.

'I can't promise you anything. But go home and get changed and I'll contact your clinical supervisor. Aunty Paula, isn't it?'

'Yes. Oh, that would be so good.'

Jill raised her hand. 'Like I said, I can't promise you anything. But I'll put it to Aunty Paula. It's not as if you're going to be nursing Dimitri again. If she gives the go ahead, when you come back, you're back here as a visitor. Clear?'

Leah couldn't stop the smile spreading across her face.

Jill turned back to Dimitri. 'And you! Oi. You, young man. You're sure this is what you want?'

He stretched out his hand and clasped hold of Leah's. She looked down, surprised at how comfortable his hand felt in hers.

'Awesome.' That amazing, radiant smile was back.

Jill laughed. 'See what healing you bring already. Now off you go until you hear from me.'

Beloved: …I found the one my heart loves. — SS ^{3:4}

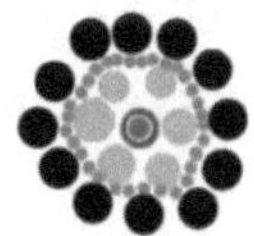

9: Leah

An amazing, radiant smile seemed glued to his face. 'I bet you didn't realise it's our three month anniversary?'

'Of what?' Leah pretended not to understand.

'Since we met.'

He looked so solemn. She shouldn't tease him, but it wasn't exactly an anniversary. They had seen each other almost every second day since returning to Adelaide, but they hadn't formally agreed to 'go out'. They'd walked on the beach at Glenelg every weekend, they'd picnicked by the Torrens River, they'd bought chocolate so many times at Haigh's they were greeted by name as they entered the store.

Leah searched his face. How lucky she was to have met such a generous, fun-loving and gorgeous-looking guy. His cousin, Kossie, had driven up to the hospital to bring him home. What a flirt that guy was. *God's gift to women?* That's what Dimitri had called him. *Hardly.* He wasn't a patch on Dimitri.

One night, Dimitri had arrived at her student quarters holding a long stemmed, blood red rosebud. A cliché? Lack of originality? Possibly. But as she watched that bud open, it reflected something inside that she had never experienced before. Dimitri wasn't shy in telling her how deeply he had fallen in love with her. For her, it wasn't as simple. Unfortunately, apprehension ran parallel to her growing love.

Her father. That jellyfish of a man. He had drained all the love her mother had for him. In the end, he had even let her die without him. Some husband.

Beloved: I held him and would not let him go. — SS 3:4

She reached down into her handbag and pretended to rummage around for a tissue. *Get a grip.* Her parent's relationship didn't have to ruin hers. Or her evening.

Dimitri looked so proud of himself. His head was tilted back, his hair surrounded by a halo of chandelier light. *You have no right to look so heavenly, you know that?* 'Actually, to be precise, it's two months and twenty-nine days.'

'So you did know!'

'Of course I knew. Aunty Paula's lecture was pretty amazing.'

'That's not exactly what I meant.' He sounded disappointed.

'Oh?' She cast her eyes around the fancy restaurant. Once an old stone cottage, each room had been tastefully decorated to create intimate dining spaces. Dimitri had booked a table with a panoramic view of the city lights. 'I didn't even know this place existed.'

'Rick's home isn't too far. Every time I pass by I've wondered what it would be like to come here with you.' Dimitri reached out and lifted her hand. 'Now I know.'

How warm and secure his hand now felt in hers.

There was another complication. There was Monday. It could be nothing.

Thankfully Dimitri would be in New Zealand. One less worry. Once he found out … now that would be a test of their relationship. If there was something to find out. It may be nothing. It could change everything.

She let go of his hand and picked up her menu. This was Saturday. She had promised herself she would keep a lid on Monday's worries for tonight.

'I wonder what the specials are.' Leah didn't have to look at Dimitri to know she had wounded him.

Her stomach growled. 'Oops, sorry!'

She felt the tension between them break. Dimitri's frown turned back to his full-wattage smile. 'That's good; it means you've been saving up to enjoy a decent meal.'

That's another thing she liked about him. He could be intense as well as laid back—all in the one sitting. He had a knack of reading her. And putting up with her.

'Absolutely. I'm tired of cooking for one. It usually ends up in a meal of two-minute noodles.'

Beloved: I held him and would not let him go. — SS ^{3:4}

Oh dear. She stared, dismayed, at the menu. The cost of a main meal could feed her for a week.

'It's my shout tonight,' Dimitri reassured her.

'Whatever for?'

She had been very careful to make sure their 'shouts' were pretty even. There was no way her student allowance could repay something like this.

'I invited you here so it's my shout. We have a lot to celebrate.'

Ignoring the comment, Leah chattered about different options. Eventually she decided on the smoked salmon and set her menu aside. While Dimitri continued to examine his, she looked around the room. White cloth covered tables as well as chairs. A large white bow decorated the rear of the high back chairs. A tealight candle flickered inside a coloured vase in the centre of each table. The cutlery looked like it could be real silver. Unlike Leah's cheap twelve-to-a-packet set. From a room somewhere out of view, soft classical music escaped.

'It's live.' Dimitri interrupted her thoughts. 'Do you like dancing?'

'I love dancing.' He had given her the space she needed. She appreciated that. No more worrying about the past or the future. Celebrations were too important.

When their plates had been cleared and they had finished their coffee, Dimitri leaned back on his chair. 'How's your reading of Aunty Paula's *Song of Songs* going?'

'I'm getting into it. I only wish I could understand the local Aboriginal language. I'm pretty sure it's the only way we can truly appreciate the richness of the text. The English version is great, but it probably doesn't do it full justice.'

He nodded. 'When you compare the Middle Eastern images to our Australian ones, the Song makes so much more sense.'

'It's disappointing that we missed out on the second half of the talk. But it did mean we got out of doing the homework.'

'Who said I didn't do any homework? I was fascinated by it all.' He grinned. 'I can tell you that in the *Song of Songs* I counted over thirty different plants or flowers and every season and element of weather. There were at least fourteen types of animals or birds and almost a dozen different minerals or jewels.'

He leaned closer. 'But that wasn't really the point, was it?'

Beloved: I held him and would not let him go. — SS ³⁴

47

'What do you mean?'

He clasped her hand. This time she didn't let go. She had to take a risk. He was far too precious to lose. As her hand rested in his, she allowed the healing and confidence of his touch to infiltrate her barriers.

'They were just images two people created to say how much they love each other.' He tightened his grip. 'I've told you how much I love you. I believe with all my heart we're meant to be together. I know I'm way not good enough for you, but will you give me a chance? I want to be so much more than just a friend.'

Leah shook her head, fighting hard to keep tears from streaming down her face. He, not good enough for her? Was he for real? If only he knew the thoughts that had spun around in her head all evening. But this is precisely what he meant. Friends could get away with gliding along the surface of communication. For couples that would never work.

Of course it's what she wanted. She just wasn't brave enough to believe it could happen. It was time to take a risk.

Mustering up the determination to keep her voice strong and steady, and eyes dry, she looked straight into his eyes. 'That's how I feel too.'

'Sweet!'

He gripped both hands. 'Towards the end of the *Song of Songs* there's a passage I want you to look up when you get home. I'll text it to you so you don't forget. The whole song is a love song, but it's not until near the end that we read how deep and powerful love really is. Nothing can get in its way. That's what I believe our relationship is capable of. And that's how I feel about you.'

'Okay.' What else could she say? He was streets ahead of her. Yet if his love was as strong as he thought it was, he would give her the time she needed to get past her fears.

'*Okay!*' A grin lit up his face. 'Let's celebrate with a dance.'

The next hour flew by and before Leah was ready, it was time to leave. 'I'm really sorry, Leah, but you know how it is. Rick and Angie are sharing their cab with me and we have to be at the airport before 5.30.'

He had been planning his New Zealand trip for as long as she'd known him. *And perhaps it made things easier ...*

Beloved: I held him and would not let him go. — SS [3:4]

48

Once again, she ignored the niggling worry. 'You're all so lucky that they held this assignment over until Rick's leg recovered.'

'I'm going to miss you. But it's only a week, and we'll pick up from where we left.'

'I'll miss you too, but I know you're going to have a great time. You probably won't get time to think about me.'

'That's not going to happen. But I will be out of range up in the mountains at times, so don't get too worried if you don't hear from me for a while.'

Leah nodded but said nothing. They may well need that space.

Her tension dissipated as they exited into the fresh air. Dimitri pressed the remote to his brand new, four-wheel drive and filled the silence with a commentary about its features. It had taken a lot of soothing over his male pride to convince him it was okay for her to be his licensed supervisor. Apparently, it was all good for him to drive Rick around in it, but not his girlfriend.

'With all your country driving,' she had encouraged him, 'it won't be for long.'

'I should have had that inheritance three years ago,' he'd complained, 'along with the down payment for my own place, the car, and not to mention the right to get my driver's license.'

Leah felt proud of him. It didn't appear to be in his nature to hold a grudge for long. There should have been a twenty-first party but, after the confrontation with his aunt and uncle, he'd decided against it. Instead, he'd spent the day with her at their special place on the beach. She'd been happy on the one hand but disappointed with his aunt and uncle. They were depriving him of a celebration just because they didn't want all of his friends to know about his grandparents' deception. It was, apparently, too much like speaking ill of the dead.

Yet the lie was tinged with mystery. Why had his grandparents felt the need to falsify his age?

Leah opened the car door and settled in.

A mystery, she determined, they would solve together.

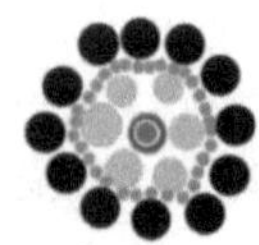

10: Dimitri

Dimitri couldn't believe the relief he felt when the plane lifted off. All his extreme caution of the past few months had paid off. As Rick's leg had healed, he'd made himself indispensible, fetching camera equipment, lugging it around, making cups of coffee. Very Greek, very potent—made properly with a briki.

Rick had choked on it at first, then enjoyed the humour of getting his 'Greek barista' to serve coffee for his clients.

Working with Rick and spending every spare moment with Leah meant he hadn't had to spend much time at home.

No one seemed in the least repentant that Yaya had lied to him. 'She loved you.' And that seemed to be reason enough for any deception. Uncle had told him about the inheritance, to Aunt Elpida's fury.

'He's twenty-one!' Uncle Spiros pointed out.

'You not act it,' snapped Aunt Elpida, rounding on Dimitri. 'You even go out with girl who is not Greek. A girl you keep the secret for shame.'

Dimitri finally lost it. 'A girl I keep secret because I don't want your son flirting, and who knows what else, every time I bring her round here! Like every other girl he's taken from me!'

'How dare you! Konstantinos is good boy.' Aunt Elpida had been red with rage. 'How you say? Chaste. He is kind and caring to girls you discard.'

Dimitri had left before he'd exploded. He'd already said far too much he regretted.

Beloved: Do not arouse or awaken love until it so desires. — SS [3:7]

The whole New Zealand trip was a blessing. Although it took him away from Leah, it also took him away from a family dynamic that had become like a powder keg waiting for a fatal spark.

As the plane took off, Rick turned to him and smiled. 'So, what's she like?'

Dimitri looked at him, baffled.

'Your new girlfriend.'

'How do you know I've got a girlfriend?'

Rick chuckled. 'You know why I took you instead of the private school kid? I checked the social media pages of every applicant to see what they were really like. Didn't want a troll on my team.'

Dimitri took a moment to process the information. 'Oh.'

Rick raised his eyebrows. 'Nothing on the internet is private, Mitri, my man. Pay you to remember that.'

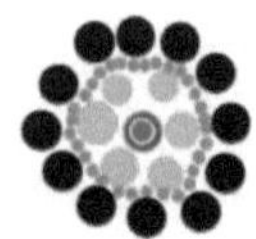

11: Leah

On Sunday, Leah tried to concentrate on finishing off an assignment. It was impossible. Her thoughts were on Dimitri. She wanted nothing more than to be with him, in New Zealand. She picked up her phone and read his message yet again.

'Love is as strong as death, its jealousy unyielding as the grave. It burns like blazing fire, like a mighty flame. Many waters cannot quench love; rivers cannot wash it away.'

Last night she had been unable to sleep as she thought about her mum. Death had reached out and taken her away. Nothing could be stronger than death. Not even love. Death wrecked everything.

If Mum were alive, they would have spent the day together. 'So you're going steady now?'

She would have cringed at the old-fashioned term. But she would give anything to hear it now.

Leah put the phone down. Her mum hadn't believed that death ruined everything. She believed that love was stronger than death. God's love. Jesus' love. The cross and resurrection. The conclusion? An invitation to experience a life full of love after death. The greatest love story of them all. That's what her mum had told her. So did the church. It was a puzzle she was still trying to sort out. And may need to, sooner than she wanted.

Time to turn the computer off. It was dark outside, and there was no use waiting any longer. Her pyjama day had to end.

Beloved: Do not stare at me because I am dark. — SS [1:6]

She switched on the shower and stepped in, relishing the warmth of the water over her body.

I'll check again. Maybe I imagined it.

Her fingers extended just beyond the axilla. Clear. She located each quadrant of her right breast and massaged the area, leaving the upper outer area until last. Finally, unable to avoid it, she pressed her fingers into her soft flesh. She knew full well what she hoped for was futile. There it was. Still present. The size of a pin head, but definitely a lump.

A cascade of water tumbled over Leah's head. It streamed into her eyes, her nose and her mouth. Her hair clung to her face, and she did nothing to stop it. She had lived in a protective haze of denial for the past few days, but the bubble had burst.

She grabbed the flannel and buried her face. Her legs buckled and she collapsed on the floor. Pulling her legs up to her chest, she found refuge behind the waterfall. Her mind picked up speed, a turbo of questions raced around in her head.

Am I going to die? Will I ever practise as a midwife?

Could she ever forgive her father for rejecting her mother? What would Abbey, her step-sister, say?

Will they cut off my breast? What about my hair?

A long, low moan escaped her. *Dimitri! What will Dimitri think? What does it matter?* Hysteria clutched her throat, and she hissed, 'I could die!'

She pulled herself up from the floor, turned off the taps and stepped out. Just like a play. Stepping out of one scene, into the next.

Except it's not a play. Mum; ill, weak and dying. That's as real as it gets.

Dried and dressed, Leah wrapped herself up in her doona and tried to sleep. That was impossible. Tossing and turning she lay awake until the birds heralded the day. Drained of strength, her body finally succumbed to sleep.

She awoke to an airless room, sunlight streaming through the windows. Within a fraction of a second she remembered.

I have a lump.

Throughout the night, her stomach had ached with the weight of anxiety. The heaviness remained, coupled with wave after wave of nausea.

Beloved: Do not stare at me because I am dark. — SS [1:6]

It's best to get up and moving. She had a doctor's appointment. Maybe, just maybe, it was nothing. Sometimes it was hormonal. That did happen.

Leah filled the kettle and grabbed the coffee. Behind the canister, her favourite muesli did nothing for her appetite. She stood waiting for the kettle to boil, stirring the coffee into the milk. Around and around she turned the spoon in the cup. The coffee changed from black to brown to cream. Her mother's voice called to her, 'Always put the milk in first. I don't like burnt coffee.'

Mum!

Life had been going so well. Thoughts of her mother no longer seared through her. And Dimitri … since she had met him, life was great.

Leah reached out for her phone, and for the hundredth time, pressed his message. From behind blinding tears she read, 'Love is as strong as death, its jealousy unyielding as the grave.' Her voice barely a whisper it now cracked. 'It burns like blazing fire, like a mighty flame. Many waters cannot quench love; rivers cannot wash it away.'

With her eyes closed tight, she mustered a prayer. 'Dear God, is there any truth to these words? Or is it just a poem? Could love ever be stronger than death? Dimitri said nothing would get in the way of his love.' She saw her mum and how strong her faith was until the end. She had believed in God's love. 'Is that what the song is about? Is that the reason it's in the bible? The *Song of Songs* is about Your love?'

She shrugged, too exhausted to think about stuff like that. Grabbing a handful of tissues, she wiped her eyes and face. Picking up her phone, she opened a new message from Dimitri.

'Hi beautiful.' Leah grabbed another handful of tissues and wiped away the flow of tears. How captivated she had been when they first met. Convinced he could have any girl of his choice, she held no illusion he would be interested in her. Yet here they were, three months later, their friendship at another level.

Through blurred eyes she read, 'You haven't changed your status yet! What's up?' A smiley face and a row of love hearts completed the message.

Her tears flowed faster and she pressed hard against her eyes with the wad of tissues. He had updated his profile as soon as he got home from the restaurant. 'In a relationship with Leah McEwen.' You didn't do that unless you were no longer 'just friends.'

Leah couldn't bring herself to change hers. How could their love go to the next level? Their relationship may well be an absolute fizzer.

Everything had changed. But not in the way Dimitri hoped. How could she explain her silence? *I haven't replied because I could be dying? My breast might have to come off? My head might be shaved?*

Would he ever call her beautiful again?

Leah focussed on her breathing. Her thoughts gradually slowed down. Yes, there was a new road ahead. She had no choice but to face it. With or without him.

Leah wiped her tears and blew her nose. She wrote: 'Miss u, Leah xxx.' It was the best she could do.

Grabbing a clean towel from the cupboard she headed for the shower.

Beloved: Do not stare at me because I am dark. — SS [1:6]

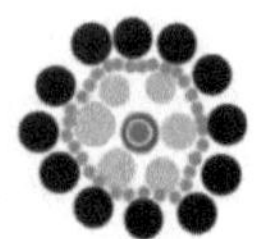

12: Leah

Leah lay in the darkness of her room on Wednesday night. This wasn't going to go away. The breast surgeon hadn't delayed and had booked her in for surgery on Friday morning. This was it. Leah lay stiff, staring up at the ceiling. Laughter from the shared nurses' lounge drifted up the passage. The TV from the room next door played the theme music from RPA.

Royal Prince Alfred Hospital. She liked the show.

Would her case make interesting viewing? Probably. Age twenty-three. No children. Breast cancer. That would do it.

Dr Jacobsen, her doctor, wasn't a likeable character. Hopefully, his surgical skills were better than his people skills.

He had thrown around options as if it were a menu. Did she want to start off with a lumpectomy? Or did she want to go for the mastectomy? Did she want the lump graded during the operation? They could proceed with a mastectomy then, if she liked. What about reconstructive surgery? Did she want that now, or did she want to wait?

It's probably just as well that he was so clinical. If he had been the warm fuzzy type she would have fallen in a heap. She had shrugged at the questions, putting most of the decisions back in his hands. Except for the reconstruction. Plastic surgery was just too much of an effort. She didn't even want to think about it, let alone have some doctor draw pictures all over her chest.

Her phone lay on the table next to her bed. There was one decision she still hadn't made. What should she tell Dimitri?

Beloved: I am darkened by the sun. — SS [1:6]

He must suspect something. Her messages were so brief. She shrugged. His phone was often out of range so there hadn't been a lot of contact anyhow. But he was back on Friday afternoon so he would have to know. What would he think of his girlfriend now?

Leah reached for her phone and found Abbey's number. She clenched her teeth. If her dad were more reliable, she wouldn't have to go through her stepfamily to contact him.

Her fingers hovered over the phone. What could she write?

She'd hardly spoken to anyone she knew. There'd been so many appointments and tests. It was hard enough coping with her own response; let alone dealing with anyone else's. Her nurse friends knew that she had a couple of days off sick. They probably thought she had a cold.

I wish.

Tomorrow night was the only night left to try to have a conversation with her dad. Leah wasn't convinced that Alison or Abbey would be overly warm with their sympathies. After all, they weren't blood.

'Hi Abbey, I need to catch up with my dad and, if possible, you and Alison as well. Sorry for the short notice but I have to do it by tomorrow night. Unless you message me that no one will be there, I'll come around after dinner; about seven. Cheers, Leah.'

It was no use inviting herself to dinner. Alison liked her routine and that didn't include Leah on a Thursday night.

Or any other night.

There was no use wasting energy being irritated. It didn't matter if Alison and Abbey hadn't welcomed her into their life. She couldn't really blame them. Alison had been a single mum. Raising Abbey on her own for most of her life had made the pair very close. They had no reason to welcome a virtual stranger into their family with open arms. Especially one that reminded Alison of her partner's ex-wife.

The rest of the evening was a haze; the next day more so. In Alison's lounge room the following night, Leah's generous feelings were challenged.

Abbey stared at Leah as if she had just announced that she had leprosy.

'Have you told that guy who's posting photos of himself in New Zealand on your page? What's his name? Dimitri?'

Beloved: I am darkened by the sun.   SS [1:6]

Leah glared at her step-sister. No privacy. 'No, I haven't told him. He's in a remote area at the moment. There's not much coverage out there.'

There was no need to justify it to Abbey.

It was herself she had tried to fool. The truth was, she had avoided Dimitri.

'Well, don't expect him to stick around.'

Leah gasped. Abbey's words peppered the doubt she already felt. 'What do you mean? Why wouldn't he?'

'Are you kidding? Guys only want one thing. If you've got bits missing ...'

'That's enough!'

Leah had never seen Alison so angry at her daughter.

'Apologise to Leah! That was uncalled for.'

Abbey lowered her eyes and muttered a strained, 'Sorry.'

Her step-mother's voice softened a little as she spoke to Leah. 'I'm sorry you had to hear that. And take no notice, it's not true.' Alison turned to Leah's dad. 'Isn't that right, Charlie?'

Leah watched for her father's reaction.

Please agree with Alison. Tell me how beautiful I am to you.

He turned away.

Why would he tell her that? He had walked away from her mum when she was most vulnerable.

Her eyes burned with the effort of blinking back tears. A spring of fury bubbled inside and she stood up. Had he deserted his wife because she had become so physically unattractive to him? It was something her mother had never known. But it was something she and Leah had both suspected.

Leah took a deep breath. She had to get out of there. She had only come because she felt she had to. The tiniest glimmer of hope that she had held for their support had flickered and died.

Abbey was right. Why should she expect Dimitri to hang around now?

This was something she would have to do on her own.

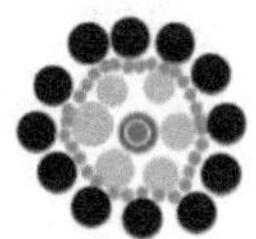

13: Leah

'Here you go, dear; it does up at the back. I'll pop back in a minute once you've finished.' The nurse scuttled from the room.

Leah picked up the white hospital gown from the bed. Between shaking hands and a brain befuddled by the incomprehensible pattern of press studs and ties, putting it on wasn't that easy. Thankfully, she had helped patients do theirs—in a past life. That's how it felt. The confident young midwife had vanished and now she was a 'dear.'

The nurse returned and straightened up the gown. 'Marvellous, well done. Now let's put your theatre cap on.'

I'm not a child.

Except that she was as powerless as a child. Since visiting her doctor, other people had taken over her life. She had seen radiographers, pathologists, receptionists, specialists, and now, hospital theatre staff.

'Sorry, lovey, but you'll have to tuck every bit of that hair under the elastic.' The nurse lifted the edges and slid the loose strands beneath the disposable cap.

Leah clamped down on her jaw. She may have to cope with hair loss. That would be almost as bad as losing her breast.

'There you go; lean back on the pillow now. The anaesthetist will be here in a minute to do a final check. Then Tim, our theatre orderly, will lead you through.'

She drew back the curtains from around the bed. 'It won't be long now.'

Beloved: I slept but my heart was awake. — SS 5:2

The nurse spun around, pushed open the double doors to the theatre and disappeared.

Leah shivered. This was totally impossible. She had landed in the same place as her mother. Her mum hadn't survived. She had gone through all this surgery. Chemo. Radiation. In the end, she had lost. They had both lost. Leah had been utterly robbed. All she wanted right now was for her mum to be here.

And Dimitri.

Eventually, she had sent him a message. 'Hi Dimitri, I have to go in on Friday for a routine test, just a woman's thing, nothing to worry about. See you soon, love Leah.'

Over the past three months, life had been amazing. He was amazing. But it wouldn't work. It couldn't work. Leah clenched her fist. She could still feel his hand, warm and strong over hers.

The chair next to the barouche was vacant. Somebody should be here. It was insane to go through such traumatic surgery with no one to support her. But there was no one.

Her father had turned away. He couldn't even bring himself to look her in the eye.

He failed her mum, now he'd bailed on her.

Leah pulled the sheet tight around her. She had left her stepfamily's house that night and stepped into the cold evening. Three cars sat in their driveway. Not one of her so-called family members had offered to drive her home.

The week had been so tough that her eyes still throbbed from crying. The bones around her eyes ached. Her skin stretched taut and dry over her face. But the tears had gone now.

Alison had called her the previous night, igniting a flicker of hope. Maybe she did have some support after all. 'When is the operation?'

'Nine a.m.'

'I just called to wish you good luck.'

Good luck? Leah had stared at her phone after she had hung up. Without any offer of support why had the woman bothered to call at all?

Leah brushed aside thoughts of the whole family experience. Negative thoughts were not what she needed right now.

Beloved: I slept but my heart was awake. — SS 5:2

60

'Hi Leah, I'm Dr Cheng.' A young doctor dressed in scrubs interrupted her musings. 'I'll be your anaesthetist this morning.'

She looked down where his hand touched her arm. Something so simple. Simple but exactly what she needed.

'I'm really sorry for what you have to go through.' His voice, confident and kind, helped soothe some of her distress. 'But I'm going to make this as easy as possible. I'll give you a pre-med to help you relax. In fact, you won't remember anything after that. The general anaesthetic will then follow.'

Over the next few hours, her life was in his hands. And the surgeon's.

Is that what she really believed? That's not how her mum had seen it. Her mum's faith wasn't perfect. 'Then it wouldn't be faith,' she had told Leah.

That's something I do have. Imperfect faith.

She wished she remembered something from going to church. But no prayers or verses came to mind. Except for the one Dimitri had sent to her phone.

She closed her eyes. *Love is stronger than death.*

The swing doors opened again and another man dressed in theatre garb came through. 'Hi Leah, I'm Tim, the orderly. They're ready for you now. Will you be alright to walk through?'

Leah nodded, and clutching the gown tightly around her, followed the orderly through the double doors. The theatre buzzed with voices and activity. She followed the orderly's instructions and climbed on to the table. The whole scene was surreal. It was better to close her eyes and block it all out. Once again she concentrated on the words. It was a new feeling. Saying a bible verse as if it were a prayer. She probably wasn't doing it right. But it's all she had to hang on to. Dr Cheng chatted to her as he took her hand. She winced as the needle penetrated a vein. The sting spread along the vessel as the medication dispersed.

'All done,' he said. 'Now count up to ten.'

'*Love is stronger…*'

Beloved: I slept but my heart was awake. — SS 5:2

61

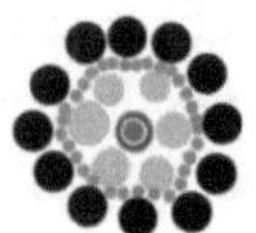

14: Leah

A hand gripped hold of her wrist. She couldn't shake it free. Her arm felt as if it weighed a tonne. She gritted her teeth and mustered up as much strength as she could and pulled. A stab of pain shot through her chest as her reward. 'Let go!'

Leah focussed. Someone was peering at her over a surgical mask. 'It's all over. Try to keep your hand still while I finish checking your pulse.'

Leah looked down at her arm. A bandaged splint protected an intravenous needle. No wonder she couldn't lift her arm.

The woman finished and laid Leah's hand back onto the bed. 'I'm Kate, your nurse for today. There's analgesia in your infusion.' She charted the pulse and clipped the file onto the bed frame. 'Your pain should ease now.'

Another stab of pain shot through Leah's chest, sucking the air from her. A groan escaped her lips.

When the wave subsided she lifted her fingers off the bed, hoping to trace the site of her pain. Where did it come from? What was she doing here? The intravenous line and attached splint were cumbersome, but she managed to lift up her hand. Her fingers crept across her upper body, over a wad of dressing. The curve of bandages extended around to her arm pit. Her fingers reached a plastic drainage tube that curled out of the dressing.

'No!'

Memories crashed through her dream-like state and her hand flopped back onto the bed.

Beloved: Listen! My beloved is knocking. — SS 5:2

Her sobs came without control. The barouche shook and rattled against the intravenous stand.

A hand pressed down on her shoulder. 'Leah, calm down, it's all right.'

It's not all right! How could something so small cause so much damage?

'I'll get you a blanket from the warmer.' The nurse's words swirled around her like a fog. 'That should make you feel a bit better.'

The warmth and pressure of the blanket seeped through her body and her muscles and mind relaxed. She slipped into a dream.

Dimitri's fingers curled around hers, drawing her away from the darkness. The cold, antiseptic environment receded and she inhaled the tangy scent of eucalyptus. With her hand warm inside his, she felt safe. He led her deeper into the Australian bushland. They traipsed beneath gum trees, their feet crunching over green and gold leaves. A kookaburra called out from a tree top. Another sang its reply. Leah zoned into their melody and her inner voices grew quiet. The choir of magpies, lorikeets and countless insects soothed her chaos. Dimitri held back low branches and shrubs for her as they wandered deeper into the wilderness. The air gradually thickened with heat and Leah let go of Dimitri's hand.

'Let's stop for a minute,' she suggested, 'and catch our breath.'

They stood shoulder to shoulder. She smiled up at him. Could he hear the pounding of her heart? After a few moments its rate settled, and the thumping quietened. Sweat trickled down the back of her neck, and her shirt clung to her back and chest. The damp was both uncomfortable and pleasant at the same time. This is where she belonged, not the air-conditioning softness of the city.

The city? Her stomach tightened. What was the matter with her? Why should that thought unsettle her? That's crazy. She ran her tongue over her gums. How had she allowed herself to become so dehydrated? She looked down at her hip. Where was her water bag? A ripple of panic came over her. No one went bushwalking without water.

Dimitri held out his bottle for her to share. She stretched out her hand, but she couldn't reach it. *Ridiculous.* The bottle was right there, but she couldn't grab it. Without moisture on her lips she couldn't even tell him what was wrong.

Beloved: Listen! My beloved is knocking. — SS 5:2

Dimitri stepped close and wrapped his arms around her. Her concern over her water vanished. He held her against his chest and then lifted her face close to his. In the darkness of his eyes, she read his harnessed passion. He bent close and their lips touched. Lush warmth suffused her body. Within moments, the warmth grew fiery but her pleasure vanished. Her chest throbbed with pain. Her mind raged with fear and confusion.

She looked around her. When had the darkness settled in? Someone pulled at her, dragging her from Dimitri's arms. He grew smaller and further away and the darkness swallowed him up. Her eyes ached and she pushed against her eyelids.

A nurse stood fiddling with her drip. Her white shirt with its blue pinstripes, and navy pants, identified her as a Ward nurse. So, she was out of Recovery.

An enormous display of bush flowers, interspersed with eucalyptus leaves, decorated a table near the window. 'No wonder I dreamt we were out bushwalking,' she murmured.

'Their smell certainly fills the room.'

Just out of reach, on the over way table, Leah spotted a glass with ice chips and a spoon. 'Nurse, can you please pass me the ice?'

She ran her tongue over her lips with the anticipation of relief.

'Good girl, I did try to give you some a minute ago, but off you went, back to sleep again.'

The nurse washed and dried her hands. 'I'm Eileen and I'll be looking after you today. Here you go.' Eileen pushed the table closer and handed Leah the glass. 'Try to keep your fluids up. The sooner we get you rehydrated the sooner we can take this drip out. I'm sure it's not that comfortable.'

Within seconds the ice water soaked into Leah's lips and mouth, bringing relief.

'Oh and here's the gift card from the flowers.' Eileen passed her the tiny card.

Without reading it, Leah knew they were from Dimitri. Clearly he had tracked her down, ignoring her attempt to play down her message: 'minor procedure.'

Beloved: Listen! My beloved is knocking. — SS ^{5:2}

A buzzer sounded out in the passage. 'I'll be back a bit later,' Eileen said, 'but just buzz if you need me.'

'Thanks.'

Alone, Leah turned over the card.

Love burns like a blazing fire, Dimitri xxx.

Leah gazed at the burnt orange and red bush flowers. She muttered the next part of that verse, *'Love burns like a mighty flame.'*

Could she dare believe him? She looked out at the dusk tinged clouds. Dimitri would be back by now, and she would have to tell him the truth.

Warm tears pooled in her eyes and the view became blurred. He could never love her the way she needed him to. Not now, not once he knew about … Leah choked back a lump that pushed against her throat.

Love is as strong as death.

Her tears spilt over and trickled down her cheeks. Reaching for a tissue, her hand shot to her side.

What did it matter how strong love was? It didn't mean *their* love was strong. Her parents' certainly wasn't. She had enough heartbreak to face. Testing the durability of a new relationship was something she couldn't … *wouldn't* … attempt. The card slipped to the floor.

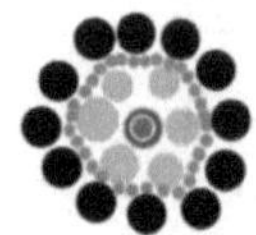

15: Dimitri

The seat belt sign beeped and the symbol switched from closed to open. All along the plane passengers unlocked their belts and stood up. Dimitri was trapped in the window seat. Rick was one of those guys who waited for the rush to ease before moving. They were going nowhere fast.

He looked out onto the tarmac of the Adelaide Airport. New Zealand had been breathtaking, but after Leah's message he just wanted to get home.

'Are you okay?' Angie had asked him.

He knew his face had probably gone pale.

'Leah's in hospital.'

'No! What happened?'

'I don't really know.' He read the message again. 'All she's said is that it's a woman's thing.' He looked up at Angie. 'What does that mean?'

He knew nothing about women's health. It wasn't something he'd ever had to think about before.

'I guess it could be any number of things. What does she say exactly?'

He read it out to her and scanned Angie's face hoping for an explanation. 'Do you have any idea what that could be about?'

'Well, it could be just about anything. Women's health issues can be very minor to serious. I wish I could be more helpful, Dimitri, but Leah isn't giving much away.'

'What do you mean by serious?'

'Look, it's no good torturing yourself. You'll soon be able to find out.' Angie looked him in the eye. 'You should send flowers.'

Lover: 'Open to me, my sister, my darling.' — SS 5:2

'I have.' Dimitri nodded. He could see Angie's sudden small start, as if he had surprised her. *I just hope I sent them to the right place. But Leah works at Queen Adelaide, and without a car, it makes sense she would choose someplace close.* 'But I'm worried no one is with her. I should have been there.'

'It can't be helped. I'm sure she's got her family or friends with her.'

He had stayed awake most of the night. From what Leah had shared, her family wouldn't exactly rally round her. He didn't really know her friends. Most of them were nursing or midwifery students. Between study and shift work they didn't have a lot of spare time. All those abrupt messages now made sense. He had convinced himself he had freaked her out at the dinner.

I mean, who messages poetry to their girlfriend?

But the *Song of Songs* had brought them together. It had seemed so appropriate. And it reflected what he believed about love.

He could sense her hesitancy. Had felt it long before the restaurant. She was scared they would end up like her parents. They wouldn't. He was one hundred percent certain of that, and was so relieved when Leah had decided to give it a try.

He looked at Angie. She had been a supportive companion to Rick on this trip. If he and Leah could have a relationship half as good as theirs, it would be fantastic. He switched his phone on as he waited for the aisle to clear.

'I'm sure you'll hear from her.' Angie smiled at him. He looked up. What was it that made him so readable to people?

They made their way to the exit stairs of the plane. Dimitri clutched his jacket across his chest against the wind and descended with care. As he made his way across the tarmac between two giant aircraft, he avoided looking up at the terminal windows. He tried to push away the thought Leah might be waiting to pick him up. It was a ridiculous thought; she hadn't asked him any of his flight details. And she was probably recovering from whatever was wrong.

He followed Rick and Angie to the luggage carousel with one eye on his phone. Finally, it connected.

'Come on you guys, our gear is coming.' Rick was waiting near the conveyor.

'We'll get you back as soon as we can.' Angie tried to reassure him. 'Even

Lover: 'Open to me, my sister, my darling.' — SS ^{5:2}

if you don't make visiting hours, you should be able to speak to someone.'

'I'll grab my luggage, then send a quick reply. If Leah's not too sick, she might get the chance to check her phone.'

He had no idea what the test entailed. Perhaps it was just a couple of hours and she would be home again. He tried to stop his racing thoughts. As Angie said, there was no use attempting to second guess anything.

He scooped up his bag as it drew near and between the three of them they collected all their photography equipment. The trip had been one of the best ever and he couldn't wait to work on some of the photos.

Once settled in a taxi, Dimitri tapped a brief message into his phone. 'Don't forget we're here,' Angie said. 'If there's anything we can do.'

Dimitri nodded but hoped he wouldn't have to call on anyone.

The taxi pulled up outside his apartment.

At last! The amount of road works, detours and traffic jams they had negotiated had been excruciating. Just when his own street lay ahead, the police had waved the taxi into a random breathtesting station. By the time he got himself over to the hospital, visiting hours would definitely be over.

'We're praying for you, mate.' Rick stepped out of the taxi to help him with his gear. 'Don't forget, give us a ring if you need us, okay?'

'Thanks.' Dimitri forced a smile. Rick had become more like a friend than a boss and he was very grateful for his support. Angie wound the car window down. 'Please pass on our love to Leah.'

'Sure thing.'

As the taxi pulled away, Dimitri lugged his bag, tripod and cameras up the stairs to his first-floor apartment. He dropped the travel bag and retrieved the key from his pocket. After having been away for most of the week, he opened the door to a place that was dark and musty. Just like his mood.

Leah hadn't responded to his message. Surely if the test had been that minor she would have had her phone on by now?

The light on the answering machine flickered against the dimness. His heart lifted. Then doubt set in. *Why would Leah leave a message on his landline?*

Easing off the camera straps he placed his equipment on the lounge suite and opened up the curtains. The fading daylight brightened the room a little. Dimitri looked at the answering machine and tried to think positive.

Lover: 'Open to me, my sister, my darling.' — SS ^{5:2}

He pushed *Play*, but when a male voice boomed from the tape, his heart sank.

'Hi, this is Mullaya from the Department of Aboriginal Reconnections. Could Dimitrios Kostos please call me on 82512098?'

A series of beeps followed and the light disappeared. One call! He replayed the message and scribbled down the number. It was undoubtedly a follow-up call to the Bilyja assignment.

He needed to find Leah. Picking up his mobile, he scrolled through his contacts for her work number. Her graduate year placement was in the Queen Adelaide Hospital. Although she worked mainly in the Maternity Ward, they had a General section there as well. It was as good as any place to start to locate her.

'You have called the Queen Adelaide Hospital. All our operators are busy at the moment. Please hold until we attend to your call.'

'Grr!' He pressed the speaker button and classical music filled his apartment. He went to the fridge. It might be a bit cool out there, but he hadn't had anything to eat or drink since before boarding the budget flight back to Australia. A solitary bottle of orange juice sat in the fridge door. He picked it up. 'Expired orange juice.'

He tipped it down the sink and turned the tap on to rinse it out. 'Oh!' Water bounced off the top of the bottle and sprayed the sink, the tiles and went all down his top. He spun around to grab a tea towel when a voice broke through the music.

'Queen Adelaide Hospital.' A nasal, bored tone didn't suggest he should expect too much information.

'Yes, do you have a patient there called Leah McEwen?'

'Maternity or General?'

'General. I think.'

'You think?'

I don't know! It's a women's thing. Does Maternity deal with those things as well?

He sighed. 'Yes, sorry. General.'

'Public or private?' the bored voice demanded.

You're kidding me!

Lover: 'Open to me, my sister, my darling.' — SS 5:2

He racked his brains trying to remember anything that Leah had told him about the different sections. To him, a hospital was just a hospital. He knew Leah worked in Maternity, but she had done a rotation through General. Wasn't the private section the one she had come home complaining about? Yes, he remembered now. She had been run ragged by answering the buzzers of wealthy female patients who had come in for a 'nip and tuck'.

'Give me a heart patient any day,' she had told him.

It's pretty unlikely she would go in for plastic surgery!

'Public or private?' the woman repeated.

'Public.' *Whatever happened to computers?*

'Wrong. Leah McEwen is in private. I'll put you through.'

Before he could respond, recorded music pumped into his ear again.

He rested the phone on the desk while he waited and flicked through a pile of unopened mail. Clearly Leah had been over to collect it for him for a couple of days at least.

Until she got sick?

An envelope with a logo he didn't recognise caught his attention. Surrounding a line of brightly coloured stick figures he read, 'Department of Aboriginal Reconnections.' He shrugged and tossed the letter back onto the pile. Probably a newsletter from Bilyja.

He tapped his fingers on the desk as he continued to hold. His eyes spotted a message on a sticky note. How could he have missed Leah's neat print!

'Mullaya, Dept. Aboriginal Reconnections called: 82512098. Love you, L xxx.'

That didn't sound like someone who wanted to break if off! Or who was really sick.

'Are you there?' The same bored voice returned to the line. 'Leah McEwen is in the Private Ward, Room 501. Unless you are her next of kin, it's too late to speak to her or to visit until tomorrow. Are you her next of kin?'

I wish.

He could always lie. But what was the use?

'No, just a friend.' *Just a friend? She's the person I love most in the whole world.* 'Thanks for your help.' He hung up. Would Leah have any next of kin visit her today? His heart broke as he visualised her, scared and alone. To think the test could be serious was more than he could bear.

The landline rang, interrupting his thoughts. Hardly anyone called him on this phone. Aunt Elpida had insisted he install it. She didn't believe in mobiles. Cost too much. He really didn't feel like speaking to her right now.

After a few rings, it went to voice mail and the same deep voice he had heard earlier spoke into the machine. 'Hi, this is Mullaya again from the Department of Reconnections. Could Dimitrios Kostos please give me a call on 8…?'

Now he was curious. Two calls, and probably that envelope, from that Department. Obviously they wanted something. He lifted the receiver. 'Hello, this is Dimitri.'

'Dimitrios Wareen Kostos?' Mullaya asked.

No one knew his middle name. Except for Aunt Elpida, and she no longer counted. He had no idea what she knew and couldn't trust if what she said was correct. He hadn't even known his full name until he received that birth certificate. He cringed at the mispronunciation of his middle name. Just because it had been misspelt like that on his birth certificate didn't mean you couldn't figure out how to pronounce it. How could you get Wareen muddled up with Warren?

'Who gave you my personal details?' he snapped.

'I'm really sorry to call you out of hours, but we've tried to reach you a number of times.'

'Mm.'

'We've been contacted by an Aboriginal woman who is trying to locate a relative.'

'Uh uh.' He shrugged, attention already wandering. *I wonder if there's a pizza in the freezer.*

'According to records, your mother, may be this woman's sister.'

Lover: 'Open to me, my sister, my darling.' — SS 5:2

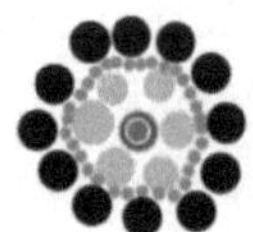

16: Dimitri

'Excuse me?' He reached for the back of the chair to steady himself.

'I know this must sound pretty strange to you…'

'Pretty strange? This is impossible!'

'Look, I know this is sudden. It would be much easier if we could talk in person. Could we make an appoin …?'

'My mother's dead.'

There was silence on the other end of the phone for a moment before Mullaya responded. 'We did know this and I'm really sorry.' His tone sounded respectful. 'We wouldn't have disturbed you, if it weren't important.'

'This is ridiculous! Did you say you're from an Aboriginal Department?'

'I am, but please Mr Kostos …'

'My family's *Greek*!'

'Please! I think it's important that we talk face to face.'

Dimitri paced around the room with the cordless phone against his ear. The neat package of grief he had tucked away since he was three years old— or *six* years old—began to unravel and his hand shook against the receiver.

'We don't have a lot of information,' Mullaya went on. 'This woman, Lucy Nader, has spent years trying to locate her sister and her search has led her to this point. If you could come in, we could go over some of her findings.' There was a pause. 'We can meet without Lucy, until we know if we have anything to offer her.'

Drained, exhausted. That's how he felt. He just wanted to get off the

Lover: my dove, my flawless one. — SS [5:2]

phone. He was sure this was just a waste of time. Best to agree so he could hang up. 'Okay, I'll give it a go.'

'That's great. How about this coming Tuesday? One thirty?'

'Yeah, all right. Where's your office?' He flicked open a notebook and jotted down the details. He could decide later whether or not to attend.

'We'll see you Tuesday afternoon then. Thank you, Mr Kostos.'

Dimitri returned the phone to its base and glanced down at the smooth olive complexion of his hands. *Aboriginal descent?!*

He knew absolutely nothing about his mother. Could it possibly be true? Could he be Aboriginal? Had Yaya and Papou disapproved of his parents' marriage, and then kept him away from his mother's people? He shook his head in disbelief. His mother had no family. That's what he had been told.

He retrieved a glass from the cupboard and filled it with tap water.

Nothing about this day had gone the way he had planned. Aboriginal Departments? Private Wards?

He was tired. Jet lagged. He just needed to sleep and he'd wake up back into his predictable, familiar world.

Lover: my dove, my flawless one. — SS [5:2]

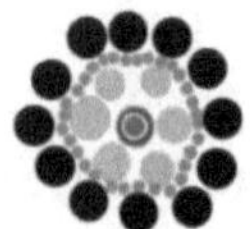

17: Dimitri

Dimitri looked up at the number on the door half way down the ward. He still found it hard to believe Leah was in hospital. Before he left for New Zealand, she had been fine.

'Whoa! Sorry.' Distracted by racing thoughts he almost stumbled into the nurse coming out.

'Leah's sleeping,' she whispered. 'Try not to disturb her.'

He nodded and paused with his hand on the handle. He slowed his breathing. He had to focus. Forget his own news. He was here for Leah.

He tiptoed into the room.

She looks terrible!

Lying still with her eyes shut, her pale face blended in with the starched linen. Strands of her long, dark hair lay matted and unkempt on either side of her.

'What's happened to you?' His whisper caught in his throat. He stepped closer and rested his hand over hers.

The door opened and he looked over his shoulder. The nurse pumped aqua gel onto her hands and came close to the bed. She stood observing Leah while massaging the alcohol cleanser between her fingers. 'It's a wonder this smell doesn't wake her.'

Dimitri hadn't really noticed the antiseptic smell. He hadn't noticed much at all. Except for how pale and tired Leah looked.

'Okay, all done.' The nurse pulled on a pair of gloves. 'I'll need to move past you to check Leah's drain. It's right where you're standing, near her chest.'

Beloved: I have taken off my robe — SS 5:3

A drain near her chest? Leah doesn't have lung trouble. Why does she need a drain near her chest? He stepped back to give the nurse space but held onto Leah's hand.

With her back to him, the nurse blocked his view as she lifted up the blanket. Leah's eyelids fluttered. They opened and her velvet brown eyes looked straight into his. She looked down at their hands and squeezed his very gently.

'The wound looks fine,' the nurse looked at Leah. 'You'll feel like a new woman in no time.'

A thought flashed through Dimitri's mind and his words tumbled out. 'You haven't had chest surgery, but breast surgery!'

Leah pulled her hand away, colour flushing her face. 'Yes, breast surgery! Unspeakable, isn't it?'

Dimitri stared at her, then down at his empty hand. 'I'm so … rry. I didn't mean …' he stammered.

'Forget it,' Leah cut him off. 'I'm the one who's sorry; this just isn't going to work.' Her voice shook and he strained to hear her. 'Nothing is the same now.'

'What do you mean? You're not making sense.' He turned to the nurse. 'What's happened here?'

'*No!*'

Leah spat the word out. She clearly didn't want the nurse to discuss her health with him. He couldn't care less about the details of her surgery. He just wanted her to recover.

'Please just go.' It was more like a whimper than a command.

'I'm not going anywhere.' Dimitri reached out for her hand but she shook it off. She turned her body away, rolling over to face the window.

'It's over.'

It's over?

'You're crying, Leah, you can't possibly mean this.' He rested his hand gently on her shoulder, but she shook it off again. She pulled the blanket tighter around her.

'Please tell me what's going on,' he begged. 'You know how much I love you. I can't bear to see you like this.'

Beloved: I have taken off my robe — SS 5:3

'Please make this easier.' She mumbled into the blanket. 'Go now.'

'She really does need her rest.'

He had forgotten the nurse was standing there, taking it all in.

He hesitated. *There's no way she means this.*

'It's all over.' Leah's voice travelled as if across a storm. 'Don't come back, Dim ...' Her voice broke.

Dim? Had she meant to call him that? Suddenly it wasn't Leah's face in front of him. It was Chiara's. He was fourteen again, and his older girlfriend was taunting him as she broke it off. 'Dim, that's what you are. I get it now why they call you and your best buddy, "Dim and Dumb". Why can't you get the picture, Dim? Go away and don't come back.'

He turned to look at the door and wondered if his legs could even carry him there. He reached the handle and looked back. Leah remained rigid, facing the window.

He left. As he made his way back along the corridor, he grasped the side rail. *What had just happened?* He couldn't believe it. She had just thrown him out. Has she found someone else? Just like Chiara had?

He approached a bend in the passage and glanced up at the mirror protecting a blind corner. Was that his reflection? Wild black curls framed his tanned face while dark eyes peered back at him. Could his features be anything other than Greek? Could he be Aboriginal as well? Impossible! Uncle Spiros and Yaya always said he looked just like his father.

What if he were Aboriginal? Had Mullaya said something to Leah when he left his message?

Did that change how she felt about him?

That's just one more insane thought. But nothing made sense. Nothing was logical.

This is ridiculous; government departments don't give out personal information. Anyway, it would be so out of character for Leah to reject him on the basis of race!

He reached the lift and pressed the button hard. Too impatient to wait for it, he looked around for the stairs. Pushing the door open he entered the stairwell and with rage ripping through the numbness of shock, he flew

Beloved: I have taken off my robe — SS [53]

down the steps.

What did he really know about Leah's character? Wasting time and money on cosmetic surgery! Did she think she would impress him by altering her appearance? Or maybe it was the new boyfriend?

A lump rose in his throat and he tried to slow his breathing. Leah was so beautiful. Surely she knew that? She was everything to him. From the moment he had seen her in Biljya, he knew there was no one else for him.

He fought down his sadness; it was easier to be angry. Clearly he was not the man she wanted. It was always the same. Always had been. Chiara was the worst, but she hadn't been the only one. Every girl he'd ever been interested in had rejected him as soon as it got serious.

Dark emotions gathered in his mind and he tried to slam a lid on them. The phone call was bad enough. Then the pain of his family's lie bubbled to the surface. Little pockets of grief burst open. Leah's rejection added fire to his sense of loss.

Stop it! Stop feeling sorry for yourself.

He pulled the door to the foyer open with a savage jerk. 'Not good enough for you, Leah McEwen? I'm off!'

Beloved: 1 have taken off my robe — SS [53]

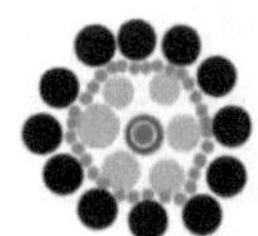

18: Leah

Leah leaned back against the pillow and closed her eyes. She was entirely spent. For over twenty-four hours, she had replayed the altercation with Dimitri. Yet it was useless to keep thinking about it. Hadn't she got what she wanted? He had stayed away.

Then why do I miss him so much?

In the corridor, muffled voices and the shuffling sound of many feet moved closer to her room. *That's Dr Jacobsen's monotone.* She pitied the poor medical students following him on his round. Her surgeon was abrupt and failed to invite questions. That had been fine with her. The less she knew, the less she had to think about.

Leah tightened her lips. That was okay before the surgery. But it was different now. Everything was different. She needed to know what he had found. And what they were going to do about it.

Her heart thumped hard against her chest and beads of sweat gathered on her brow. She reached for her glass and almost toppled it off the bedside locker. Gripping it with two hands, she managed to lift it to her lips and moisten her mouth. She leaned back on the pillow yet again. Even simple tasks sapped her energy.

Leah cast her eyes over her room. Clean and modern. The privacy was really an illusion. It would be shattered any moment now. As part of a teaching hospital, even private patients were the subject of group discussions. She wasn't really a private patient anyhow. It wasn't affordable on her income. She was just fortunate the hospital provided this option for their own staff.

Beloved: must I put it on again? — SS [53]

The muffled tones cleared, heralding the team's arrival outside her door. Her body trembled and she clutched the blanket closer to her chest. What she wouldn't give to vanish right now.

The door swung open and her room swelled with a crowd of innocent-faced aspiring medicos. She focussed her attention on the specialist who acknowledged her with a nod. He turned his back and faced his students. Leah swallowed back a wave of irritation. Not the friendliest of doctors!

Focussing on the back of his balding head, she avoided eye contact with anyone else. His monotone continued as he gave a rundown on the implications of breast cancer for younger women. Her stomach gripped with annoyance as much as anxiety.

He flicked through pages of her medical file with careless ease. How could he be so flippant? Those pages described her. It wasn't a work of fiction or an academic paper. This was all about her and her life. Closing her eyes, she tried to retreat from the scene. A few moments passed and the page-turning stopped. An eerie feeling hung over the room and she opened her eyes. All fidgeting by the students had ceased.

The doctor held the pathology report and without a trace of emotion, he studied the results. Every muscle in her body tensed. That flimsy piece of paper detailed her biopsy results.

She pulled the blanket up around her shoulders. For over twenty-four hours, an insistent voice had competed for her attention over all thoughts of Dimitri. It screamed at her now.

You have lymph node involvement.

Her pulse throbbed beneath her wound. The extensive dressings could mean nothing else. What she was about to discover was how much.

Multiple pairs of eyes burned through her silence, watching for her response. *You can't disclose these to me in front of a crowd. Please, don't be so callous.*

'Excuse me.' Leah licked her lips, her voice cracking. 'Wh … wh … what was that?'

'I'm sorry,' the dispassionate surgeon repeated, 'multiple lymph nodes were affected, so we had to remove your entire breast, including all the lymph glands. We'll try chemo and maybe some radiotherapy as well.'

Beloved: must I put it on again? — SS [53]

She looked down at her hand. His fingers barely touched her skin as he patted it. With a watery smile he added, 'Let's hope we've got it all.'

A rush of blood pumped through her ears and explosions clapped inside her head. Bile rose from her stomach and she stared at him, unable to believe his insipid attempt at comfort and reassurance. He averted his eyes and turned back to the group. His tedious voice picked up his lecture.

Each word pierced her like a spear as he went on and on. Leah could hardly believe it. He said something about the size of the tumour and the grade of cancer. His message jumbled around in her brain and he might as well be speaking another language. Acid burned her throat and she had no hope of verbalising any questions.

Leah felt sure that less than a minute had passed before the group turned away and traipsed out of the room. Less than a minute to turn her life upside down. She stared at the door left ajar. What did she expect? That one of the students would stay behind to hold her, and to help gather up the pieces of her shattered hope?

Where is Dimitri? What on earth have I done?

Beloved: must I put it on again? — SS ^{5:3}

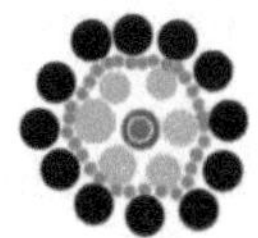

19: Leah

'You can't go home on your own.'

Leah stopped. Those nurses had eyes everywhere. Did she really think she could just stroll out of the ward? Plastering on a smile, she turned around. 'The doctor said I was well enough to go.'

Eileen leaned over the counter of the nurses' station. 'Oh, did he just?'

Leah felt herself relax slightly. This nurse had been kind to her. With her British Liverpool accent and gentle humour, she had lightened the trauma of her hospital stay.

'And did he ask who you're going home to? Or how you'll be getting yourself there?'

Leah stiffened again. 'It's all good. My friends will look out for me.'

'And these are your nursing friends? The ones who come and go in the Nurses' Home?'

You know very well that they do. Don't you think I don't know how crazy this is?

Leah tried to hold her own as she stared straight into the nurse's eyes. Discharge planning was such a nurse thing to do. At Uni, she had to do a whole assignment on it. Now she was on the receiving end. *Don't they get it?* These questions were designed to create a care plan. All they did was show up the holes. Her student accommodation was a terrible option for post-operative recovery. Especially for health needs as serious as hers. Her friends were great but they were hardly ever there.

Beloved: I have washed my feet — SS[53]

Leah continued to glare. If she acted strong, maybe she would become strong. Eileen waited for her response. After a minute Leah shrugged. 'There's no room at my dad and his partner's house.' The truth was she hadn't been invited. And if she had, she wouldn't have gone anyway. Leah sighed and lowered her eyes. 'You've met my dad.'

'I sure did.'

Her face flushed. All the staff would have heard about her dad by now. He had only visited once, and that was enough. He had staggered down the hospital corridor in an alcoholic state, yelling out her name. How grateful she had been that Security had arrived within moments and removed him.

'You're right, lovey. Keep away from him just now. I just wish you wouldn't be leaving here on your own.'

'I'm used to it.' At least she had been until Dimitri came into her life. Leah straightened her shoulders. She didn't need help from him. 'Thanks for all your help, Eileen. If I ever get past this graduate year, I hope I'll be as good a midwife as you are a nurse.'

'Of course you'll get through this year! You've already overcome so much in your life, and with more strength than some people twice your age.'

The phone rang and Eileen turned around to answer it. Leah took the opportunity to head towards the exit. When the outside doors slid open, the air refreshed her face. Out of her cocoon and back into the real world.

Except that I'm minus a breast.

Leah moved towards the taxi rank but after a couple of steps everything around her began to spin. She dropped her backpack and reached out to the post to steady herself.

'You don't think you were going to escape that easily?' Eileen's voice came from behind. The nurse's arm felt strong and warm as she braced Leah's back and healthy shoulder. 'I'm sorry I can't be taking you home. Unfortunately, it's not in my job description. I can help you into the taxi, though.'

Leah allowed herself to be steered toward the front of the queue of taxis.

'Don't you go forgetting you've had a general anaesthetic. That's enough to be knocking you out. And that's beside the surgery.'

Leah hadn't realized that she might feel a bit light-headed simply because of the anaesthetic.

Beloved: I have washed my feet — SS[53]

'Do you have a driver's licence?'

Leah nodded. 'Well, don't you be thinking of driving. It takes about six weeks for it to be gone from your body.'

Her finances hadn't stretched to a car yet, so that wouldn't be a problem. Pain still throbbed along her arm so she couldn't imagine herself driving anyway.

Eileen helped her into the taxi and stretched the seatbelt out and across her body. 'Make sure you keep your arm up on the pillow.'

Stop fussing, Leah felt like saying. *That's what my mother is for …* She blinked back the tears.

Eileen lowered her voice and spoke gently. 'When you come back for your follow-up appointments, make sure you drop into the ward. I want to see how you're getting on.'

Not trusting herself to reply, Leah just nodded.

'To the nurses' accommodation,' Eileen told the driver. He grunted. It was less than a block away, but it was the only way Leah could get there. With a brief smile at Leah, Eileen closed the door and waved.

As the driver pulled out of the rank, Leah said, 'Glenelg beach, please.'

The driver looked up into the rear vision mirror. 'Are you sure? You don't seem like you're up to a trip to the beach.'

'I'm sure.' She leaned back onto the headrest and closed her eyes.

Glenelg was their special place. Maybe if she went back to what she knew from before, everything would feel okay. Even behind closed eyes her world felt woozy. She knew she wasn't thinking straight. But she needed to be somewhere that was life-giving.

Leah opened her eyes again. How awful if she were to be car sick! When the taxi approached the beachfront, the sea didn't look very inviting. Its grey waves and frothy caps forewarned her of the bite to the air, yet it was perfect. The power of the sea was the change in its moods. And today's mirrored hers exactly. The taxi slowed to a halt, the driver doing his best to drop her close to the walkway.

Leah shuffled along the jetty, holding onto the rail. The wind beat against her body with such ferocity, she could barely stay upright. Her eyes watered from the air as much as they did from grief. Her tears felt good,

Beloved: I have washed my feet — SS[53]

tumbling freely down her cheeks, bothering no one. At the end of the jetty, a family gathered around a fishing rod and bucket, congratulating each other with their catch.

Barely a week ago, she had envisaged a future like that with Dimitri.

Leah's nose ran and her eyes ached. Her mind raced with questions. Should she have called Dimitri from the hospital? Would he have come back? Had she been the stubborn one?

She reached into her pocket and pulled out her mobile.

A few taps on the screen and they would connect. But why would he respond now? He'd made no effort so far. Didn't this prove her point? He wanted nothing to do with her.

Rage erupted from a place so deep it scared her. One tiny, treacherous lump had led to all this! Cancer had crept not only into her breast but to every part of her life. Just as it had stolen her mother, it had stolen Dimitri.

No, it hadn't. He had turned and fled!

She knew her anger was irrational but she didn't care. She grasped the rail as fury seized her. Down below, the waves rose and crashed, releasing their passion against the wooden posts.

Leah held the phone tight against her palm. Drawing back her arm, she aimed the phone at the crest of an incoming wave and hurled it into the ocean.

Her link with Dimitri was now severed. Leah turned away from the stunned family and dragged her feet back down the jetty.

Beloved: I have washed my feet — SS[53]

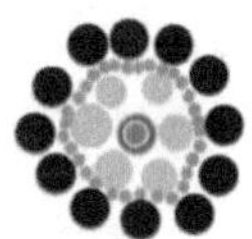

20: Dimitri

Dimitri held the photographic paper up to the safety light in Rick's dark room. He winced and tossed it onto the pile of rejects. So much for the thrill of watching his subject emerge onto the paper. The quality was shocking. Just like all the others. The only image he could produce was in his mind. There was Leah, ghostly pale, blending into the hospital linen.

He looked down at his gloved hand. It might be covered, but the bare, empty feeling where she had snatched her hand from his was still there.

He picked up another negative and slid it into the tray. He stared at the second hand sweeping the timer. The endless replay cycle in his mind was stuck on Leah's parting words. 'It's all over, Dimitri. Please don't come back …'

In his dreams, she wasn't in hospital. She was in a crop duster. 'Run, Mitri,' she cried. 'Don't forget the wombat. Please don't come back.' Then the plane had exploded. Those last moments with her had become tangled with his final memories of his parents.

Glancing down at the picture, he groaned. The ranges deserved better subtlety and contrast in colour. Getting up at dawn to capture the light should have been worth his while.

He reached up, pulled on the cord and the dark room became flooded with light. This is why computer programs were invented. Despite his muddled thoughts, he grinned. His digital camera could never produce that satisfying smell whenever he opened a fresh tub of film.

He leaned back in his chair.

Beloved: My lover thrust his hand through the latch-opening — SS 5:4

'Please don't come back.' The more he thought about it, the more he was sure Leah's eyes weren't saying the same as her lips. But where did her heart lie? With her eyes or her lips?

He slid back the chair and stood up. He was tired of the inner arguments. It was over, and he probably would never find out why. He hadn't called her. Not for a week, anyhow. But it was too late by then. He didn't blame her for not answering.

She could have called you.

'Stop it! '

The room he loved closed in on him and he had to get out. As he peeled back his gloves and snatched off his face mask, the acrid and metallic odour swept up his nose. He pushed open the black door and stepped into clean air.

He slid open the window behind Rick's desk. He'd felt a deep sense of satisfaction when Rick had given him a key to his suburban sandstone studio. It had almost soothed the ache in his heart. *Almost.*

Please don't come back.

The morning sun had already warmed the glass and it relieved his cold hands. A neighbour revved up his car and pulled out of the driveway. A pair of magpies warbled out to each other from the gums on either side of the street. It was time he stepped out of his own little world.

The phone rang and he jumped. Talk about getting lost in his own world! Phones, making him jump! He stared at it. What if it was … it couldn't be … don't be stupid. She doesn't have this number. *But she knows I'm apprenticed to Rick …*

He settled his breath and resolved to keep his voice steady. 'Hello?'

'Hey Dimitri, how's it goin'? Got yourself a nice sunrise yet?'

'Still working on it.'

'What's the matter, mate?'

Dimitri sighed. Trust Rick to pick up on his mood straight away.

'How's Leah?' Rick pressed on. 'Angie tells me she invited you both to dinner but she hasn't heard from either of you. And you haven't answered any of my texts. Is everything okay?'

'I'm okay but …' He knew he may as well tell Rick the truth. Get it over with. 'Leah and I have… we're not seeing each other any more. It seems like I've blown it.'

'I'm sorry to hear this, really, but ...' Rick sounded hesitant. 'Well, it may just work out to your benefit. I wasn't going to offer this to you because of Leah, but ... well...'

Dimitri waited.

'*Outback Tours* were really happy with our landscape work in Bilyja. They've offered us a bigger contract. They want more photos for their tourist brochures and stuff. We gotta go up way past the Flinders Ranges, deep into bushland.' Rick sounded almost boyishly enthusiastic as he warmed to the idea. 'To do the job properly we need to stay up there for a decent time. Maybe even for a couple of months. Angie's coming and can help with some of the equipment. I think it would be good for your portfolio.'

He said nothing. This offer should have really excited him. To go bush and rough it; sleeping under the stars and all that. That was heaven. But he felt nothing.

He only half-listened to Rick explaining the details of the contract. He picked up a framed picture of himself with Leah at Glenelg Beach. Her wind-blown hair swept across his face and he heard his own laughter as she protested to Rick she wasn't ready for the take. The day had been freezing and the wind crazy. He could taste the salt in the air as the waves sprayed their foam against the jetty.

'You got all that?' Rick concluded his monologue.

'Yes, yes of course.' Dimitri replaced the picture and grabbed a pen. 'Just wait a minute and I'll find something to write on.'

He rummaged around in his backpack and pulled out a small notepad. The first page had a date and time scribbled across it. His appointment with that social worker! He'd clean forgotten it. He flipped open to a new page and forced himself to concentrate on Rick's instructions. He jotted down the details. 'I need to attend to some business first. But then, sure, count me in.'

'Yeah, all right mate, but we need to be ready to leave first thing Saturday morning.'

'No worries.' Dimitri hung up.

A breeze tiptoed through the slight opening of the window, playing with the skin on the back of his neck. At the same time, he experienced a strange stirring in his spirit. He picked up the photo again and this time looked into his own rich brown eyes.

'Could it be true?' he whispered. 'Was my mother Aboriginal?'

He replaced the photo and reached for the envelope Aunt Elpida had opened. His birth certificate had resulted in more questions than answers.

His eyes scanned the details about his mother. Maria Pearl Kostos. He hadn't even known his mother had a middle name. Her place and date of birth, and Aboriginal status were all stated as Unknown.

Aunt Elpida had refused to discuss it. 'Yaya didn't want to talk about your parents and we should respect that.'

Dimitri's chest tightened. *This is nuts.* This code of silence had surrounded him throughout his childhood. But his grandparents had passed away. It had to stop.

It was getting more and more difficult to maintain his respect when he visited the restaurant. After he had tried to confront his aunt, Uncle Spiros had taken him aside. 'Yaya, she believed your mum was, eh, how you say …? Illegitimate? Back in the old country this is very shameful. Besides …' He raised his eyebrows. '… they had a girl already picked out for your dad to marry. But your father, he was too modern for all that way of doing things.'

He couldn't even find solace in his cousin. Kossie had left for a tour of Europe and they had hardly heard from him. Too many girls keeping him busy.

He bashed about the studio, looking for his keys. 'Some government department barges into my life and does my head in!'

Well, maybe it was time to look at other options. His family wasn't going to tell him much. And if he did start this search, he might not like what he found. He had a perfect image of his mother and it might vanish.

But that's all I have of her. An image.

Grow up! It's time for some proper answers.

Whatever he and Leah had was over. He had his own life to sort out.

This Aboriginal thing was either relevant—or not. He had to find out. It was stupid not to have turned up for the appointment with Mullaya.

He reached for the phone and keyed in the Department's number.

Beloved: My lover thrust his hand through the latch-opening — SS 5:4

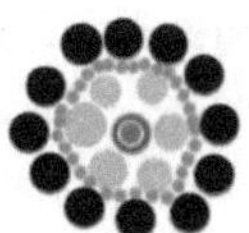

21: Dimitri

Dimitri threaded his way through shoppers and city workers, trying his best not to get bowled over. People shoved past him, rushing to get to their destination. Everyone talked or laughed at the top of their voice, either into their mobiles or to friends as they hurried past. It was as if they were competing with the noise of the traffic.

He reached the main road and pressed the button at the pedestrian crossing. Traffic flew past, ignoring the slow speed limit. Talk about noise pollution. Not to mention the smell! Diesel fumes poured out the back of buses and trams. He hated coming into town. What a dumb place to set up an Aboriginal office.

The light flashed green and he stepped into the crossing. Reaching the other side, he had no idea which way to turn.

He should have washed his new jeans before wearing them! His skin itched against the hot denim. And then there was the dumb decision to wear a white starched shirt. He didn't dare look for sweat marks. Hopefully he could trust the vanilla and cinnamon deodorant to keep any odour at bay.

Please. Now I'm thinking like a TV commercial.

His toes rubbed against the sides of his leather ankle boots. He had wanted to look cool and smart. *Cool?* He imagined what Kossie would say. *You look like a cowboy, cuz.*

He had tried to tell himself this meeting wasn't momentous. But he couldn't remember feeling this nervous about anything before. He had so many questions about his past. *But what if I don't like what I discover?*

Beloved: my heart began to pound for him. — SS 5:4

What was the use of worrying? It was probably all a mistake; a complete waste of everyone's time.

He reached into his back pocket and retrieved the notepaper with the address. Within a few minutes, he'd located the multi-storey building and entered the foyer. Looking up at the directory, he found that the Department of Aboriginal Reconnections was situated on the twenty-second floor.

He shook his head. Whatever happened to the Outback? An Aboriginal office in a skyscraper? He stepped into the lift.

'Going up.' The computerised voice added another level of plasticity to the whole experience. The elevator sped past each floor with hardly a shudder. He tried to calm his racing thoughts but within seconds the voice announced, 'Twenty-second floor,' and the door slid open.

Dimitri stepped out in a daze. The door closed behind him and the lift descended. He rotated his neck trying to loosen his collar.

'Wow!' Stunned, he stood staring at an Indigenous Gallery. Aboriginal art filled every corner of the office space. An intricate mural covered the wall. Profiles of kangaroos, wombats, koalas and emus were in-filled with thousands of colourful dots. He remained still, trying to get his bearings. A gentle thumping vibrated from the walls and he strained to hear the echoing of a didgeridoo through a speaker. He took a breath. The beat had a calming effect and he looked over to the reception desk.

An Aboriginal flag hung across the front of the counter. 'The large yellow circle in the centre symbolises the sun.' A familiar voice interrupted Dimitri's musings.

He looked up. In his shock, he hadn't even noticed the man behind the counter.

'The black above the horizon represents the sky,' the burly man continued, 'the red beneath the horizon is the earth.'

'Yes, I've read the explanation before but I must admit I had forgotten.' Dimitri collected himself. 'I'm Dimitri Kostos. I have an appointment with Mullaya.'

'Yip, that's me.' The man's face broke into an exuberant smile. 'It's great you came this time.' He extended his arm across the counter. Dimitri liked the man's firm shake. 'Take a seat while I go find Monnie. She should have finished her lunch break by now.'

Dimitri sat down on an armchair in the empty waiting area. He selected a magazine titled *Connections* from the glass table. The preamble on the cover described the magazine as a collection of articles about generations of family dispersion. His tension returned and he focussed on slowing his breathing. Replacing the magazine without flicking through it, he wondered why he had come. Surely this whole new world had nothing to do with him?

'Keep it,' Mullaya appeared.

'No. It's okay.' Dimitri cringed. He hadn't meant to be so abrupt, but he wasn't so sure he wanted a souvenir of this visit.

'There are some great photos in there.'

Dimitri frowned. Had they done some kind of background check on him?

Mullaya smiled which irritated Dimitri further.

'I recognised your name from the coverage up at Bilyja. The work was good.' He gestured towards a small office. 'Come in, and welcome to my chaos!'

Files littered his desk. While Mullaya shuffled through the various piles, Dimitri stared at a notice board covered with photos. Elderly white-haired men, wrinkled toothless women, healthy-looking youths, mothers and young babies and bright-eyed children smiled proudly into the camera. They captured snippets of life stories across the generations.

His gaze settled on to a well-rounded middle-aged woman. Definitely not Aunty Paula, but she certainly bore a resemblance. Leah's face flashed through his mind. She had slipped into the Aboriginal community so easily. What he wouldn't give to have her with him now!

He shook his head. People can be deceiving. Hadn't she just rejected him on the basis of his possible heritage? *No way, that just couldn't be true!* There's got to be something else …

'Here it is.' Mullaya picked up an orange manila folder.

Dimitri stared at the file and said nothing. He couldn't speak. His mouth had dried up and he licked his lips. His lower back and tailbone already felt numb against the plastic chair.

'As you know,' Mullaya began, 'we've been contacted by a woman called Lucy Nader who has been trying to locate her sister.'

'It's been a tough journey for her. She's had to break one of our strong Aboriginal traditions.'

Dimitri looked up at him, relieved to steer the focus away from himself. 'Culturally it's taboo to speak of the dead by name. If there were any other way of checking links she would have done it.'

Dimitri rubbed sweaty palms on his jeans. He wasn't sure where Mullaya was going with all this.

'Lucy believes that at some stage her sister's birth name was hyphenated to include Maria.'

A lump rose to Dimitri's throat. His family had so rarely referred to his mum he had no idea what she liked to call herself.

'Around the time of your mother's birth, government policy allowed the removal of many Aboriginal children from their homes. They had the belief that Aboriginal family life wasn't good enough for their welfare.'

Through the pain in Mullaya's voice, Dimitri witnessed a glimpse of history he had never reflected on before.

What if his mum had been affected by that policy? What must her childhood have been like?

Dimitri tried to steer his mind away from those thoughts. At the moment, everything was pure hypothesis. If any of this were relevant to his mum, then he would face the tumble of change to his life full on. *But it's a huge if.*

'I reckon there would be thousands of women named Pearl or Maria in Australia!' He heard the protective hardness in his own voice. 'I don't get why you think this has anything to do with my mother. I already told you on the phone that our family background is Greek!'

'Please. Bear with me.' Mullaya removed a printed email from the file. 'Would you mind if I read this to you? Lucy sent it, hoping you would come to see me.'

Dimitri nodded. Mullaya leaned forward, his elbows resting on the desk.

'To Dimitrios, I've spent many years tracking down my younger sister.

Beloved: my heart began to pound for him. — SS ^{5:4}

It's a long story and it would be so much better if I could share it in person. Briefly, when she was four years old, she was taken away from our family. I found information about a Mr and Mrs Alvarez, who fostered a little girl from an orphanage near our settlement. That little girl's first name was recorded as Maria and her middle name was the same as my sister's. The date of birth in the orphanage record book correlated to the day she was registered; backdated by four years. I think there's reasonable evidence that the girl they fostered could have been my sister. I want to give my sister back her identity. She has her own name and date of birth. It is etched on my mother's heart and every year another scar is added to her wound.'

There was no getting away from the grief. Even if he couldn't feel it for himself, Dimitri empathised with this family. He looked up at the collage of photos on the noticeboard. How could a government policy be so cruel to pull a child away from its mother? It had left that little girl with huge gaps in the history of who she was. Just like the gaps in his own life.

Mullaya continued reading. 'Eventually I found marriage records in South Australia between a Maria-Pearl Alvarez and a Dimitrios Kostos. I was unable to find this couple and finally tried death records. They both died on the same date, in the Northern Territory.'

Mullaya paused and Dimitri looked away. An image of a mangled bi-plane flashed into his mind. He felt the heat, inhaled the smoke, saw fire rip through it. He shoved the intrusion from his mind. It was hard enough to cope with in his dreams; he didn't need it during the day. He wanted Mullaya to stop. Yet he wanted to know more.

'I'm really sorry, Dimitri.' Mullaya rested the paper on the desk. 'I can hardly imagine how upsetting this is for you.'

Dimitri stared at the floor, trying hard to release the image from his mind.

'This is really hard for both you and Lucy,' Mullaya continued, his tone comforting.

Dimitri nodded, acknowledging the serious steps Lucy had taken in her search. Clearly she had some information about his parents. But did any of it identify his mother as Aboriginal?

He looked around the office and exhaled. This was an Aboriginal department. It was up to them to do the hard work to find this out. Mullaya picked up the paper and went on. 'After this I discovered that six years before their death they had a son named Dimitrios Wareen Kostos. The baby was born in a small town near Bilyja in South Australia.'

Bilyja! And six years old! Dimitri's stomach tightened. No wonder Aunt Elpida had panicked.

This Lucy woman knew how old he was before he had. He'd spent six years of his childhood with his mum and dad and knew virtually nothing about it. He clenched and unclenched his fist. This wasn't the time or place to process all the issues.

Mullaya had paused. He probably had been reading the struggle on Dimitri's face again. He cleared his throat and continued, 'I know my search may have led me down the wrong path. I have never been able to find a birth certificate or adoption papers for this child, Maria. She might not even have been Aboriginal. But if you could meet with me, I can explain more. My mother is still alive but very frail. She's had a hard life because of it all. The best gift I could give her would be closure so that she can at last find peace. Kind regards, Lucy Nader.'

Kind regards? What if this all turned out to be true? His mother's sister! They could have a relationship. Kind regards could morph into an endearment of affection. On behalf of his mother!

He quelled the spark of hope. Instead, he honed into a growing annoyance. These were his parents Lucy had researched. She held more information and documentation than he ever had.

'I've never even seen their death certificate. I wouldn't have a clue which date they died. And yet Lucy does.'

'Please, Dimitri, relax. There has probably never been a reason to question your background before.'

True. You have no idea what control my grandparents exerted. I thought I did. But I had no real idea. Dimitri sighed. 'I've only just got my birth certificate. My mum's surname, before she was married, was Alvarez.'

The background noise of the open office space filtered through to their room. Life carried on. Someone tapped away on a computer keyboard. A

Beloved: my heart began to pound for him. — SS [5:4]

94

phone rang out. Peals of laughter escaped another interview room. The noise added to Dimitri's chaos. His thoughts scattered around in all directions.

Mullaya sat back and said nothing. Dimitri took the opportunity to gather his thoughts. He visualised the unbelievable picture of a small child taken from her family. *What did 'taken' mean?* How terrified she must have felt! How utterly alone she must have been. Dumped into a new world without the person who loved her most! He knew her sadness first hand.

'But it still doesn't necessarily link her to Lucy's sister.' He felt himself growing cautious. 'How likely do you think it is that Maria-Pearl Alvarez and Pearl Nader is actually the same person?'

'Given the amount of effort Lucy has put into tracing her sister, she must think there's a pretty high chance. If you met her, I'm fairly sure she could tell you a lot more.'

Mullaya placed the sheet of paper on the table in front of Dimitri. 'Children who were removed and placed in a "white" household were often renamed. At age four it may have been too hard for Pearl to answer to a new name.' He grinned. 'It could also highlight the tenacity and determination of this little girl to hold on to her identity. Her adoptive parents may have reached a compromise and used a hyphenated version.'

Dimitri was already chasing another thread in his mind. 'Like Lucy said, I was born near Bilyja. I was up there recently. If anyone knew my parents, wouldn't they have recognised the name "Kostos"?'

Mullaya shrugged. 'As I said, it is taboo to speak of the dead. So it's possible the local Aboriginal people may have known your parents but not been willing to talk about them. Despite all the white settlement, the land there has been owned by the same Aboriginal community for generations. On the other hand, the non-Aboriginal population has been transient, so there may not be any white folk up there who knew them.'

Dimitri stretched out his legs in an attempt to break the tension gripping his body. He knew that with the glimmer of hope came the risk of crushed expectations.

Leah's face came to mind. Was there any connection between her rejection and his potential Aboriginality? He looked closer at Mullaya.

Beloved: my heart began to pound for him. — SS [5:4]

Maybe he should ask him if he had disclosed any information to her during his phone call? No way! It was hard enough to have a social worker digging around in his past. His current life was nobody's business.

Anyhow, that's such a crazy thought! What about privacy and confidentiality? There was no way a government worker could disclose that kind of information.

Dimitri's thoughts tripped over each other. He knew he had to discontinue this interview. He was desperate for information about his mum, but none of his fantasies had included anything like this. He needed time to process everything. He cleared his throat and stood up.

'Thanks, Mullaya, I guess I've got a lot to think about …' His voice trailed off, unsure what the next step could be.

Mullaya stood and extended his hand. It felt firm and encouraging beneath Dimitri's own rigid fingers. His voice held compassion.

'I understand your distress; there is a lot to think about.' He picked up the email and handed it to him. 'Take this and read it over. I'm sure Lucy would be more than happy for you to reply. On the other hand, I could go ahead and arrange a meeting here where I could introduce you to each other.'

Relieved that Mullaya would take the lead, he nodded. 'That would be good.' He knew he owed Lucy the chance to talk through her story. Organising it himself was more than he could manage.

'Good on you, Dimitri. I'll work out a way for the three of us to get together. Lucy's from interstate, so I'm not real sure how long this will take.' He held Dimitri's eyes, his expression solid. 'It means a great deal to someone who is trying to bring separated family members together.'

'Of course.' Dimitri followed Mullaya out to reception. 'I'll wait to hear from you.'

On the way down in the lift he glanced at his arms. He ran his hands over his skin. What if he were Aboriginal? Would that open the door to more racism? Was there any possibility at all Leah had rejected him on this basis?

Leah! She was the only person he wanted. *What's happened to us? I thought we were made for each other.*

He pushed aside the burning desire for her. Clearly he had been misguided about their relationship. Get out of the lift first! He looked up at the Adelaide hills circling the city. So much had happened since they had gone there for dinner.

Love stronger than death? Perhaps not, after all.

Dimitri shrugged off his melancholy. The hills stood guard at the roads leading into the Outback. If Leah could move on, so could he.

Rick's invite to go bush looked like a positive option.

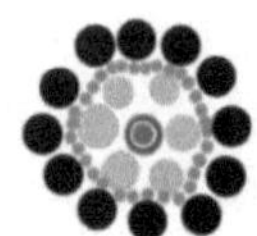

22: Leah

Red mud drizzled down the coach windows. Despite the jarring as the bus lurched across potholes, Leah felt a smile creasing her face. The desert teemed with life: the rain had enticed dozens of brolgas to gather in puddles, attracted by unfolding green shoots and emerging insects. The elegant birds stretched their necks and responded to the disturbance of the bus with a series of croaks. Leah grinned at their indignation. *How great it feels to be alive!*

Her oncology nurse had encouraged her to use the scalp cooling system to minimise hair loss. The results had been astounding. Definitely some thinning, but she had managed to retain the length. Months of chemo and radiotherapy had been ruthless and degrading. Not having to cope with baldness as well had made it all so much easier to cope with.

Ouch! Another pothole; another jar. She adjusted the compression bandage beneath her cotton sleeve and massaged her arm. *Returning to Bilyja so soon after the treatment is probably not the wisest move. Was there a place more rugged or remote to work?* Yet, it was the isolation that had attracted her. Away from the hustle of the city, she hoped to regain her peace.

'You're our new nurse, aren't you?'

Leah spun around. A girl around ten years old rested her arms over the back of Leah's seat. 'I'm going to be a nurse when I grow up.' The child's smile filled her face.

'I think that's a great idea. You can come back here after your training.

There'll always be lots of work for a nurse.'

The girl nodded. 'This is my country. I'd want to stay with my own people. It would be too hard to leave my family for too long.'

'And your people would love to have you as their nurse too.'

As welcoming as the community were, she knew she would always be an outsider—a visitor. As if to prove her point a dilapidated sign post appeared at the end of the T-Junction. *Welcome to the Shire of Bilyja.* An arrow to the left indicated *Town Centre.* The arrow on the right stated *Permit Holders only.*

Aunty Paula had secured a permit for her. Leah knew it was a way to ensure visitors acknowledged and respected the value of the community's traditional ownership of the land.

The coach veered off to the right and Leah grasped her side.

'Are you okay?'

Leah nodded, her teeth gritted. 'I'm fine.'

The bus straightened up and returned to its previous speed.

'Do you know how much further it is from here?' she asked the girl. It seemed a lot further than she remembered.

The child shrugged. 'The driver will try to get us there by sunset or it'll be too dark for him to see.'

Sunset! *Two hours of dirt track to go!*

'We should make it by then.' The girl's radiant smile was back. 'So long as we don't hit a 'roo.'

A kangaroo! Leah groaned. Dimitri had told her that it was likely Rick's car had rolled while avoiding a 'roo. Driving at dusk was a bad idea. She'd seen enough dead wildlife strewn along the sides of the road, hit by vehicles. A kangaroo could damage a vehicle irreparably.

Please God, protect the kangaroos from us, and our bus from the kangaroos! She shuffled herself on her seat trying to make herself more comfortable.

'My name's Krissie.'

'I'm pleased to meet you, Krissie. I'm Leah.'

'What happened to your boyfriend?'

Leah took a deep breath. 'My boyfriend?'

Beloved: I arose to open for my beloved. — SS [5:5]

'I saw you walking with him in town. He was nice. He went out to help his mate who rolled his car.'

Leah laughed. 'There is no privacy out here, is there?'

The beaming smile got wider. 'Nope.'

'He recovered very quickly. So did his boss, Rick. He didn't stay in plaster for very long and he's back at work.'

At least I think they're okay; I wouldn't really know. 'Are you going back home for the weekend?' Leah deflected the conversation before her heart felt another stab.

Krissie nodded. 'I can't wait. I don't really like staying in town. I miss my little brother and sister but there's no other way I can do school.'

'That's hard. Who do you stay with?'

'My aunty.'

Krissie went on to tell Leah all about her school, family and community life. It didn't take long for Leah to realise Krissie was a proverbial chatterbox.

She found her concentration drifting … inevitably back to Dimitri. *What's the point of thinking about him? Thoughts won't bring him back.* They only deepened her heartbreak.

It's insane to miss him so much. Throughout the darkness of all the chemotherapy, she had remembered his declaration. *Love is stronger than death.*

But he'd never got back to her. She rotated her stiff shoulders and neck muscles, and repositioned her arm on her travel pillow. The swelling under her armpit had almost disappeared and although a little bit sore it was much more manageable.

'We're here!' Krissie interrupted Leah's day dreaming. She grabbed her school bag and stood up. 'Nice talking to you, Leah. I'll see you 'round.'

'Yes, nice talking to you too.' Leah smiled. The last hour had gone so fast. She doubted Krissie had noticed her lack of attention. At least she hoped so.

Unscrewing her bottle top, she sipped some lukewarm water. Closing the lid tight, she told herself that this was where her memories and feelings for Dimitri would stay; locked away securely inside, unable to spoil her stay here.

Dozens of children laughed and waved as they raced alongside the bus, eager for outside visitors. Leah shuddered as mangy dogs also barked their welcome.

Beloved: I arose to open for my beloved. — SS [5:5]

They drew to a halt and the children surged to the front, jostling to be the first off. Leah sat back and allowed each of them to alight. Butterflies gathered in her stomach. This was a bit nerve-wracking. Commencing her first post graduate placement as a Registered Midwife was hard enough. But she knew she arrived with a lot of personal baggage. Although the doctor had cleared her for work, she hadn't told Aunty the full story of her illness. *Well, I'm here now and I'm going to be the best new midwife ever!*

She stepped from the bus straight into a puddle of red mud. 'Eeh!' The squished earth seeped through her best toe sandals. *Serves me right for wearing city shoes!*

A broad smile lighting up her face, Aunty Paula pushed her way through the crowd. 'Welcome back to Bilyja.' She opened her arms and enveloped Leah in a hug.

Leah swallowed back a lump. Aunty's warmth and wisdom oozed through her embrace. *How great it feels to be held like that.* Leah was conscious of her own bony frame, yet if Aunty Paula noticed, she ignored it.

'We're gonna have a celebration big time for you tonight!' she declared. 'You're our special guest.'

Leah protested, 'I'm only here for a contract …'

Aunty Paula kept hold of Leah's arms and stepped back. Her eyes perused Leah's face.

She knows. She knows I've come back to heal.

Aunty Paula smiled, displaying her set of beautiful white teeth. 'While you're here, Bilyja is your home. So, we are going to welcome you home.' She let go and swung around. In the local language she directed a pair of teens to retrieve Leah's bags from beneath the coach.

Leah smiled. If anyone could help her to recover peace within her body and spirit, she knew Aunty Paula was her first choice.

Beloved: I arose to open for my beloved. — SS 5:5

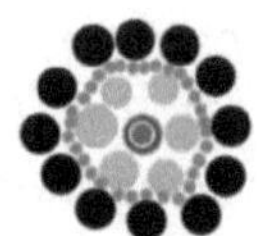

23: Leah

'Come on, hon, let's get some food into you.'

Dusk had fallen, so Leah and Aunty Paula shone their torches on the path ahead of them. Even before they reached the common ground, the smell of barbequed meat tantalised Leah's nose. 'I didn't realise how hungry I was!'

Aunty Paula led the way towards a large gathering of women around a fire. The men hung around their own fire on the opposite side of the oval.

'Good to see you again, Leah,' one of the women called out.

'Where you been, eh?' Another came over and greeted her with a warm hug.

'Thanks, it's so good to be back.'

The women reshuffled their circle and made space for the two of them. Leah looked around the group. Unlike barbeques at home, this group hadn't segregated into old and young. There were women and girls of all ages enjoying each other's company. Some of them would be related, but Leah knew she would never be able to work out how. On her previous visit she had learnt the cultural definitions of grandmother, mother, sisters, aunts and cousins were so different from her own she no longer tried to figure it out. What she did know was that family ties were very strong and could be traced back many generations.

Leah recognised a girl about her own age. Rosie passed her a plate from a pile on the table. 'Here you go.' She winked. 'I guess you haven't had barbecued kangaroo for a while, since those city prices are so high.'

'Absolutely.' Leah picked up a pair of tongs and helped herself to a decent serve of steak. 'This looks delicious! It's been hours since I last had a decent meal and I'm starving!'

'I won't offer you any kangaroo tail. I remember your reaction last time!'

Leah pulled a face. 'Yes, I remember too. Boiled kangaroo tail! Sorry, I draw the line at that!'

'It's very good for you.' Aunty Paula winked. 'Lots of protein.'

'Here, have some potatoes.' Rosie scooped two from a tray with a serving spoon, and put them on Leah's plate. 'They've been baking in the ground most of the day.' A collection of bush tucker was set out on the table as well. Leah had enjoyed most of it the last time she had come. 'I see you have another of my favourites.' Leah pointed to a plate of witchetty grubs. 'No way!'

Rosie laughed. 'Like I said last time, they taste just like scrambled egg.'

Leah shook her head. 'Now native fruit, that looks good. Especially the wild oranges and desert apples.' After piling up her plate with food she settled herself on a rock next to Aunty Paula. Everywhere groups of people laughed and ate. Leah found herself relaxing, soaking up the atmosphere.

'This is in honour of you comin' back to us,' Aunty Paula reminded Leah.

Leah flushed. 'You having me back here is the honour.'

'We like havin' folk up from the city. It's important you go back and tell people about the Aboriginal way. There's a lot of ignorance down there. A lot of people don't know that culture like this is still alive.'

Leah nodded. She had known hardly anything about Aboriginal culture before coming up last time. Except from academic papers at Uni. Being permitted to soak it in as a living experience—almost too awesome to explain.

A rhythmic, nasal chant announced the start of a dance. A group of men, women and children had converged on the centre of the ground. The dancers' painted bodies and faces were a spectacular contrast to the darkness. Hundreds of tiny chalked dots illuminated the bridges of their noses and cheeks. Black charcoal and white paint decorated their torsos and limbs. Decorated didgeridoos and clap sticks maintained a throbbing beat. Leah felt the earth vibrate as their feet pounded the ground.

She sat mesmerised as Aunty Paula interpreted the ancient stories

Beloved: my lover had left; he was gone. — SS [5:6]

behind the movements and chants. 'Many of these folks have come up from the cities to stay for a while.' Aunty swept her arm over the array of groups. 'They come lookin' to find out more about their people. It's very important that they learn, so that we can pass down the richness of our culture.'

She pointed Leah to a vacant space near the campfire. They moved closer. Stretching out her cold hands towards the fire, Leah relished the warmth spreading along her fingers and into her palms.

'We've given you an Aboriginal name.'

Leah stared at Aunty Paula. Her throat constricted and words wouldn't come. It was an honour beyond anything she had ever imagined.

The women in the circle around them beamed their approval.

Aunty nodded. 'We've decided to name you Marrawi.'

'Marrawi,' Leah whispered.

'Where my Grandma comes from, this is the name of a native bird. In English the bird is known as the *Peaceful Dove*.'

'Peaceful Dove?' Tears welled up and she had to blink them back. They couldn't have chosen a name further from the truth. If they only knew the distress she carried deep inside. She dropped her head and spoke in a whisper, barely audible even to herself. 'I have no peace.'

Aunty rested her hand over Leah's. 'You will grow into the name.'

Leah stared through the flames and the harmonious chanting faded into the background. The fire flickered against the black sky, causing shadows to dance in front of them.

Aunty Paula sighed. 'I know what it's like to lose your peace.'

Leah looked up at her. Aunty's eyes were too difficult to read behind the light reflecting on her large glasses.

'Fire is a strong part of our Aboriginal culture. Without it we have no warmth, no cooking and no place to gather.' She paused, her gaze fixed on the orange flames dancing before them. 'For a long time I just couldn't look at fire without this real bad pain in my heart.' She sat motionless, her face seemingly bewitched in the shadow of the flames. 'My tiny newborn baby, she died in a bush fire.'

Leah gasped. 'Oh, Aunty Paula, I'm so sorry!'

Beloved: my lover had left; he was gone. — SS [5:6]

Aunty nodded and continued in a slow, soft voice. 'It was a long time ago. We didn't even give her a name because that would mean we could never speak of her again.'

A breath of wind blew smoke into Leah's eyes and hair.

'I could never smell this smoke without the pain. It was time for me to give birth.' Her trance-like voice broke into sudden animation. 'Mate! Those pains came quick. I could hardly move more than a few steps. Smoke came over from a bush fire not far away to the east. All my people were collectin' their things; they knew that wind could carry those flames right near our place.'

Leah clasped her hand to her mouth.

'I crawled to a bush and my baby wouldn't wait,' Aunty Paula went on. 'She slipped out and I grasped her tight to my chest. Giant flames came so close they devoured our house. They moved on their path within seconds leaving behind a black mess. The whole time, I rocked our daughter, holding her head against me. When I dared to look at her, I heard wailing from far away, but it wasn't far away, it was my own. That first breath of hers killed her.'

Leah reached out for Aunty Paula's tough, wrinkled hand. 'What a terrible, terrible tragedy! I'm so sorry!'

'Hon, you are right. It was a terrible tragedy. For a long time I was angry with everyone. Including myself. Most of all I was angry with God. Like a lot of people when bad things happen, I'm cryin' out to God; how could You have let this happen?' She looked straight into Leah's eyes, and against the darkness her crooked white teeth flashed as, incredibly, her face broke into its usual smile. 'It was the end of who I was. I was never the same person. Which meant it was the start of somethin' new.'

Leah said nothing. She had been given back her life. How much more of a new beginning was there? Yet, without Dimitri …

She drew up her knees and hugged them to her body. She was well-practised in reining in her thoughts about him.

The dark figures danced on. She knew they would continue until dawn. Guitars had now joined the ancient instruments, strumming the same calm beat continuously.

Beloved: my lover had left; he was gone. — SS 5:6

'At some point I needed to be reconciled.' Aunty's voice blended in with the atmosphere. 'And to be reconciled means to forgive. Whether it's forgivin' ourselves or God, or one particular person. The bush fire; that was a natural disaster; they're not really God's fault. So there was no one to forgive. But there were other times …' Aunty Paula's soft voice dropped even lower. 'Aboriginal people; we had to forgive a nation.'

They sat without speaking, watching the dancers. Leah mulled over the statement. Several minutes passed before Aunty spoke again. 'It's lack of forgiveness and reconciliation that destroys our peace.'

So this is where the conversation was going. Did Aunty know how much turbulence she carried inside? Was the name Marrawi chosen to challenge her?

'But you don't know what's happened! Dimitri walked out on me. He promised me his love but at the first test he disappeared.'

Aunty Paula looked straight into Leah's eyes. 'From what I remember of that young man of yours, he really took to the *Song of Songs*. I reckon he thought of himself as the Lover and you as his Beloved. I can't imagine him walking away unless there was a good reason.'

I told him to go—but that's not the point. If love really is as strong as death, he shouldn't have given up at the first sign of trouble.

'The *Song of Songs* isn't about a perfect relationship. You remember what I said on the second night? Those two were definitely in love, but it didn't take them long after the honeymoon to run into trouble.' Aunty shot her a penetrating look. 'Go back and read the Song again. This time start with Chapter Five, Verse Three. That's when everythin' begins to fall apart. It's a song about love, yes, but also about conflict and ultimately forgiveness and reconciliation.' Her voice gentled. 'Things could still work out between you and Dimitri, Leah, if that's what's in God's plan for you.'

How am I supposed to know? Leah looked up at the Southern Cross and wondered if Dimitri had kept the promise they had made to each other: at the end of each day to trace the configuration of stars and send a blessing to the other. *Oh, what a stupid thought. I told him to go. It's over.*

'Just remember that no matter what happens between you and Dimitri,' Aunty's voice drew her back, 'you are each loved by the greatest Lover of all.'

Beloved: my lover had left; he was gone. — SS 5:6

Weariness settled over Leah, and she knew Aunty Paula wasn't expecting a reply. Was it even possible for her to forgive Dimitri? To forgive herself? For them to be reconciled?

'There's been a lot of rain out here.' Aunty Paula flashed Leah a last smile as she heaved her body up from the ground. 'But there's more to come. A flood can devastate. But it can also replenish.'

She rested a hand on Leah's shoulder. 'I'll see you in clinic in the morning.'

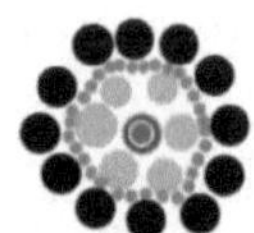

24: Dimitri

Dimitri poked dust over the twigs to smother the camp fire. Nothing tasted as good as smoked steak cooked over an open flame. He grinned. The smoke also reduced, but did not quite eliminate, the buzz and bite of mozzies as they attempted to feast on his blood.

He cleared a place to settle for the night and grabbed his swag, wrapping it around him for warmth. Rick and Angie had set up a two-person tent a few metres away. Dimitri much preferred to sleep out under the open sky.

Stretching his legs under the warm cover, he crossed his arms behind his head and stared up at the sky. His sleepy mind traced the five stars of the Southern Cross. Where was Leah? They had promised to 'meet' at the close of each day, and trace the cross in blessing for the other. He'd wondered, even as he'd suggested it the first time, if it was more religious than romantic. Had that been one of the things that had scared her away? Had she forgotten him?

Of course she has, vlakas.

He tried to block out the familiar knot of tension whenever his thoughts strayed towards her. Rolling over, he faced the gentle glow of the remaining embers and welcomed the creeping numbness of sleep.

A low crackle warned him the fire had not been completely extinguished. His body felt too heavy to drag himself up and check it out. Chatter emanated from the opposite side of the campfire. 'They'll do it.' He peeked through half-open eyes and watched a group of adults sitting in a circle. Part of him realised he was dreaming. Or was he? It all looked so real. He had been here before.

Lover: How beautiful you are, my darling! — SS [4:1]

In the middle of the group a baby wombat waddled about on its four stout legs. He watched, fascinated, as a beautiful woman reached out and drew the creature close. As her fingers combed through the thick fur behind its ears, he felt the soothing massage himself. Her voice reached him, soft and strangely familiar. 'My wombat, my precious wombat.'

The spell broke as something dragged him from beneath her hand. He struggled free and escaped into bushland.

Not this again. I don't want to run away. I'm too tired.

Throwing a look over his shoulder, he saw the creature's enormous teeth as its jaws dripped saliva.

It's getting closer!

Its heavy body shambled after him, crashing through the bush on all fours.

Faster!

He urged himself on, but the ground was hot. His feet burned and he could barely lift one after the other.

The slow, heavy creature panted right behind him.

Get away from me you … what are you, anyway?

It looked like a monstrous dog, but its awkward body ambled like a bear.

Dimitri ran deeper into the untamed bush. His skin stung as his arms, neck and face scraped against the overhanging branches. His feet felt like they were on fire.

Finally he saw a red flickering light ahead. If only he could reach that clearing, he could lose the creature.

Help!

He tripped over a fallen tree. One foot was caught in a tangle of roots. He was trapped. Moist hot breath stirred the hairs behind his neck as he turned to stare into beady red eyes. One lethal claw stretched onto the white bark of the fallen gum. Dimitri pulled at his boot, but it was shackled to the undergrowth. The second claw reached over the trunk and the monster crouched, ready to pounce.

Sweat poured down Dimitri's face while the pounding of his heart thumped against his eardrums. His own breathing came in short, frantic gasps. With a sudden jolt he sat bolt upright …

Lover: How beautiful you are, my darling! — SS [1:15]

… alone.

Dimitri looked down at the twisted mess of his swag. With shaking hands he freed his legs. Wrapping the swag around his shoulders, he staggered closer to the dark red coals of the dying campfire. It wasn't so easy to shake free the image of the giant…

… *wombat!*

The nightmare was as persistent as that of his parents' death. They seemed to be linked but he'd never quite understood how. If only he remembered during the nightmare that the creature was a wombat, he wouldn't be so frightened. But he never ever did.

Who was the woman in his dream? Her voice sounded so familiar, but she remained elusive. His fingers gripped the swag, hoping to stop the shivers taking over his body. He slowed his breathing, allowing the sounds of the night insects to calm him. He sat there for a long time, until he felt totally numb, both in body and mind.

Woven through all his thoughts were images of Leah. Clearly his desire for her was not going away. He shouldn't have let her go so easily. Even if she had pushed him, he could have been stronger. He had quoted that verse to her and he had meant it. *Love is stronger than death.*

But he had never tried to prove it.

There were other verses. They all made Dimitri think of Leah. In fact he had tortured himself by reading them until he knew many of them off by heart. What was the use of that if he couldn't share them with her?

Should he track her down? See if she'd changed her mind? He gazed into the hot coals and pushed aside all the negatives. Instead, he focussed on one of his favourite images from the Song. '… my dove … my beautiful dove, let me see you, let me hear your voice.'

Dimitri sighed. He needed to get to sleep or he wouldn't be up to seeing or hearing anything, let alone photographing it. He covered the coals with dust one more time and ventured back to his clearing.

He had almost drifted off to sleep when he was jolted by a sudden realisation. All the people around the fire had been Aboriginal! He had been dreaming this dream his whole life but he had never noticed it before.

Lover: How beautiful you are, my darling! — SS 4:1

110

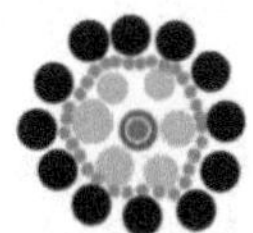

25: Dimitri

'Pull over.' Dimitri thumped the back of Rick's seat.

Rick shot him a curious glance in the rear vision mirror as he pulled the car to a halt on the gravelled edge of the road. When the engine purred to a stop, the silence enveloped them. Dimitri reached across to the passenger side and retrieved his camera and tripod.

'Comfort stop. I'm just going back up the road a bit. You never know what there might be to photograph while I'm there.'

Rick's brow furrowed in an odd look. 'Okay, but this is a five minute break, all right? I'd rather not be following semi-trailers in the dark.'

'No worries.'

Rick grasped Angie's hand and they crossed the road and seated themselves on a fallen log.

That was close. He'd almost made a fool of himself. But how could he have asked Rick to stop to photograph a *road sign?* Then again, if it was an entirely accidental subject no one would question it.

He reached the diamond-shaped sign and stared up at it. A silhouette of a koala, kangaroo and a wombat warned drivers to look out for native animals crossing the road. They had driven past dozens of these signs rising up from the sides of the road. So why did they pester him?

It was the wombat. It invariably stirred weird feelings. Yet Dimitri wasn't sure they were actually feelings. More like memories. *But memories of what?*

He focussed his camera on the sign and took a series of pictures. Snapping the camera lens shut, he stood still and breathed in the leisurely quiet of the bush. As he exhaled, he tried to release his growing unease. 'Ridiculous.' He turned away from the sign.

Dusk was settling in and their parked car appeared as a shadow against the red-limned sky. Rick and Angie were sitting close together on the fallen branch of a gum tree. They appeared deep in conversation, clearly unaware of his internal struggle.

He stood and watched the fading daystar capturing the glint of their blonde heads. He and Leah had hair as dark as theirs was fair. They would be an eye-catching foursome. How cool it would be to share a trip like this with Leah!

As he gazed at his friends his heart ached. Hope for a relationship with Leah was futile. He had blown it for good. Shaking off his introspection, he called out, 'C'mon guys, let's go. It'll be dark soon.'

What was that?

He froze. The sound of scurrying at his feet warned him of an animal nearby. Wary of snakes at the end of a hot day, all his muscles tightened. Without moving his head, he lowered his eyes. With a mixture of relief and delight his body relaxed. In the dimming light the silver grass had softened. Amidst its stems appeared the hairy face of a foraging wombat.

Dimitri didn't hesitate. He snapped open the tripod, adjusted the camera and clicked shots in quick succession. The wombat raised its curious face. 'Wow!'

As the wombat turned, he could see a tiny infant peering out from the rear-facing pouch in its mother's belly. Refocussing the lens, Dimitri panned the camera as the wombat moved off. The effect would highlight the pair in the foreground while keeping the bush to a blur.

You're kidding me! A car roared towards them, shattering the tranquil moment. It zig-zagged across the road, straddling lanes, until the driver managed to slow it down. The wombat squealed and Dimitri looked down at his feet. *I'm blocking it from its burrow.*

He stepped aside but the wombat dodged around him and bolted towards the other side of the road.

'Stop!'

The car was only metres away and, within a fraction of a second, there was a sickening thump.

Lover: Your eyes behind your veils are doves — SS ^{4:1}

'Dimitri! Step back!' Angie screamed.

The brakes screeched again and he lost his footing, landing face down on the rocky ground. His hands burned as they skidded along the gravel while trying to break the fall of his camera. The driver regained control and drove off, leaving the foul vapour to stain the air.

Furious, Dimitri hoisted himself from the dirt and brushed away gravel from his jeans and smarting hands. 'He didn't even stop!' He spat out grit embedded around his mouth.

He picked up his camera and quickly checked it. Relieved that it appeared to be undamaged, he laid it on the grass next to his fallen tripod. He strode to the centre of the road.

'Dimitri!' Angie raced over with Rick at her heels. 'Thank goodness you're okay!'

'I thought you were a goner!' Rick patted him on the back.

Dimitri said nothing. He knelt over the distressed wombat, lying on the bitumen. Its hairy body shuddered. The lifeless infant was a tiny mass of blood and matted fur.

'Don't people read signs?' Dimitri thundered.

'These two have had it!' Rick shook his head. 'Let's get ourselves and them off the road.'

'It's all my fault!' Dimitri whirled to face him.

Rick looked down at the wombat. 'You weren't the one driving like a maniac!' He shook his head again. 'It didn't stand a chance.'

'I disturbed her. And she wanted to get back to her burrow.'

'That driver was being an idiot. No one takes corners at that kind of speed. It's just lucky you weren't the one hit.' Bending down, Rick was about to pick the wombat up by the scruff of its neck. 'Come on, help me move it.'

'Don't!' Dimitri grabbed Rick's arm. 'She's not quite dead and those claws could go right through to your bones! Once they're latched on they won't let go for anything!'

'We can't just leave them lyin' here!'

'Angie!' Dimitri called over his shoulder. 'Could you please fetch me the plastic tarp from the trunk?'

A couple of cars approached, slowing down to drive around them. When Angie returned, Dimitri grabbed the tarp and threw it over the

Lover: Your eyes behind your veils are doves — SS [17]

wounded wombat. It was barely alive but still struggled against the plastic. The two men waited for another car to pass, before carefully wrapping it under the creature. They took an end each and dragged the bundle to the side of the road.

'Whew, this thing weighs a tonne!' Rick cried as they freed it from the blood and dirt-stained tarp.

Dimitri looked down. 'I think it's dead now.' Sadness overwhelmed him. 'At least they both died together. The joey would have been too vulnerable to be left without its mother.'

Like me.

He went cold. He looked up to check if he had spoken out loud. It seemed not. Rick's attention was on Angie, who looked a bit pale. *For heaven's sake, I've got to pull myself together! Where had that insane thought come from?* The thick wall he had created around the loss of his parents had begun to weaken, and he didn't like it. He had never considered himself an orphan, and he wasn't about to start now.

Drat Mullaya and his Department! *Everything was going along fine, until they butted into my life.* 'C'mon, let's get out of here. It's getting dark.'

They slid the tarp from under the dead animals, covered them with loose branches and turned back towards the car. Dimitri sat in the back seat and stared at the road ahead as it merged into the horizon. He was glad no one spoke.

After a while, Rick glanced in the rear vision mirror. 'Dimitri, you're really upset about this. More than is reasonable. What's up, mate? '

Dimitri said nothing. He knew he was probably over-reacting, but he didn't know why.

'You've seen hundreds of animals lyin' along the sides of the road; all hit by cars.' Rick wasn't going to give up on the questions. 'What's got into you this time?'

They passed another sign, barely visible against the darkening sky.

'I'm not really sure.' Dimitri sighed, hesitating. 'I think maybe because it was a wombat.'

'What difference does that make?'

He shrugged. 'I have no idea, Rick. It just does.'

Lover: Your eyes behind your veils are doves — SS 4:1

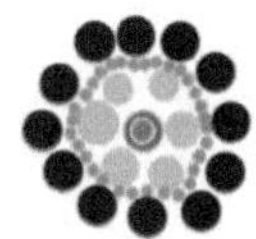

26: Leah

'Hey, you! Nursie!' Matt's voice boomed above the noise in the clinic.

That man is so irritating! Leah struggled to be civil to the community's jack-of-all-trades. While everyone else couldn't do enough for her, Matt seemed to take great delight in baiting her.

'The boss said to get yourself over to the Gorge Camp, now, Nursie. They've got some kind of emergency.'

'Do you know what the problem is?'

'She didn't give me the juicy details.'

Leah couldn't tell how serious he was. His waterproof hoodie covered his expression. Not that it was ever easy to read. His ginger beard, moustache and mass of unkempt hair covered most of his features. No wonder the children called him 'the bear man'.

Why did she let him get to her so much? She stared at him, determined to appear unflustered. After all, an emergency could mean just about anything.

Matt shrugged. 'Maybe she said a birth. Don't know more than that. Aunty Paula can't go as she's up at the Station, fixin' up the jackaroo's broken leg.'

A birth! Now it was time to panic. Leah had delivered her quota of births required to register. But none without supervision, and definitely none outside a hospital. Let alone one without an emergency response team available at the press of a button. The local women were encouraged to travel into town a couple of weeks before their due date to be close to the hospital.

Beloved: if you find my lover — SS 5:8

Leah shuddered as she felt his stare roving up and down her body.

'She told me to take you there.' He spun around and walked away.

Leah stared at his departing back. Matt made her feel very uncomfortable, but she knew Aunty Paula wouldn't send her out with him unless she really had to.

Washing her hands, she hurried into the store room to grab her yellow rain jacket and medical backpack.

'Sorry!' She almost stumbled over Graham, the Aboriginal Health Worker, as she exited the room.

'No worries, Leah. Now, I heard what Matt said. You've never been out to the camp before, eh?'

Leah shook her head.

Graham smiled. 'Since the wet season has really set in, we've got plenty of water now runnin' into Alawara Creek. There's a lot of people camped out there for the fish.' His grin broadened. 'It's good tucker. Anyway, about the emergency; I've already called into town for the ambulance for that jackeroo.' He frowned. 'I hope they send it out straight away; that road won't stay open much longer. It'll be flooded soon, I reckon.'

Leah's heart skipped a beat. Aunty Paula had already told her that, with water rising on the road connecting them to the highway, it was only a matter of time before they were cut off from outside help. If the patient needed evacuation by road, it had to be done as soon as possible.

'There's a birth kit in the bag, including a portable heart monitor,' Graham went on.

Leah tried to concentrate. But another distracting thought went through her mind. She had planned to mail Dimitri a letter. But she had been too busy.

Procrastinating, to be precise.

She argued with herself. There was no internet access to send him a message online. She no longer had a mobile and, even if she did, she didn't have his number anymore. The satellite phone was always a bit dodgy even if she did manage to locate his home phone. Snail mail to his home address had been her best option. But she had sat, chewing her pen, not knowing where to begin. And now it was too late. The priority for the ambulance drivers was the patient; not a nurse who wanted a letter dropped into town.

She refocussed on Graham. 'Thanks, I'll head off straight away. Hopefully, we'll be back before too long.' Leah slung the pack over her shoulder and hurried over to the car pool. Matt stood waiting for her, leaning up against the lone fuel pump.

'Can't take the comfy car today, lovey.' He unfolded his arms as she approached. 'The track's washed out and it's pure bog out there.' He pointed to a quad bike. 'It's my trustworthy steed for you and me today.'

Leah looked at the cumbersome four-wheel bike, wondering what she would do if her patient needed to be transferred.

'Don't worry.' Matt clearly read her concern. 'When Paula's finished with the ute, she'll send someone over with it.'

Leah shuddered. Every now and then he dropped Aunty's title. Another sign of his lack of respect for people.

He grinned. 'Meanwhile, looks like you're gonna have to wrap your delicate arms around my waist.'

Leah ignored him and hung the pack over the luggage rack.

'You gotta lean deeply with the bike and let those hips and feet of yours steer the bike with mine.' His voice seemed to have gained a sleazy edge.

Matt passed a helmet to her, his sweaty hand lingering on hers for just a few seconds too long. Leah restrained herself from snatching the helmet away. It would be an arduous few hours and they needed to work together for the sake of her patient. Slipping the helmet over her head, she adjusted the chinstrap, snapped shut the buckle and closed the protective visor. Then she swung her legs over the seat behind Matt.

The engine responded to his persistent revving and Leah clung to the back of his rain jacket as they took off.

The bike swerved around puddles and bucked like a wild horse over mounds of red clay, avoiding rocks jutting from the ground. They weaved in and out between the gum trees, avoiding the water that had pooled near the roots. Birds scattered in response to the engine, yet their wide wings never dipped far from the puddles. Despite her spine and kidneys taking a pounding, Leah felt exhilarated. Cool air poured through the helmet's vents, providing

Beloved: if you find my lover — SS 5:18

welcome relief from the stickiness produced from the ever-present humidity.

A wall of stony cliffs soon appeared, stretching across the breadth of the horizon. The quad navigated boulders and clumps of wild grass as they approached a narrow valley. A layer of greenery spread across the gorge and Leah knew they must be close to the creek where so many locals had set up camp.

As the bike roared into the clearing, a spectacular flock of pink and white cockatoos surged into the air, settling like confetti in the foliage of a massive gum tree. A group of dogs raced to meet them, barking their welcome. As they stepped off the bike, a young girl approached, a toddler clinging tightly to her hip.

'Krissie!'

'Leah, I'm so happy you're here. My mum, she's got a lot of pain. You got to help her.'

'Okay, we'll try our best.' She scanned the area, surprised by the absence of adults. 'Where is everyone?'

Matt answered instead. 'The women are back in the clinic, surely you know that? It's baby health day.'

Leah flushed as he stated the obvious. 'What about the men?'

'Fishin',' Krissie replied. 'My dad's still not back from the clinic. He went to get you, 'cos Aunt Shirl said Mum was sick.' She shifted the toddler higher up her hip. 'But I know these things. My mum, she's havin' a baby. I seen it before. My dad told her she was supposed to go into town for it, but it come too quick.'

Leah smiled. She wasn't sure how much she would have known about a baby's birth when she was ten years old. 'You're going to make a good midwife.'

Krissie's face lit up. 'You think so?'

'You've made a good start already. Now, I want you to lead the way.'

Leah retrieved the backpack from the bike. Reaching out her hand, she held Krissie's. 'Come on, Matt, you're part of this. I may need another adult.'

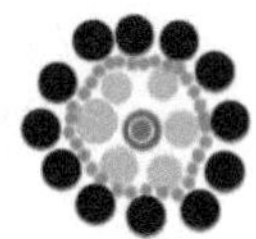

27: Leah

Leah realised by the look on Matt's face that she'd got her revenge.

'No way! This is women's business. I've got no place there.'

'That's true, but I may need some help and it looks like you're it.'

With a shake of his head, he recovered. 'Well, I have delivered a few lambs in my time; I suppose it's not much different.'

Leah knew she was taking his bait. 'Matt! You won't be doing any of the delivering.'

He responded with an irritating smirk.

Leah tried appealing to a better nature she wasn't sure he had. 'Please be discreet, for Krissie and her mum's sake.'

He snapped at her. 'I'm not totally out of my depth, lovey.'

His unexpected response threw her. 'Come on, let's go.'

They hurried towards a group of shelters made from tree branches and covered with bark. *Very practical.* Leah ran her gaze over them. *When it rains, the water will just flow off the A-frame.*

Krissie stopped at one of the temporary dwellings on the periphery of the cluster.

'Stay near the door,' Leah instructed Matt.

Parting the leaves of the entrance, Krissie beckoned Leah inside. 'Mum! Leah's here. You know; the new midwife.'

New midwife! 'New' is right.

Krissie let go of the natural curtain and turned to wait outside.

Beloved: Tell him I am faint with love — SS 5:8

Blinking, Leah's eyes gradually adjusted to the dim shelter. The whites of two pairs of eyes shone against the darkness. A young woman semi-squatted, her armpits supported from behind by an older woman. Even as a new graduate, Leah recognised the moans of established labour.

'Thank goodness you got here,' the older woman cried. 'Young Jeannie here, she started bleeding soon after her pains started. I sent her hubby to you mob for help.'

Great! Bleeding in labour and no obstetrician, anaesthetist, paediatrician or anyone!

Leah removed her raincoat, opened the backpack and grabbed a towel. Unrolling it onto the foam mattress on the floor, she scattered the contents of the medical kit over it. Pulling on a pair of disposable gloves, she unzipped a small case and retrieved an electronic foetal heart monitor. When Jeannie's cry settled, Leah knelt close to her.

'Hi, Jeannie. I'm Leah, a midwife. I'd like to listen to baby before your next contraction.'

Jeannie attempted a weak smile then looked down as a gush of dark red blood trickled down her inner thighs. Leah took a deep breath to calm her own racing pulse before switching on the monitor.

This is serious stuff! She gulped and pushed aside a flicker of panic. *This mother and baby could actually die!*

She scanned the monitor across Jeannie's abdomen. A sound like a galloping horse filled the room. 'Wonderful!' Leah wasn't sure whether she was reassuring herself or the mother. 'Baby's heart is racing just the way it should be.'

Jeannie's groans commenced again as another contraction gripped her.

The older woman moved closer. 'I'm Shirl, her Aunty.'

Leah nodded. 'Jeannie still needs you to support her, so I'll have to call Matt in to help with the actual birth. I've already asked him to respect your privacy as much as possible.'

'It's not custom to have a man in here,' Shirl sniffed.

A scream escaped Jeannie's clenched teeth and her face turned red as she began to involuntarily bear down.

'But,' Shirl relented, 'I s'pose we don't have much choice at the minute.'

'Matt!' Leah bellowed.

His silhouette blocked the light as he stepped into the cramped space.

'Come over here and pass me whatever I ask,' Leah instructed.

Obediently he stepped over her crouched legs.

'First pull on a pair of gloves.'

Jeannie thrashed around as another contraction took hold.

'The baby's coming now!' Leah exclaimed. The crown of the baby's head was just visible. 'Hang on a minute, don't push. I just need to check for the cord.' Leah's fingers felt around the neck, and she groaned. *I don't believe this.*

She turned to Matt. 'Clamps!'

A very large man, Matt was struggling with the tight gloves. 'How am I supposed to get these things on?' He threw them aside and fumbled through the equipment. 'What do clamps look like?'

'This cord is tightly around the baby's neck and will strangle it if I don't clamp it off ... No!'

The woman screamed and gave another push.

'No!' repeated Leah. 'Don't push yet!'

Feeling a nudge on her elbow, she looked down to see a pair of bootlaces in Matt's outstretched hands. Amazed and thankful for his quick thinking, she grabbed the laces.

'Cut one of them in half...' She indicated a pair of scissors with her shoulder.

In the absence of clamps she knew the laces were essential to prevent bleeding from the cut cord. In a gap between labour contractions, she tied the three laces around the umbilical cord.

'Scissors!'

Matt placed them in her outstretched hand. Leah cut the cord between two of the three ties.

'Okay, Jeannie, you're doing well. Just give a small push before the next contraction comes.'

As Jeannie pushed, a black-haired head emerged. Leah watched its little face as it rotated itself slightly to the right. She placed her hands

Beloved: Tell him I am faint with love — SS 5:8

gently on either side of the baby's head and guided the shoulders out, one at a time. With a rush, its wet slippery body followed.

Jeannie relaxed back into Shirl's embrace and Leah lifted the baby onto its mother's abdomen. Cupping her hands over the tiny chest, she was relieved to feel the lungs expand, followed by a loud lusty cry. 'You have a girl!'

'We gotta another girl, Jeannie, d'ya hear that?' Shirl kissed Jeannie's head, tears already running down her exhausted face.

'Pass me a towel, Matt.'

Matt fossicked around in the backpack until he found a small hand towel and handed it to her. While Leah patted the baby to dry off some of the fluid, Shirl cleared a space on the mattress.

'Come on, girl, have a lie down now.'

Without moving the baby off her abdomen, Jeannie shuffled her way onto the mattress.

Leah hovered close. 'That's right. Keep your arms over her and she'll know she's safe and still close to her mum.' She grabbed a syringe and prepared an injection. She knew she had to give it to aid removal of the placenta and prevent further bleeding. Still she took a moment to watch in wonder as Jeannie and her baby bonded. The tiny newborn snuggled into the warmth of her mother's chest and crept up towards the breast, opening her mouth like a baby bird waiting for food. Jeannie directed her nipple into the hungry mouth.

An unexpected pang of jealousy ripped through Leah's moment of peace. Would she ever experience the intimacy of feeding her own baby? The only sound in the room came from the baby, smacking her lips as she suckled. Turning her back on the surreal scene that enfolded the mother and child, she focussed her attention on delivering the placenta. As she had done so many times over the past months, Leah snapped shut her emotions, keeping her pain buried deeply inside.

After a moment she became aware of Matt, standing transfixed, stroking his beard, deep in thought. She was surprised he didn't appear shocked or traumatised by all the drama. It was as if he were recalling a past experience from another place and time.

Beloved: Tell him I am faint with love — SS 5:8

Ridiculous! Leah scolded herself. Yet his demeanour seemed so out of character. Leah shook her head. Who was she to judge character?

Dimitri's stunned face came back to her, as he discovered she had undergone breast surgery. Why had he found it such an appalling procedure? She would never have guessed that part of his character existed when they first began dating.

Jeannie groaned and drew her knees up towards her chest. Leah turned her attention back to her patient. 'It's okay, Jeannie; it's just the afterbirth ready to be delivered.'

'I'm out of here,' Matt announced. A flash of daylight lit up the room as he parted the makeshift curtain.

Leah turned before he left. 'You were a great help, thanks.'

He gave a slight nod and, with heavy boots minus their laces, stomped out the door.

There's more to this guy than he lets on. Maybe I need to make more of an effort to get to know him. A shocking, bitter thought startled her. *What for? The last thing I need out here is another guy to remind me I'm damaged goods!*

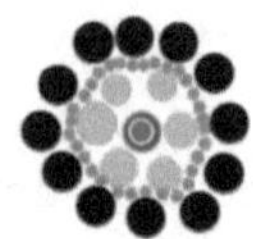

28: Dimitri

Dimitri threaded his way between the outdoor customers of Kostos Café. Normally it was a scene he loved. But today his nerves were stretched. He really didn't look forward to the conversation he had planned. But it had to be done.

He entered the café and wondered how the diners could hear one another. Six months ago, he would have laughed at anyone suggesting he'd prefer the quiet of the bush to the bright music and laughing chatter of customers. Hilarity filled the room, cutlery clattered against plates, bottles clinked against glasses. Cups settled on saucers. The coffee machine revved over the top of everything.

'Dimitri! Good to see ya, son!' Uncle Spiros greeted him from the counter with a broad grin.

'It's good to be back.' He joined his uncle at the counter. 'Got a minute?'

Spiros poked his head into the servery where hunks of lamb were being sliced from a rotisserie. 'Giorgio! Go fetch Elpida. You be telling her our young Dimitri's here!'

Dimitri inhaled the charcoal smokiness of the roasted meat. As it rotated he watched the oil drip into the base. This restaurant, the Greek food and music, was all part of him. It was all he had ever known. He straightened his shoulders. But it wasn't the whole picture.

That was the problem.

A customer stood at the counter waiting to pay. 'I just finish here, son,' Uncle said. 'Take a seat, eh?'

Dimitri wandered over to a spare table near the window. His uncle's thick accent and broken grammar always amazed him. The family had migrated over fifty years ago. He looked up at the black and white family photo hanging behind the counter. Papou and Yaya and young Spiros stared into the camera, a giant ship in the background and their trunks at their feet. His own father was born in Australia, ten years after they had immigrated. He remembered how often his grandparents had told him they had left their country hoping for a better life for their children and grandchildren. Looking into their unsmiling faces, he read their sadness and uncertainty of leaving their homeland. His grandparents would never return to Greece. They would never see their parents again.

Well, I know what that feels like.

His vehemence startled him. Losing his parents had never been something he had blamed his relatives for. This whole birth certificate thing … and the conversations with Mullaya …

He slowed his breathing. Being irritated with anyone would not achieve his aim.

He sat back in his chair and zoned into the contemporary Greek rhythm blaring through speakers. His classmates had always ribbed him for loving Greek music. They'd been the reason he'd downloaded *Zorba* as his ringtone; he wasn't going to give in to their mockery.

He tapped his fingers to the beat. Thinking of school reminded him of one thing he didn't have to worry about anymore. Once he had learnt the truth about his age, he'd just never gone back. There had been the potential for a huge fight with Aunty over not finishing his last year, but Rick had smoothed it all out by offering him a full apprenticeship.

'Dimitri!' Aunt Elpida emerged from the doorway of the living quarters.

Dimitri grinned. How could he stay cross at this short, plump woman dressed in black, complete with apron and headscarf? She might as well have just stepped out of the family village in Greece.

He stood up. 'Tia!'

Aunt Elpida bustled over and smothered his cheeks with kisses. He wondered if it was her affection that had attracted his uncle. He had travelled back to Greece and had returned with Aunt Elpida as his bride.

Lover: your hair is like a flock of goats — SS [47]

125

'Dimitri! You back! Is answer to prayer.'

'It was a great trip, Tia. Fantastic weather. We got some amazing photographs.'

He averted his eyes. How could he come home and make small talk when there were so many issues she refused to discuss?

'I get you something to eat, eh? You want some meat maybe?' She nudged him. 'Some sweets, eh? Some baklava?'

He glanced over at the pastries on the counter. He adored Aunty's home-baked sweets—baklava, that was his favourite. Layers of rich, sweet pastry with chopped nuts and sweetened syrup. His mouth watered, but he shook his head. This was a business meeting. He didn't want to linger.

It occurred to him she might be distracting him. 'Thanks Aunty, but I'm not staying that long today.'

It was as if she hadn't heard him. She pinched his cheek, just as Yaya had done since he was a small child. 'We gotta fatten up those skin and bones!'

When he didn't answer, she sighed. 'I'll bring ya some coffee, eh? You always liked your Aunt Elpida's coffee.' She patted his hand and headed back to the counter.

Before long, Spiros made his way over, bearing two glasses and a bottle of water. 'So!' He lowered himself into the chair opposite, pulled out a handkerchief and mopped his balding head. 'These old ovens! One day we buy a modern one and I won't have to sweat all the time!"

Dimitri knew his uncle would never replace his traditional wood stove, despite the constant perspiration it caused him. Customers came from across town for the succulent taste of their homed baked yiros and roasted meat.

Dimitri decided to jumped right in. 'Tio, I need to ask you something.'

'Sure, kid, what you want?'

There was no subtle way to ask. 'I know a lot about Dad since he was part of your family. But I know nothing about my mum. Where did she come from?' He held his uncle's gaze. 'Nobody ever talked about her while I was growing up. Now you and Aunt Elpida are the only ones left who can tell me.'

Spiros stared for a moment, then shrugged. 'Why you wanna know? Your mother, she's gone; no good to stir up trouble.'

'Trouble for who? Papou and Yaya have both gone now.' Dimitri was careful to edge his determined tone with respect.

Spiros took a handkerchief from his shirt pocket and wiped the back of his neck. He muttered in fast incomprehensible Greek.

Dimitri leaned forward. 'Please, Tio! I need to know!'

Aunt Elpida delivered a tray of three short black coffees and a plate of Greek pastries. Uncle Spiros mumbled at her in their own dialect. Dimitri understood enough to know she had been asked to leave them alone. With a frown, she picked up a baklava triangle and a coffee. 'You come to church at Easter with us, Dimitri?' She smiled. 'You come with Leah, eh? She very nice girl!'

That's not what you said before. Anyone who isn't Greek isn't good enough for me …

As she left, Uncle Spiros poured them each a glass of water. 'Your dad …' He gestured around the café. '… he hated this place!'

Dimitri looked at the simple welcoming decor. With its whitewashed walls, arches, wooden tables and chairs and framed prints of Greek islands, it had come a long way since his dad lived here. He had seen early photos of it when it wasn't such a glamorous place. It had started as a corner store in a neighbourhood mostly inhabited by European immigrants. It had taken nearly thirty years of hard work to build up the business.

'He never liked to stay inside. That little garden out the back was the only place he happy. His tomatoes were perfect. And the herbs …' Uncle kissed his hands and raised them. A gesture Dimitri knew was one of approval. 'So nice to get them fresh; the rosemary, and then the mint, they fill the kitchen with their smell when we cook.'

'And my mother? Where did they meet?' Dimitri refused to be side-tracked.

Spiros ignored him and talked on. 'Our life was too hard. Work, work, and work! No time to play like other kids at school. When we come home, we help here. I was fifteen when your dad was born. He was Yaya's favourite. So when he say he was going fruit picking, she cry and yell, but it was no good. He was twenty-one and that's what he wanted.' Spiros picked up the glass of water and emptied it in one gulp. 'Our father, he get so mad, he throw plates all over the floor. I hid in the cupboard I so scared!'

'Did he go to Bilyja, where I was born?'

'Not right away. He no write much, but he sent a postcard saying he hate fruit picking. Another boy, he told him about work some place out in the middle of nowhere with cows and sheep.'

'This was Bilyja?'

'I think somewhere near there.'

'Near my mum's family?'

'I dunno, son. Like I say, he no write much.' His voice grew hard. 'English wasn't our best subject. We hated school. The other kids, they call us wogs and dagos! I never finished school, I had to stay here and help and translate for my parents.'

Dimitri pushed aside a feeling of anger. He wasn't sure if it was because of the racist taunts or the injustice his uncle had experienced. He fiddled with the fork on the table. His uncle loved to tell rambling stories that took forever to get to the point.

'Your dad, one day he send a letter and he say he got married! He say she's not Greek, she's Australian. Yaya, she gets so mad! Now it was her turn to throw plates on the floor and against the wall!' Uncle leaned back in his chair. 'Many Greek parents still arranged marriages. They no want their own culture to get lost. My mother, she already knew a good girl for her son.'

Dimitri's heart went out to Yaya as her plans for her favourite son's life and his marriage fell apart. Yet what he really wanted to know was about the woman, his mother, whom his father had chosen himself.

Uncle Spiros smiled. 'Next you were born, out there in the middle of nowhere. Our mother, at last she very happy. Another grandson!' The smile widened. 'Yaya, she proud of your name too, after her father, Dimitrios.' He shook his head and frowned. 'We no sure about your middle name, Wareen. But he say in his letter that his wife, your mother I mean, she chose it.'

'My mum chose it? Why? Didn't my dad ever tell you?' His frustration escalated. 'Didn't anyone ever ask? It could have been important. What if was her father's name?'

My grandfather. My other grandfather that no one considered finding out about.

Uncle picked up a spoon and stirred his coffee slowly. 'I'm really sorry, Dimitri. If Yaya or Papou knew, they never told me. I forgot you even had a middle name until that birth certificate arrived.'

But you knew how old I was. That was a different issue and he shelved it. It wasn't the reason for this talk and he wasn't about to be side-tracked.

'They never came down here.' Uncle sighed. 'They always say "soon", but their work made them so busy. Then one summer they buy tickets for the train to come and visit. Your Yaya! Everything got cleaned and she get all the beds ready.'

Dimitri could imagine Yaya's whirlwind of washing and dusting and polishing. He smiled at the thought.

'We all come to meet you at the station and we so happy!' Uncle looked away.

Dimitri didn't need him to tell this part of the story. He knew what happened next.

'But the train came and everyone got off.' Uncle's face clouded over and his voice grew sad. 'You all lived so far away you had to catch a plane to the train. We dunno why that plane crashed. Something went wrong; we dunno know what really happened.'

Dimitri remembered his first encounter with Yaya. He recalled clinging to a social worker while Yaya tried to take hold of him. He didn't want to go with her: she was a stranger. She was sobbing and talking a funny language and she smelt funny. His own mum didn't smell like Yaya.

He had since come to recognise the aroma of garlic, and other ingredients from her prolific cooking.

He remembered being strapped into a car seat belt. When the engine started up, he had kicked and tried to escape. His screams drowned out all attempts to settle him down. The further they drove, the further they carried him away from his parents. All he wanted to do was get back to the plane where he last saw them.

He would never forget that feeling of gradual disconnection, especially from his mother.

He clenched his hand into a fist. *I was six!* All these years, he thought he had imagined the trauma of leaving his home behind. *Three years old!*

Lover: your hair is like a flock of goats — SS [4:7]

How did anyone fall for it? How could they even think I'd forget that part of my life? They tried, but it's in here. All six years of it.

Dimitri swallowed back a lump. It was time to ask the critical question. Keeping his gaze steady, he looked straight into Uncle's face. 'What culture did my mother belong to?'

Dimitri read genuine bewilderment in Uncle's eyes. 'Culture? Whatcha mean?'

'You know, like you and Aunty are Greek. What background did my mum come from?'

'Like I told you, Australian.'

'What do you mean, Australian?'

'Australian, you know, not a migrant like us.'

Dimitri lifted the ice-cold glass to his mouth. He swallowed a mouthful and rested it back on the table. 'Uncle Spiros, was Mum Aboriginal?'

'Where you get that idea from?'

'*Was she?*'

Uncle shook his head. 'Son, I'm sorry. I really don't know.'

Dimitri's frustration bubbled over into a torrent of questions. 'What do you mean? You *must* know; you were an adult when I came here. Why was Dad's family chosen to care for me and not Mum's?'

Uncle Spiros took out his hanky again and wiped the droplets of sweat from his forehead. 'You gotta believe me, Dimitri. It's true. When Papou and Yaya come back from the welfare, they say your mum had no family. My mum and dad, they make it sound like she was illegitimate. Your Aunt Elpida had a big fight with them that day. She say that everyone has a family, but Yaya told her if she wanted to stay and live here, she was not to talk about it again.'

Blood rushed to Dimitri's face. 'What made Yaya think my mum was illegitimate? And even if she was, did it really matter?' He shook his head, barely able to contain his frustration. 'Anyway, it wouldn't have been my mother's fault!'

'I know, I know, but there was another reason for them not to talk about her.'

'What was that?'

'Yaya, she blame your mother for your father's death.'

Lover: your hair is like a flock of goats — SS [4:1]

'That's crazy! It was a plane crash. How could that be her fault?'

Spiros nodded. 'I know, but Yaya thought if he didn't marry your mother, he would have come home and then he wouldn't have been in that plane.'

'It sounded to me like Dad was happy out there, whether he was married or not!'

'That's right, but she no want to believe it.' Uncle wiped his forehead again. 'When you came here, Elpida, she says to me your eyes are dark, but different to ours. She says they must be your mum's eyes and she wondered where she came from and why our Dimitrios didn't ever say. Like I told her, Dimitri, it doesn't really matter now, does it? We're your family.'

'I should have asked Yaya more questions before it was too late!'

'Don't blame yourself! Yaya was a strong woman and whatever she say, well, we all had to listen, eh? She loved you so much and she no want you to feel sad about losing your mum and dad.' Uncle looked up as a family entered and waited to be seated. 'I gotta go, kid. I'm sorry I don't have anything more I can tell you.'

Dimitri knew that he had unravelled as much as he could from his uncle. He pushed back his chair and stood up. 'Thanks, Uncle; I appreciate what you've told me.'

Uncle Spiros grinned and slapped him on the back. With that gesture he closed the door on the topic. 'Like Tia said, you bring Leah to Easter service, eh? Then here for nice party.'

Dimitri forced a smile. 'Thanks, Uncle, for talking to me. Please say "bye" to Aunt Elpida for me.' He was negotiating his way to the door when he stopped and went back.

'Why did Yaya lie about my age, Tio?' He suspected that Yaya's intention included blotting out his memory of his past. Maybe to protect him from grief. Or from knowledge of his heritage.

Uncle Spiros hesitated. 'I think she get it in her head your mother's family would try to get you back. Steal you from us. She worry that the social worker think a Greek restaurant no good place for small child. But one day she figure the social worker have no idea how old you really are, so she come up with plan. She keep saying you too young to go away. Just a baby. Need a stable life with big, fat, happy Greek family. The movie helped.'

Dimitri almost laughed. 'And then the lie took on a life of its own.' At least he now knew that Tio and Tia knew nothing about his mother's background. *Absolutely nothing.* Any knowledge had died along with Papou and Yaya. He had no choice but to meet again with Mullaya.

Lover: your hair is like a flock of goats — SS [4:1]

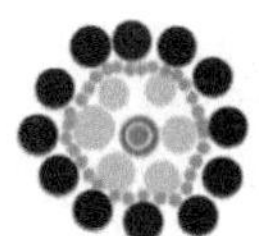

29: Leah

Leah dangled her legs over the edge of the flooded waterhole. She relaxed as, all around her, children laughed and splashed each other.

'What's the matter, Nursie?' Leah jumped as Matt's sneering voice broke into her thoughts. 'Scared of the water?'

'What are you doing here?' She turned to face him. A cigarette protruded from his lips, drooping near his fuzzy beard. She waved her hand to stave off the wafting smoke. 'You shouldn't be smoking near the children.'

Matt exhaled a circle of smoke.

Leah glared at him. 'Anyway, what are you doing out here? You know men aren't supposed to hang around while it's the women's turn!'

'Well, I ain't seen you go swimming. Not that I've been lookin' or nothin'.' He laughed. 'Can't swim, can ya?'

Leah flared at him. 'Yes, I can swim. I got into the school squad, in fact!' She recoiled from his stare, crawling over her from behind his sunglasses. It was none of his business why she didn't go in. She turned back to watch the children. If she could concentrate on the ripples of water tickling her toes perhaps she could ignore his annoying presence.

'Let's see ya do it then!'

A shove between her shoulder blades toppled her into the water. She lost her balance as her left side weighed her down and she was dragged beneath the surface. As water gushed into her ears, Matt's coarse laughter gradually receded. She needed to propel herself back up. Bubbles escaped her clamped lips. Her feet searched frantically for the bottom. *Where … ?* She was running out of breath.

With a burst of determination, she used the strength of both legs to kick her way up to the top. She took a gulp of air. Her right arm throbbed and she found herself being dragged below the surface again. A rock jutted near the edge. She snatched at it with her left hand and pulled herself across it.

'Get out of here!' she screamed.

Matt watched her, a smirk plastered on his face. After a moment, he shoved his hairy hands into the back pockets of his jeans and sauntered off towards a thicket of salt bushes.

'Here, grab my arm!' Aunty Paula stretched her arm towards Leah.

Gripping hold of Aunty Paula's wrist, Leah allowed herself to be pulled from the rock and across the water to the edge.

'That nasty snake!' Aunty cried. 'I won't waste my breath on him, but I'm gonna get on to Graham. He's an elder, and I reckon he'll have a bit to say. I'm sorry you had to go through that. Are ya all right?'

Leah spluttered, coughing out a mouthful of water. Cradling her right arm across her chest, she was unable to slow the throbbing beat of pain.

Aunty Paula frowned. 'You don't look too good. Here, take my towel, and let's get you behind these rocks and get those wet things off.' Passing her the towel, Aunty wrapped her arm over Leah's shoulder, and steered her around the pile of boulders. 'I'll stand close by, so sing out if ya need anythin', all right?'

Leah's teeth chattered and she could only nod. After Aunty had disappeared, she wrapped the towel around her. Her body trembled and she collapsed onto the ground. Tears mingled with the water dripping off her hair and onto her face. She needed to get out of her wet clothes. She unfastened the buttons of her dripping shirt, removed it and put it over a rock to dry. The blazing sun would dry her clothes within minutes. Her fingers fumbled with the hooks of the bra strap until it came undone.

Her soaked cotton prosthesis fell out onto her hand. She stared at the breast-like shape cradled in her palm and her throat constricted. The pain throbbed against her windpipe as she struggled to hold back a sob. All the humiliation of the past few months gathered behind her throat, bursting to

Beloved: My lover is...outstanding among ten thousand. — SS 5:10

be expelled. She couldn't hold it in any longer. A long sob escaped and she snatched up the towel, trying to muffle her cries. Tears continued to roll down her cheeks, building into a steady stream. She made no attempt to keep them under control. It was too hard.

'Here's another towel, lovey.' Aunty Paula called to her from behind the rocks, but Leah couldn't answer. After a few moments, she sensed Aunty's presence, and she looked up into her dark eyes. 'Aw, hon! What is it?'

The woman's empathy and gentleness broke through to Leah. It was time she trusted somebody. She had been fighting this on her own for far too long. Carefully she withdrew her towel, partially revealing her scarred flesh on the flat, empty wall. She couldn't look at Aunty for the shame that choked her. Through her lowered eyelids she felt Aunty's eyes trace the scar that took the place of her breast.

In place of my breast! How cruel is that?

Turning slightly, she revealed the extent of the scar stretching almost to her back. Leah needed someone to see what she saw every day, and to accept what she herself found so hard to accept. After a moment she mustered a skerrick of bravery and looked up at Aunty. There were tears streaming down the older woman's face.

Aunty Paula came close, settled herself on the ground and took Leah's hand. 'Cancer?'

That's all it took, that one forbidden word. Leah lowered her head, unable to reply through chattering teeth. Instead of words a dam of tears burst and her sobs escalated. Her mind vacillated between anger, anxiety, fear, grief and disgust.

Disgust. Leah forced herself to form the word, to keep it in her mind without shying away. Isn't this what Dimitri would have felt if they had stayed together? *There.* She had finally admitted it. As she thought of him, and their broken relationship, she wept harder.

The comfort of Aunty's presence eventually quietened her inner chaos. After some time she glanced up. 'I must look a state!'

'You got a right to look a state, lovey; you've been through a bad time.' Aunty squeezed her hand. 'But maybe you feel just a little bit better now. Sometimes we just need to get it all out.'

Leah nodded. The whirlwind of emotions died down, replaced by a diffusion of numbness through her body. If it wasn't for the pain in her arm she might have known peace. It throbbed in time with her pulse.

'Come on, kiddo, would you like me to give you a massage? Just show me where it hurts.'

Leah wrapped the other towel around her chest and allowed Aunty Paula to knead the taut muscles in her right arm. Gradually the ache began to subside and Aunty Paula began to sing a traditional lullaby. The tender rhythm calmed her, and it didn't matter that she couldn't understand the words.

'My mother would sing it to me as the night drew closer,' Aunty whispered.

Leah allowed the rhythm of the massage and lullaby to calm her. 'Thanks Aunty, you don't know how much ...'

'Shh.' Aunty put her fingers to her lips. 'You deserve it. Now, I'll leave you alone while you get yourself dressed. Those clothes look like they're dry already.'

Aunty Paula moved away and Leah gathered up her clothes. After getting dressed, she settled herself against the rock. Overhead a magnificent gum tree extended its arms to provide shade. A flock of cockatoos peeking between the leaves could be mistaken for white cloud.

Leah gazed up at its ancient branches and strong smooth trunk. She wondered how many people had sat and poured out their stories beneath it. Surely it could tell so many tales? The trunk stood stark, illuminated white, and she knew that, as the evening shadows approached, it would stand ghost-like against them.

She thought of her mother. Her mother's faith found God everywhere. Surely she would have said God is like this tree. He was ancient, steadfast and offered shade from life's heat through contact with the right people.

The flock of cockatoos rose up from the branches, their squawking protest breaking the peace. Leah looked around, certain she had heard footsteps on the other side of the rocks. She shuddered. *Don't be so highly strung.* Within seconds the birds descended, settling onto the branches of the lone tree, covering it like white spring blossom.

'They've come home for the night.' Aunty Paula returned and extended her hand to Leah. 'Come on; it's time to move on.'

Beloved: My lover is...outstanding among ten thousand. — SS ^{5:10}

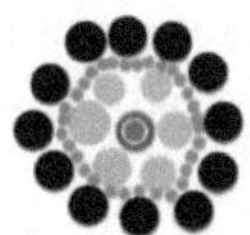

30: Dimitri

'Come on, Dimitri, sit down and try to relax. You're starting to make *me* feel nervous.'

Dimitri paced up and down the interview room, ignoring Mullaya's gesture to settle into one of the three armchairs. 'Sorry.' He managed a rigid smile. 'I know I can't keep still. But why do you think Lucy is so late? She's changed her mind?'

Maybe that wouldn't be so bad. Adelaide is a long way for her to come, for something that might just come to nothing.

'I know what you're thinking. But it doesn't matter if there's no connection between the two of you. Lucy is looking forward to meeting you, no matter the outcome. There is no way she'll change her mind. Come and sit down and have your coffee. She had an appointment this morning, so she's most likely just been held up.'

Dimitri sighed, settled himself into a chair and wrapped his hands around the mug.

'That's better. I know this is nerve-wracking for you, but I'm sure everything will be just fine.'

'*Just fine?* I'm about to meet a stranger claiming to be my ...' He faltered. *This is an insane situation to be in.* '... my deceased mother's sister!'

'You're doing an amazing thing for someone and that means a lot. Remember, I'll be here to support you, no matter what happens today.'

'I know that, you've put up with all my protests and procrastinations

Lover: descending from Mount Gilead — SS [47]

so far! You were given an appropriate Aboriginal name. Mullaya means *companion* and *friend*, doesn't it?'

'You've been doing some homework!'

'I'm making a start!'

'Good on you. Many Aboriginal parents give their children a traditional name as well as a non-Aboriginal one, even if they never record it on the birth certificate.'

I wonder if my mum gave me an Aboriginal name. Whoa, hang on a minute with that thought! This whole Aboriginal thing might have nothing to do with me at all.

A secretary poked her head into the room. 'Lucy Nader is in the waiting room.'

Mullaya flashed Dimitri a reassuring smile, 'Okay, mate?'

I suppose. He nodded.

'Wait here, I'll be back in a minute.' Mullaya left the room, leaving the door slightly ajar.

A warm, confident and deeply guttural voice drifted into the room. 'So sorry I'm late! I was invited as a guest lecturer at the uni and there was an Aboriginal student who wanted to chat after the lecture.' She lowered her voice. 'Is Dimitri still here? He must think I'm so rude!'

'He's doing okay,' Mullaya reassured her, 'and he's waiting through here.'

Dimitri stood up and relaxed his neck muscles, his eyes focussing on the door. Eagerness seeped into him, replacing some of his tension.

Mullaya led Lucy into the room. 'Dimitri …' He inclined his left hand. 'I'd like you to meet Lucy Nader.' He turned to Lucy. 'Lucy, this is Dimitri Kostos.'

Her smile radiated across her ebony face, filling her cheeks and accentuating dimples which expressed a sense of humour. She glowed with confidence, and gave the impression of enjoying life and people. He hadn't imagined for a moment she'd look anything like this. The Lucy in his mind's eye had good reason to be bitter at the world, and had sadness and grief dominating her life. Instead, she emanated hope and longing, as well as determination and strength.

Her hair was neatly brushed back off her forehead and clipped loosely at the top, allowing its waves to flow down her back. The light captured a hint of grey in the dark curls, aligning her age with tell-tale wrinkles in her toughened skin.

He felt Lucy was sizing him up, even as he took her appearance in. He hoped he would pass her scrutiny.

'I'm so happy to be here, Dimitri.' Her voice expressed genuine warmth. 'This is a great day for me, one I have waited and prayed about for so long!'

Dimitri swallowed back an unexpected lump in his throat. What if she was disappointed? What if he wasn't the nephew she sought after all? He slipped his hand into his trouser pocket and touched a tiny photo of his parents' wedding.

An annoying pang gripped his stomach. This was something else his grandparents had kept back from him. All these years and he had never set eyes on it. If it hadn't been for his conversation with Uncle Spiros, his uncle wouldn't have been prompted to search for a keepsake amongst Yaya's belongings.

He had examined the photo so frequently he knew her every feature. He still wasn't sure if his mother had been Aboriginal—the black and white photo could have been that of a woman deeply tanned by the Outback sun. He could see at once that Lucy bore no resemblance to her. His mother's face was long and triangular, her nose broad and sharp. Her smile was shy and subtle and her hair light. Perhaps the long curls were similar, but were they enough to match them as siblings?

Dimitri extended his hand to Lucy's. 'It's a great honour to meet you. I can't even imagine what you've been through trying to locate your younger sister.'

A glimmer of sadness spread across Lucy's face and she nodded. 'It's true, and you've had your share of grief too.' She looked over to Mullaya. 'I have been given just a few details, but I hope you'll feel free to share more with me.'

They settled into their chairs and Lucy accepted the offer of a cup of coffee from Mullaya.

'Just before I leave you two alone for a minute, I want to check if you are both comfortable mentioning your relatives by name?'

Lucy flashed a smile. 'All good with me.'

Lover: descending from Mount Gilead — SS [41]

'And me,' Dimitri replied.

'I thought it would be, but I do have to check. It's definitely part of our culture not to mention the name of people who are deceased. But, in this Department, it's almost impossible to do any research unless you do.'

He left the room and Dimitri turned to Lucy. 'You said you were at the uni this morning. What did you do there?"

'I'm an anthropologist and at the moment I'm lecturing at the Western Australian University. After my sister was stolen from us, I promised myself I would solve the puzzle behind the perceived differences between the black and white Australian populations.' She laughed. 'Here I go, in lecturer mode! What about yourself? How do you make a living?'

'I've got an apprenticeship in photography. The company specialises in landscape work. It suits me as it gives me the chance to get out of the city. After a few weeks in town, I start to feel stifled and just want to go out bush.'

'Do you have a favourite place? I mean it's a huge land we live in. Believe me; I've travelled over half of it trying to trace my sister.'

Without doubt, Bilyja held the most meaning for him. He was born somewhere in that region. He loved the rustic copper and stark landscape. He had met Leah there. *Leah* … Bilyja was a painful place to remember. 'No, not really. Tell me where you're from.'

'My mum and dad's family came from Pearling Bay as far back as they can remember. It's a small coastal town not many people have heard of. I don't really know that much about my dad's people. I was about six when he died while working out on a boat. He drowned while fishing; big companies, they didn't care that much about diving gear and safety precautions back then; especially for Aboriginal workers.'

Dimitri felt a catch in his throat. *Six … she'd been six when she'd lost her dad.*

'After a couple of years, my mum, she married again. My step-father had some whitefulla heritage. That's why my sister was so much at risk. Soon after she was taken, my brother Kev was born. Mum was terrified they would come and steal him as well because his skin was just as fair as my sister's was. So we moved down to the city and lived with our aunty. She thought it would be a bit safer there.' Lucy shook her head and gave a short laugh. 'They weren't too worried about me; I'm as full blood as you get.'

Lover: descending from Mount Gilead — SS [4:1]

Questions spun around Dimitri's mind. *What does she mean, 'after my sister was taken'? Who took her? How was being fair-skinned relevant? What did she mean about her brother Kev? How could someone just come and steal a child?*

When Lucy paused, Dimitri settled on a cautious response. 'What happened to your dad when you went to the city? I mean, your step-dad, sorry.'

'No worries, I always called him "Dad". Anyway, he stayed behind because he had a good job as a deep-sea pearler. Mum never actually said, but I know she believed Dad partially blamed her for what had happened. That's not fair, because the men were away working at the time and there was nothing the women could do. Their relationship was never the same. He sent money down to us when he could. This really helped subsidise the measly pay Mum received from factory work.'

'It looks like you two have started to get to know each other.'

Dimitri turned around, surprised he hadn't heard Mullaya return.

Lucy laughed. 'I'm a good talker, aren't I? It comes from years of standing up the front, telling stories to students, helping them to learn about our people. Forgive me for jumping ahead.'

'No!' Dimitri said. 'Please continue.'

'Like my mum, not a day has passed where I haven't remembered that awful day when they came for my little sister.' Lucy stood up and walked over to the window.

Dimitri watched her closely as she looked down at the city traffic speeding by. After a minute, he realised he was holding his breath. As he exhaled, he offered up a prayer for Lucy for courage.

Turning around, she looked first at Mullaya, then at Dimitri. 'I can still hear my aunts shrieking at their kids.' Her voice took on a trance-like quality. 'I was almost ten at the time and that day is as clear to me now as it was back then. I'll never forget the way mothers screamed at their children, "Quick! Run! Hide!" I stood at the edge of the camp, watching everyone. But I was frozen, too scared to move.'

She looked aside for a moment. Dimitri held his breath.

'Adults swooped upon the smallest children like the great eagles. Some

Lover: descending from Mount Gilead — SS [4:1]

snatched up two, or even more, in one scoop and raced towards their huts. From the branches up in the top of the gum tree, a leading cockatoo shrieked out its warning. The whole flock rose in the air and flew away, high in the sky as one white cloud. Dogs went crazy, barking and chasing people as they scattered. Mothers shoved aside the kangaroo skins flapping over the entrances of our temporary huts, and disappeared inside. The dogs had no one left to chase and ran off into the bushes. It felt like every living thing had vanished.'

Lucy took a deep, rasping breath. Dimitri felt as if his throat was constricted as he stared at her.

'Everybody, that is, except us. My mum's tummy was huge with a new baby inside and we had no chance to run away from our camp fire. My little sister clung onto her, sobbing into mum's chest. "Sit!" Wrenching my arm, my mum forced me to the ground. "Your skin … it's gotta be darker!" Mum scooped up a handful of charcoal from the cool fire and mixed it with the kangaroo fat we used for the cooking. I had never seen her hands shake so much. After rubbing the black powder and fat together, she grabbed my head between her two strong hands. "Keep still!" Then she picked up that greasy slime, and slapped it all over my face. I tried to pull away from its sticky paste, still warm from breakfast. Mum kept rubbing it in, all over my cheeks, my forehead and my nose. "Close your eyes!" she hissed. The foul smell of animal grease made my churned-up stomach even tighter. Mixing more powder and fat she hissed, "Your arms! Your hands!" She kept rubbing it into me. "If they see ya, they'll know ya Full Blood for sure."'

But surely, if Pearl was fair, then it was more logical to … Then it hit Dimitri. *Her mother was scared of losing both her daughters. Lucy would have had to carry Pearl into hiding and they would have both been taken.*

'My throat felt like it was choking me,' Lucy went on. '*Who* would know I was Full Blood? What *was* Full Blood, anyhow? Then the noise of an engine broke through the stillness of the camp. I had been aware of the noise but hadn't registered what it was. It had sounded like a swarm of bees buzzing in the silence, getting closer. I looked up and saw a great cloud of red dust follow the ute towards our site. It moved so quickly until it got so close its petrol fumes nearly made me throw up.' Her eyes were winking

Lover: descending from Mount Gilead — SS ⁴⁷

with unshed tears. 'My mum tried to rub that paste onto my sister's face too. It was impossible to drag her off our mum's chest; she was clinging to her like a baby koala. I'll never forget the horrible fear and desperation in my mum's eyes as she shoved me and yelled, "Run! Hide!" I tried to stand up but my legs wouldn't hold me. I could only crawl on my belly. I felt like a hunted snake. Our place was too far away. All I could see was a clump of spinifex. I crawled over the dirt, desperate to reach the mound of grass. The trail of dust settled as the car slowed to a stop. The engine went quiet and a huge blackfulla stepped out. *A cop!* I could feel flies crawling over the tears and grease on my face. I bit down hard on salty lips so I wouldn't scream out. I didn't even know what I was afraid of, but I knew something bad was happening. The policeman fixed his slouch hat in place. I still remember its metal badge catching the sun. Underneath the wide leather brim, I watched his wrinkled and tough face. To me he looked very big and mean.'

Lucy was quiet for half a minute.

Dimitri glanced at Mullaya but he simply sat, unmoving, waiting for Lucy to start again.

'A tall, pretty lady moved away from the passenger door. Her skin was like the moon. That's what I thought—even paler than my sister's. I watched her lime green dress with yellow pinstripes swish around her ankles. My throat ached so bad from keeping my crying in, but now I had to stop myself from giggling. The woman's hair, the colour of dried grass, was piled high on top of her head. It looked just like a bird's nest, and she looked like a lorikeet. Carefully she looked over our row of little shelters. Her head turned, straight towards me. I froze. My mind was shivering. Could she see me? *Was* I a Full Blood? The stones sounded funny as the Lorikeet's high heels crunched over them towards my mum. The cop hitched up his khaki shorts over his fat belly and followed her. "She's from the Government," he growled at my mum. The Lorikeet's language sounded strange and the policeman had to change her words into our own. "Your little girl's gonna be better with us ... she's not Full Blood, you know that ... White homes are good ... she'll go to school ... get to talk properly ..." That's what he translated. My legs were numb and cramped. I wanted to get up and scream questions. "What's Full Blood?"'

Lover: descending from Mount Gilead — SS [47]

Lucy sighed heavily. Dimitri could see how much the story was taking out of her. 'My mum said nothing; that's how I knew she must have been real scared. The huge cop went back to the car and stuck his hand into the open window and took out a bottle of Coke. My tongue licked my lips. I'd tasted ice-cold Coke once. I wanted to grab the bottle and let its bubbles sink into my sticky, grease-covered tongue. The cop fiddled with his keys until the lid fell off, landing on the ground. I watched the bubbles turn creamy as they fizzed up to the top. When he returned to Mum, my sister squirmed free and lifted up her tiny arms to grab the bottle. The Lorikeet bent down and picked her up. She took the bottle and held it to my sister's mouth. Grease ran down my cheeks and behind my neck. It dripped into my face and dry mouth. Flies continued to buzz and crawl all over me. I desperately wanted to jump up from my stiff legs and lift up my hands as well. The cop stood and I could feel his eyes looking over every house. My teeth chattered as I thought he would see me peeking out behind this tiny bush. He said something to the Lorikeet, fixed his hat in place again, and headed back to the car. The Lorikeet followed him, still holding onto my sister. Her high heels ground the earth again, quickly this time, like tiny explosions. My sister's light brown curls bobbed up and down as she guzzled her soft drink and moved further away from us.'

I bet you've never drunk Coke ever again. Dimitri ran his tongue over his own lips. *Because that's what they used to take your sister.*

'My mum screeched and tried to hoist herself up from the ground. But the Lorikeet pulled open the back car door and, with my sister clinging to her, climbed in and pulled it shut. My mother's wails merged with the sound of the car engine. I sprung up from the dirt and watched the pillow of dust that followed the car which held my sister. I wanted to run and catch the car, but everything in me felt dazed and slow and all I could do was stand and stare and watch it get further away. Women burst out of their huts, their little kids crying and still clinging to their parents' hips and necks. The mothers screamed and wailed as they ran over to my mum. The old men came out too. They just stood, silent, like I did, on my mound of sand watching that car disappear into the white man's world. It was like a

Lover: descending from Mount Gilead — SS [4:7]

144

slow motion dream as I looked over at Mum and saw her pathetic empty arms. My aunty wailed, "You sold her!" But another one cried, "They stole her, you mean."' A fine pulse was visibly throbbing at Lucy's throat. 'My mother's wail is carved so deeply into my heart.'

Dimitri sat transfixed, struggling to transport himself back from the past. After almost a minute, Lucy broke the silence. 'It probably seems crazy, but I've kept this all these years.' She retrieved something from her jacket pocket and placed it onto the coffee table. When she moved her hand, Dimitri stared at a bent coke bottle top.

A faded bottle top; that's all Lucy had to connect her with her little sister. At least he now had a photo. He really should show her the photo. But he couldn't bring himself to. The picture was definitely his mother. But there wasn't any evidence to say it was Lucy's sister.

'This is just devastating, Lucy, and I'm really sorry for you and your family. But …' Dimitri didn't want to sound rude but he wasn't sure.

Lucy nodded. 'I can't blame you if you can't relate to it, but I'm just asking that you bear with me for a bit longer. I've examined lots of records and drawn conclusions. I may have been following the trail of a Maria-Pearl Alvarez whose origins have nothing to do with my family.' She looked over to Mullaya. 'However, with the amount of research the Department has done, I don't think so.' She paused as if selecting her words carefully. 'Still there's only one way we'll know for sure. That's to find someone who knew her.'

How do you propose to do that? As far as he knew, the only people who knew anything about his mother had died. His father was gone. And any information his grandparents might have had had died with them.

Lucy went on. 'So, my next move is to go back to the place where Maria-Pearl and Dimitrios died. And the place you were born.'

'Bilyja? You want to go to Bilyja?' *I should have guessed—that would be her next obvious move.* But it was a waste of time. No one even knew which part of the Bilyja area his parents were buried, let alone lived. The region around the tiny town consisted of thousands of square kilometres of desert. The only thing he was reasonably sure of was that they hadn't been townspeople. He'd rung back to ask Joey at the hotel. And Joey knew everyone; he had been there forever. Joey had asked around but no one recalled a plane crash. It would have been impossible for an event like that to go unmarked in the memories of locals in a small Outback town.

Lucy folded her arms. 'I know it sounds like a long shot. So has this whole journey. But I'm not giving up now.'

Mullaya turned to Dimitri. 'I've spoken to an Aboriginal Elder up there. She's pretty confident that, if your mother was Aboriginal, the community would know.'

Heat rushed to his face. 'I didn't even consider asking the Aboriginal community.' Talk about being caught up in his own familiar world! To check with Bill but not even consider Aunty Paula.

Mullaya shook his head. 'Don't be hard on yourself. It's still early days for you. But I agree with Lucy. The next move has to be to get in amongst the Aboriginal community and start to make connections; build relationships.'

'I've been monitoring the weather up there,' Lucy said, 'and right at the moment the whole region is ringed by flood waters. No one can get in or out. But as soon as the water recedes, I'm going up there.'

Of course!

Dimitri looked at the other two quickly to see if he had spoken aloud. For the first time in months, hope suffused his thoughts. How could he have been so … *oblivious* …?

Bilyja would *have* to be where Leah had disappeared to.

It made sense now. All his messages had gone unanswered; clearly there was no internet access. Even satellite communication might be difficult. He tried to keep his smile from spreading across his face. Just maybe it wasn't totally over.

'Dimitri.'

He looked up quickly. *How long had Lucy been talking?*

'Why don't you come to Bilyja?'

Dimitri looked into Lucy's eyes, trying to register the invitation. Only it wasn't Lucy's eyes that he gazed into. It was Leah's bright green and lightly flecked eyes, filled with eagerness. He gulped. 'Yes. I would love to.'

Lover: descending from Mount Gilead — SS 4:7

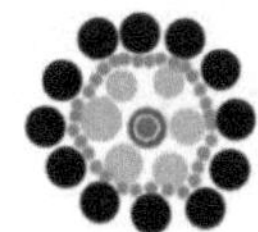

31: Leah

Leah stood like an animal stunned under the beam of headlights. The urge to throw up penetrated her trance and she gripped her stomach, slowed her breathing. The wave of nausea subsided.

Stumbling through the room to her bed, she rocked her body back and forth. A moan throbbed against her throat. Her jaw clamped shut. If she released it, it would be a howl echoing across the desert like the baying of a dingo.

Perhaps it would be powerful enough even to reach Dimitri.

Dimitri. *Stop it! He's gone!*

This was supposed to be in the past.

Please God, not again! Not… not… not again.

Leah left the house in a rush and made her way to clinic. The chaos of children, dogs, and even birds, were a noisy din beating against her ears. Everything remained the same, yet everything had changed.

'You look like you've seen a ghost!' Aunty Paula greeted Leah.

'You don't know how true that is…' Her voice came from a strange place. It functioned all by itself.

Aunty Paula's eyes searched hers. Leah never could hide from her gaze.

'Come on, let's start the day with a cuppa.' Aunty took control. 'The others can set up the clinic.'

They sat out on the back veranda, each leaning against a wooden pole. With a mug of warm coffee clutched between her hands, Leah stared out across the plain. Shrunken puddles lay still scattered across the land. The deluge of rain had sourced new life and a magnificent regrowth of vegetation extended beyond the pools. How secure was her own connection to life?

'I reckon we could get that plane in pretty soon. It must be almost three weeks since any of us left the site.' Aunty Paula broke into Leah's musings. 'It's about time you had a week or so off.'

What would she do with a week off now? She had looked forward to doing normal things like meeting up with other nurses, going shopping, attending church, and eating fresh food. And, best of all, getting onto the internet. Maybe even check if Dimitri has sent a message … *Stop it!*

This next trip into town promised only to be a frightening and lonely experience. Her throbbing headache beat in time with the pulse still pounding in her ears. Closing her eyes, she puckered her forehead and massaged her temples. Aunty Paula said nothing but her presence emanated the calm Leah needed. She swallowed back the blockage in her throat and cleared away a crack in her voice. 'I've found another lump.'

'Aw, kid! That's just awful!' Aunty Paula put down her cup and moved closer, wrapping her arm around Leah's shoulders. The weight of Aunty's arm brought comfort, drawing Leah out of her cocoon.

'I'll come in with you to the hospital. You won't have to do this alone, okay?'

Leah broke away. 'I'll be fine, Aunty Paula; I know how much you hate going into town.'

'Take no notice of my ravings; it's not that bad in there, really. Besides, I got a couple of people comin' up from the city to meet me. So I got no choice anyway, eh?' Aunty looked away, focussing on the clouds overhead.

Is that a hint of uncertainty in her voice? Leah dismissed her speculations. She was in no state to second-guess anyone right now.

'Yep, I reckon that sky will stay clear for the next few days at least.' She turned back and rested her hand over Leah's. 'You get yourself back home and get some rest. We'll manage all right here. I'll buzz the hospital and let them know we're comin' in.'

Beloved: His head is purest gold — SS 5:11

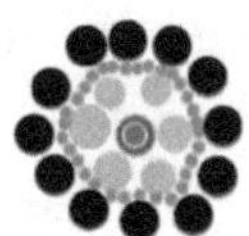

32: Leah

When evening drew near, Leah headed to the airstrip. She eyed the water markers. The water had receded; mud clung to where the flood had peaked. If she had wanted to head here only a few days earlier, she would have had to wade rather than walk.

Her stomach tensed. Krissie had delivered a message from Aunty Paula earlier that day. The strip had been considered safe for landing and take off. By tomorrow morning she would be back in town. On the medical treadmill.

Walk! Don't think.

She trudged along the edge of the strip, her hiking boots lifting up the soft golden mud. This could be the last chance she had to take a nightly walk.

It was odd how the smell of evening meals and the bantering of gathered families never once made her feel excluded. She was a visitor, yet she was welcome. At that level she belonged. Still, she needed to withdraw as well. The deserted strip had always afforded her the peace she needed to quiet the voices of her busy day.

Beads of sweat formed on her forehead. Although the sun was lower in the sky, the humidity hadn't decreased. Up ahead, the windsock inhaled a miniscule breeze, its limp tail just swaying from side to side.

In the quiet, her anxieties about her health gathered but she managed to keep them at bay. Instead, Dimitri crept into her thoughts. She knew now she could never put thoughts of him totally aside until she'd seen him once more. He'd said his love was stronger than death. It was time she put

Beloved: his hair is wavy — SS 5:11

it to the test. What did she have to lose? If he wanted nothing to do with her, she would move on.

If?

Who am I kidding? She wasn't good enough for him before. With the possibility of another scar it would be even worse.

Leah settled herself on a wooden bench. The spectacular landscape stretched endlessly, merging into the sky, aglow with the orange, red and yellow of the sinking sun. A continuous chattering of insects replaced the chorus of water birds from earlier in the day. Leah enjoyed the cool breeze dancing against her calves as it played with her loose skirt.

"How beautiful you are my beloved! Oh how beautiful!"

Beautiful? Like a knife, the word stabbed deep into her soul and she felt almost physically sick. This was a verse from the *Song of Songs*; a declaration by the Lover to his Beloved.

How could anyone possibly see me *as beautiful any more?*

Her eyes swept the world around her.

This is beauty; the sky, the land, the rain, the chorus of birds, insects and wildlife. These make up the beautiful song of the Outback. Not me.

Her throat throbbed as she tried to hold back a cry of sadness, yet deep inside she became aware of a tiny whisper: 'You are even more beautiful to Me than these.'

A flick of a match from the shadows broke the moment. The foul odour of cigarette smoke permeated the fresh air. *Matt!* His menacing laugh shattered her moment of solitude.

'Do you think I don't know all about you?' He moved towards her.

Her heart thumped and her body froze. She braced herself for humiliation.

The wooden slats sank as he settled himself on the bench. His shoulders touched hers and she inched away. He reeked of tobacco but there was also a touch of alcohol on his breath.

This is a dry zone! You are such a total …

What was the use? Her mouth had clammed up and she could form no words.

'You told Aunty your little secret.' The alcohol made him creepier than usual. Petrified, she remained immobile.

Beloved: his hair is wavy — SS [5:11]

'That's why your fancy man ditched you, isn't it?' His tawdry voice sent a shiver down her spine. 'Why else would a scrumptious chick like you return to Wild Nowhere Land?' He blew a puff of smoke into the air and tossed his cigarette butt onto the ground, stubbing it out with his heel. His hand free, he pressed it firmly onto the middle of Leah's back. Her body stiffened but still she couldn't move. His fat fingers crept up her spine. 'But I'd have you, what you got or ain't got makes no difference to me.' He sniggered. 'After all, there's nobody else who wants you, is there?'

He pulled her close, murmuring in her ear. 'Better with me than stuck on your own the rest of your life.'

His words seeped into her broken heart. He was right. Dimitri didn't want her. It was pathetic to cling to some hope that they'd get back together.

'So what do you say? You and me; an item, eh?' He pressed his hand harder onto her back.

The physical pressure broke through to her seduced mind. With a rush of strength she shook off his hand, stood up and stared straight into his face. 'Don't you ever come near me like that again. My business is my business. You hear?'

Leah spun around and fled across the strip, jogging all the way back to her place. Once inside, she bolted the front door and leaned back against it. She doubted he would follow her. But the run had done her good. Cleared her head. She steadied her breathing, willing her racing heart to slow down. Eventually the darkness in the house settled her and she moved away from the door and lay down on her bed.

I need to pray! I need to get back. You've been stolen from me, and I need You back. It's the only way I'll ever get through this nightmare. As she continued to work on slowing her breathing, a familiar and comforting presence began to settle around her.

Aunty Paula's words came back to her. 'The *Song of Songs* is God's love song to you.'

"All beautiful you are, my darling; there is no flaw in you."

Leah grabbed a slim-line torch from her bed-side table and picked up her bible. Flicking through to the *Song of Songs*, she found the verse underlined. It came from chapter four; the pinnacle of the love story; the royal wedding. Her eyes moved carefully across the text and she felt like she was reading it for the first time.

Aunty Paula had told them that the *Song* could be interpreted as an analogy of God's love for His people, but this wasn't really an abstract poem to be read between two lovers. Yes, there had been wonderful moments when she and Dimitri had quoted it to each other. But it had so much more. It was a description of how God saw her; His perfect bride, with no flaw!

How could she turn away from His gaze of love, and focus on the superficial, negatives about herself?

I didn't even give Dimitri a chance to accept me. I didn't give myself a chance to accept the way I am. I've just run away, up here to Bilyja.

Like Eve, in Genesis, hiding in shame. That is so illogical. God saw her as perfect. It was time she saw herself like that.

Beloved: his hair is wavy — SS 5:11

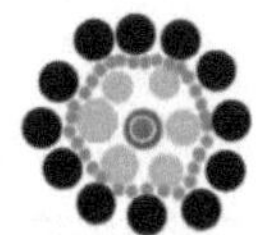

33: Leah

'It's the plane! The plane is coming!'

Children had lined up along the airstrip since first light. Leah was pretty sure the arrival of the plane always caused a stir. But this was also the first contact with the outside world for weeks, causing even more excitement.

She stood up and raised her hand to her eyes, watching the plane draw closer. Parents yelled to the children above the noise to keep back. They pulled the cheekier ones aside by their windblown clothing.

Aunty Paula's smile was reassuring as she came and dropped her bags next to Leah's. The plane landed at the other end of the airstrip, splattering mud everywhere, including its own windows. It taxied to a halt, its heavy wheels yellowing as they created muddy trenches.

Leah grimaced as the noxious smell of fuel brought with it the intrusion of the outside world. When she stepped out of the plane on the other side of the desert, a whole world of challenges would face her.

Aunty Paula gripped her hand and spoke close to her ear. 'Don't forget, I'm right here with you. There's no goin' it alone, right?'

Not having enough energy to shout above the noise, Leah just nodded.

Four passengers alighted and Leah's mood lightened.

'Jeannie!' She stepped forward to greet the mother and new baby girl. 'So sorry you were stuck in town all this time! How are you doing?'

'Okay.' Jeannie's smile was shy as her downcast face fluttered up. 'We were stayin' with my aunty and she was real happy to see the two of us.'

'Can I have a cuddle of your little one?'

Beloved: and black as a raven — SS [5m]

Jeannie carefully handed her the baby, swaddled in a bundle of cotton wraps.

'She's just beautiful!' Leah cooed.

'I called her Leeya, like you. Hope that's okay?' Jeannie's gaze dipped down again.

'Jeannie! That's so special.' Leah's eyes threatened to spill tears and she gripped the baby's tiny fingers. 'I'm absolutely honoured.' She passed the little girl back to Jeannie and, after a quick hug, looked away. She had no idea whether she would ever be back to see her namesake.

'Got room for me, mate?' Matt yelled at the pilot.

Leah swung around. He had come up behind them, his backpack slung over his shoulder. 'You heading into Bilyja town?'

'Why are you coming?' she blurted out.

'Why are you?' His sleazy drawl irritated her as usual. 'I need a drink. Haven't been to a pub in weeks, and I need a cold beer!'

Luca, the pilot, observed them with a shrug. 'Should be okay, Matt, but come and weigh in to make sure.'

When Matt stepped off a set of scales, he turned to Leah again. 'Go on, my fair one, why are you going? Can't cope with bein' away from the big lights, eh? Or are you missing your boyfriend?'

'You leave her alone,' snapped Aunty Paula.

Leah shook her head, tired of secrecy. 'I need to see a doctor,' she said simply. 'It's personal.'

He raised his eyebrows and his face softened. With his large, coarse hand he stroked his beard. Leah wondered if, beneath that bawdy exterior, there was a touch of human kindness. The moment passed and he shrugged, swung his pack onto the scales, while Leah and Aunty Paula turned and clambered into the plane.

Finally they were in the air, and Leah relaxed back into her seat to enjoy the view below. She was amazed at how it had come to life. The torrential rains of recent weeks had transformed the barren landscape into a virtual floral show. Birds of countless breeds and colours gathered near hundreds of shallow water holes.

'It's just magnificent!' she called to Aunty Paula over the noisy single engine. The breathtaking distraction helped her slow her turbulent mind.

The flight lasted for less than thirty minutes, cruising into the small airport far too soon for Leah.

Beloved: His eyes are like doves — SS ^{5:12}

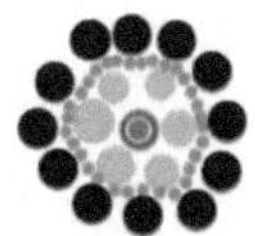

34: Leah

Leah sat on the bank, mesmerised by the golden reflection of the trees on the river. The last time she had been here, it was with Dimitri. For a romantic riverside lunch in beautiful downtown Bilyja. She smiled. There had been nothing romantic about warding off mosquitoes from a dry river bed. So much had changed since then.

She shifted uncomfortably. The biopsy had hurt. The local anaesthetic wasn't quite deep enough. Leah tried not to replay the events of the morning. She was just so thankful that Aunty Paula had stayed with her. She folded her arms, cradling the painful area over her chest.

The recent flood had swept branches and debris up along the riverbed. The doctor had sent the pathology down to the city for testing. It could be a week before she got the results. A week before being swept up in the health system. Or not.

Meanwhile she was determined to make contact with Dimitri. There was free wi-fi at the nurses' home. But she needed to figure out what she would say. There was so much.

'You think you're too good for me, eh?'

Before Leah could turn, Matt heaved himself down to the bank and snuggled up to her. He pushed her hard against the trunk of the tree, his arm pinning her chest. The foul odour of alcohol and tobacco blew across her face and his voice spoke close to her ear. 'Well, you're not.'

'Get away!' His arm dug into her fresh wound and she struggled to free herself from his grip.

Beloved: His eyes are like doves — SS 5:12

She squirmed to free her neck and turned to look him full in the face. His eyes were red and crossed and he drew closer to her face, his lips barely a centimetre from hers. 'Dreamin' of Prince Charmin', eh?'

Leah recoiled from his putrid breath. His arm weighed heavily into her wound but her voice froze, failing to produce the scream of terror she needed.

Heavy footsteps approached them from behind and Matt sat forward, startled. With his weight off her, Leah could breathe again. But he gripped tighter onto her wrist, burying his head into her neck. She gagged from his rancid breath. His fingers dug into hers, warning her not to cry out. Leah willed the person not to pass and leave her alone with Matt.

The footsteps stopped just metres away. Matt let go, stood up and mocked her with a bow. 'Tomorrow, same time, same place, my precious one?'

He moved past the bystander, mumbling, 'Nice piece of work, ain't she, mate?' His sleazy laugh echoed across the water. 'Hands off, though, she's all mine!'

Matt stumbled away, but Leah's face burned with too much shame to turn around. Holding her breath, she willed the stranger to walk on and leave her alone. The footsteps drew nearer and stopped.

'Leah?'

The incredulous whisper sent goose bumps along the back of her neck.

Blood drained from her face and she remained still. His voice, as quiet as it was, rang with familiar magic. Yet it couldn't be him. Why would he be here?

'Leah?' Low and urgent, his voice now carried a trace of uncertainty. Her mind refused to function, and she sat protected in a bubble. If she turned and was wrong …

Beloved: His eyes are like doves — SS ^{5:12}

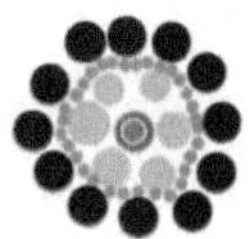

35: Leah

His presence remained, bold and unmoving, and taking a deep breath, she turned.

Here was the face of the man her dreams had never forgotten. Her fingers ached as she restrained herself from reaching up and taking hold of his face. They ached to trace every familiar line on his beautiful bronze skin.

Dimitri? She mouthed his name, her voice lost.

His eyes looked as shocked as she felt. She held his gaze and watched them fill with longing and passion. He beamed a smile and she had no doubt that his delight matched hers. Joy bubbled from inside and she recovered her voice. 'What are you doing here?'

Thud!

Dimitri spun around. On the path near the edge of the park, Matt had stumbled. He picked himself up, waved and staggered away. Dimitri turned back to Leah. A shadow had crept over his face. As if a blind had been pulled down, his eyes lost their warmth.

His voice sounded flat. 'I'm sorry to have disturbed you and your friend.'

Leah scanned his face, seeking a clue for his abruptness. 'My friend?'

'That guy, he was a friend of yours, wasn't he?'

Heat crept into her face. She wanted to shake him and yell, *How can you possibly think that sleaze could be my boyfriend?* Her mind grappled with the see-saw of emotions.

'You're shaking; are you all right?'

The familiar ring of compassion to his voice stung her again. How could his tone contradict the disdain she had just read in his eyes?

'Do you mind if I sit down?'

'Go ahead.' Leah nodded. *This isn't the way I'd planned it. It's all going wrong. Yet here he is … in Bilyja …*

Dimitri lowered himself onto the place Matt had just vacated. How could two men make her feel so vastly different? Her arms ached for Dimitri's to enfold her as they had always done in her imaginary reunions. Instead, her hands gripped the grassy edge to settle their trembling and to curb her overwhelming desire to clasp hold of his.

'Are you sure you're all right?' he asked again.

She nodded, but her jaw clamped, withholding a string of questions.

They sat by the river in silence. In the great gum trees on the opposite bank, magpies called to each other. They seemed to be making up for her silence. A flashback of a football game she'd gone to with Dimitri a lifetime ago tumbled into her thoughts. The Magpies versus the Crows. She had been surprised at how much fun they'd had cheering for opposite teams. Back in those first early days of going out, their only conflict was casual and meaningless.

Dimitri leaned forward with shoulders slumped, his despondency unmistakable. Leah imagined the warmth of her fingertips diffusing the strain of his neck muscles.

But her hands remained locked. The tension felt like it would break her apart. *Has he come here to look for me? Why now?*

Tears built up behind her eyes and she had to stare hard at the flakes of the paper-bark gum tree to stop their flow.

Was this a second chance?

The Lord alone knew how terrified and lonely she felt to face another cancer scare. Yet if she couldn't tell him about her illness back then, how could she now? Why would he consider going out with her again?

She took a deep breath. 'So, what brings you to Bilyja?'

He didn't answer immediately. *Is he figuring out how to choose his words?* After a moment, he picked up a stone and threw it towards the water. It skipped across the top and disappeared beneath a ripple.

Beloved: by the water streams — SS 5:12

'I came up to meet someone.'

'You came to meet someone?' *I don't believe this!* He had chosen one of their special places to meet someone else! Fury pumped through her. '*Who?*'

'It's not what you think, Leah.'

'What do I think?'

'I came up to Bilyja with … a friend. We hope to find some information about our families.'

Her body lost some of its tension. 'Are you related?' He had been born in the area, but as far as she knew he had never found any family from around the region.

'It's a long story and I really want to explain it to you.' His eyes recaptured some of his joy. 'But I'd rather do it properly.' He hesitated.

Leah held her breath. She would love to sit and listen. She had lots of time.

'Will you have dinner with me?' His words tumbled out. 'We can talk it over then.' He looked over his shoulder for a moment. There was an edge to his voice. 'That is, if you're not too busy.'

She ignored the insinuation and chose to smile. 'I'd like that.'

'Fantastic!'

'What about we try that little place just along from the nurses' home?' His smile was as gorgeous as ever. And he hadn't lost his sense of humour.

'The Red Ochre?' she asked. 'Unless you mean something other than the *only* restaurant in town.'

'That's the one. Are you staying in the nurses' home? I'll come and pick you up.'

Too much like a date. She wasn't ready for that just yet. 'No, that's fine. I'm okay to walk. It will still be light and it's only a few streets away. What about seven?'

'Sounds good. I'll book it, if you like? It's only small and it might fill pretty quickly.'

Leah searched Dimitri's face. Despite his light-heartedness, something about him had changed. He seemed more mature. Maybe this family matter was significant. He certainly wasn't interested in giving her the short version.

'Are you going back there now?'

'Sorry?' Leah realised he had kept talking.

He beamed that cheeky smile again. 'If I can't walk you home later, I'm offering to do it now.'

It was hard to keep a straight face. And there was no harm in taking up the offer. 'Of course.'

She stood up and looked again at the light dancing on the river. No one ever knew what may turn up in the current of life. They walked back along the path, side by side. Dimitri's arm brushed hers. How easily she could have slipped her hand into his!

At the exit, Dimitri turned to face her. 'You've done something to your hair.'

His words ripped through her. *Could he tell? Did she look ugly?* She recalled how her mother's loss of hair coincided with her dad walking out on them.

Dimitri must have sensed her reaction. 'I'm sorry, I didn't mean anything. You look different, that's all!'

She turned back to him, trying to gauge his tone.

'It looks kind of cute.' His smile appeared genuine. 'Brushed back from your face like that, it shows even more how pretty you are.'

They walked the few metres to the sandstone building of the nurses' home in silence.

'So, I'll see you at seven?' Dimitri asked.

'That's fine.'

Not trusting herself to linger under the veranda, Leah fumbled for her keys in her bag. 'Catch you later.' She opened the front door and stepped inside.

Her eyes took a moment to adjust to the gloom in the parlour. As she settled herself on the sofa, she heard his footsteps slowly fade into the distance.

Did that really happen? Was that the reunion she had anticipated? How could it feel so awesome, yet so painful?

The old grandfather clock chimed once to indicate the half hour. *Time is predictable.* It ticks away the minutes and days and years while we are still stuck trying to control what happens to us. Yet we never know what life will bring us. Or for how long.

They had to talk about what had happened. Whatever the outcome, she would just have to deal with it. They owed it to themselves and to each other.

Try telling that to the nerves tightening in her stomach.

Beloved: by the water streams — SS [5:12]

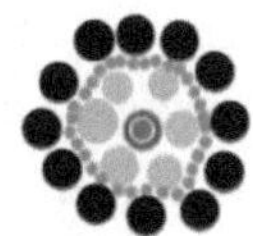

36: Dimitri

Dimitri fiddled with the candle centrepiece. Delicately hand-painted lilac holders featured on all the tables. A slight aroma of lavender emanated from the wax, adding to the intimate mood. His eyes strayed to the clock; again. *What if she doesn't turn up?* He should have insisted on escorting her. But then it would have seemed as if they were going on a *date.*

Was it a date?

He still couldn't believe it. There had been an outside chance Leah had come back to the Bilyja area. *But to actually be in town!* And to meet her like that; face to face! What was the chance of that?

He rotated his shoulders hoping to shake off some of his tension. It probably wasn't that much of a coincidence. After all, Bilyja wasn't exactly the most populated place. He should have been more prepared. He had rehearsed so many things to tell her on the day they met. And, when the moment came, he couldn't remember a single word.

His face flushed and his heart beat faster. He couldn't help the poison of jealousy seeping through his veins. *How could she possibly go out with a guy like that?* The sleaze was all over her like a rash. And he'd had more than a few too many drinks.

Dimitri exhaled. Did I ever know the real Leah at all? Was it all an act? Was she a chameleon who knew just how to get the most out of a guy?

He stretched and relaxed his fingers. It didn't matter. He still loved her! How hard had it been to restrain himself from holding out his arms and hugging her tight to himself!

Lover: You have stolen my heart — SS 4:9

'Lost in your own thoughts?'

'Leah!' Dimitri pushed back his chair and stood up. 'Sorry, I didn't see you come in.'

His chest tightened for the second time that day. She was so beautiful! He loved the way her smile brought her face to life, spreading to her eyes.

'It's so good to see you.' He reached out and wrapped his arms around her. There. He had done it... carefully, gently. Not to scare her off.

And she felt so good. A bit too thin maybe, but holding her felt good, really good. She hugged him back. Maybe not the biggest one she had ever given him. But she hadn't pushed him away. He stepped back.

Their eyes met for a second before she looked away. 'It's all those hours you spend on your own in the bush; you forget the rest of us.' Leah fussed around settling herself in to her chair, her voice overly bright.

Not true! If only you knew how many of those hours I've spent thinking about you.

They chatted lightly before picking up their menus and scanning through the options. A lanky teenager in a skimpy top and short skirt bounced towards them for their order. 'Hey, I didn't know you two were up our way again.' The waitress grinned and chewed her gum. 'This place could do with a bit of romantic gossip!'

'Hi, Mel, good to see you, too.' Dimitri glimpsed Leah's heightened colour just before she hid her face behind the menu. *Awkward! Mel means no harm, but really ...* 'We'd love a jug of water,' he hinted.

'Oh.' Mel turned back to the counter.

He picked up his menu again and checked the daily specials. Mel returned after a minute, settling the jug of water in the centre of the table.

'Ready to order?'

'Thanks,' Leah replied. 'I'll have the warm chicken salad.'

'And I'll have roast of the day.' It wouldn't compare to Uncle's chargrilled lamb or pork.

'No worries.' Mel held out her hand for their menus. 'Shouldn't be too long.' She winked at Leah and turned back to the counter.

'That's the trouble with a small place,' Leah said. 'Everyone knows your business.'

Lover: You have stolen my heart — SS 4:9

'In a way I'm hoping that's going to be the case while I'm up here.'

Leah raised her eyebrows. 'So, what brings you to Bilyja?'

'It's a long story …' Unable to restrain himself, he leaned closer. 'I've missed you!'

'You could have come back!' Leah returned.

'You made it clear that you didn't want me around!'

Her eyes flashed. 'I thought you loved me! But at the first sign that I'm not the woman you imagined, you leave me to face everything on my own!'

'What do you mean? You *told* me to go! That surgery; I know it was your choice, and you didn't have to explain it to me, but …' Her eyes pierced through him. He saw at once this was a sore point; one best avoided. He took a different tack. 'You're right. I should have come back, but the timing was all wrong. I think I just got it mixed up with my own news …' He trailed off again, his words sounding lame even to his own ears.

'*Timing*? I had no choice when to have it done!'

Her glare burned into him. Dimitri's heart ached with desire to reconcile with her. But wasn't she forgetting something? She had rejected *him*.

Leah fiddled with her glass and when she spoke her voice had lost its fire. 'I had to go in as soon as they had a bed available.'

Her hand trembled as she lifted her glass to her lips and a dash of water spilt onto her hand. He grabbed his napkin and wiped the back of her hand. His fingers tingled; his desire to hold hers was unbearable. If it wasn't for that infuriating image of Matt snuggled into her on the river bank …

'I'm sorry, Leah.'

'It's okay; it's just a few drops of water.'

'No, it's not okay!' He couldn't hold back. He leaned forward and took her hand. 'I didn't mean about the water, I mean everything. You're right; I should have tried harder to find you! It was just that I thought we loved each other and I was so angry you could just break it off. I should have given you a chance to explain.'

Leah snatched her hand from his. 'You wanted to give *me* a chance to explain? Did you think you may need to explain why you allowed me to push you out so easily? I was so sick and down, and I needed you to be

Lover: You have stolen my heart — SS 4:9

bigger and stronger than me. Had I become so unattractive to you that you were happy for the excuse to walk away?'

What? How is it my fault that I did exactly as you asked? Dimitri ran his fingers through his hair, completely frustrated and confused by the exchange. He threw one last card into their argument. 'Besides, I couldn't be sure if you wanted to keep going out with someone who might turn out to be Aboriginal.'

'What?'

Dimitri's mind spun as thoughts came from all directions. If Leah knew nothing about his Aboriginal journey, then why *did* she break it off? Or if she did know, why would she pretend not to? To protect her racist action? *This is nuts! Just spit it out.* He watched her closely. 'While I was away there were some messages from Mullaya in the Department of Aboriginal Reconnections. Maybe you had a chat to him.' He knew he was fishing and he wasn't sure if Leah even knew about Mullaya. Kossie had, though, and he might have told her.

Leah shook her head. 'I don't think I've ever heard of him. What are you talking about?' Her face had gradually paled and she looked so incredibly vulnerable. How could he ever have accused her of being racist? Her response sounded flat. 'I was organising a hospital stay. I was too busy to even think about anything else.'

Or anyone else. Even me. He slowed his breathing but his chest continued to throb. *So Mullaya wasn't the reason. Was it Matt?* That 'friendship' hadn't taken very long to get going. There were two guys she had met in Bilyja. He grabbed his glass. His hand shook.

And she had chosen the other one.

Lover: You have stolen my heart — SS ^{4:9}

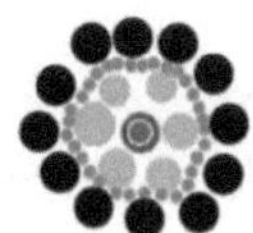

37: Dimitri

'Tell me what happened.' Leah broke through the surge of despair. 'Have you had contact from your mum's family?'

He stared at her. If she wasn't interested in him, how could she sit there and listen to his story? *Maybe this wasn't about him, after all. What if this is about her?* What if something else was bothering her? And, like she said, he hadn't been there for her?

She was doing his head in. Leah's gaze had settled on his face, waiting for him to go on. He sighed. He had nothing to lose any more. He leaned forward to tell her about the Department of Aboriginal Reconnections and their work bringing together Aboriginal families separated by previous government policies. He described his interview with Mullaya, followed by the meeting with Lucy. 'I have no idea if this is relevant to me. I'm convinced that Maria-Pearl Alvarez is my mother but not that she's necessarily Lucy's sister. Still, it's opened up a whole world I knew nothing about.'

'That's so incredible, Dimitri! After all those years of wondering who your mum is and why you had no contact with her family, your questions might finally be answered.'

'Warm chicken salad for you.' Mel arrived, setting the plate before Leah. '… and roast lamb for you. Enjoy your food … as well.' Mel grinned and walked away.

Dimitri reached his hand across the table. 'Last time we came here, you offered to say *Grace*. Do you feel comfortable doing it again?'

Lover: my sister, my bride; you have stolen my heart — SS [4:9]

Leah nodded and gripped his hand. 'Father, you brought us to Your banqueting table and Your banner over us is love. Please bless our food, our conversation and our evening.'

'That was so beautiful,' he whispered. 'I mean, *Amen* …'

Leah smiled. 'Amen.'

'So, you still read from the *Song of Songs* then? Is that verse about His banqueting table and banner of love still one of your favourites?'

Leah steered the conversation in a different direction. 'You must think there's a reasonable chance there's a connection between you and Lucy's stories; Bilyja is not exactly a brief journey from Adelaide.'

Why doesn't she want to talk about the Song? Was it possible that last time he had put her off? All that talk about love being stronger than death and setting him like a seal on her heart … Sure, it *was* a bit corny … *Was that what had ended it?*

He shook out his serviette and described Lucy's tragic story, of Pearl's removal, over dinner.

Leah shook her head. 'It's so hard to believe there was a time when people thought it was okay for a child to be snatched from the arms of its mother! Aunty Paula has told me so many stories like that. People come up from the city, trying to retrace the steps of missing family members. So many of them have no idea which family line they belong to.'

'When Lucy and I met at the Department …' Dimitri took her lead and focussed on his retelling. '… Mullaya laid out a map of Australia and traced the journey they think Pearl made.' He explained again how Lucy had come to her conclusion that his mother and her sister were the same person. 'But the only way we'll really know is to meet someone who has met Maria-Pearl, and can vouch for her Aboriginality.' He paused, sighing. 'And my question will be answered. Am I an Australian Aboriginal?'

Her eyes searched his and tears slipped down her face.

'You've carried that question around all these months and I've never even known.'

'Would you have cared?' *There.* He'd said it. There was no power behind his question. Just a flat-out question. Did she care? Or not?

Lover: my sister, my bride; you have stolen my heart — SS ^{4:9}

'How can you even ask such a thing?' Leah picked up her handbag and fumbled inside until she retrieved a tissue. She wiped away her tears and cleared her throat. 'So this is what brings you to Bilyja?'

What could he say? That was the truth. He hadn't thought to come looking for her up here. Not until Lucy invited him to be part of her search. He wished he had, but he hadn't, and couldn't pretend any different. He nodded.

Leah's face remained unmoved. But her jaw definitely tightened.

'I'm really sorry, Leah …'

'Excuse me; I'm going to the bathroom.' She stood up, slung her handbag over her shoulder and turned away.

As she retreated, her shoulders squared in determination and she held her head high. He slumped back in his chair. *Why had he been such a vlakas?* He could have come to Bilyja months ago to seek her out. Why had it mattered so much what she thought of him?

Leah was right; he had seen how weak she was in the hospital and he had walked away. He had thought only of his own need for her acceptance as he faced questions that rocked his identity.

He pushed away his plate. His appetite had disappeared. Matt or no Matt; he would fight for their relationship to be rekindled. He sat back and waited for her to return.

Lover: my sister, my bride; you have stolen my heart — SS 4:9

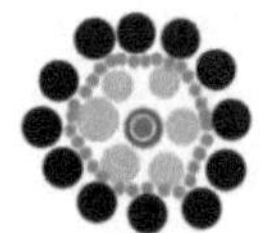

38: Leah

Leah bypassed the bathroom door and headed for the exit. Her throat tightened and her breaths came in short, frantic gasps. *I'm hyperventilating!* Her legs shook and she held onto the wall as she made her way out the door. The chill of the night air cooled her face and her airway relaxed. She eased herself down to the ground, beneath the curtain of a weeping willow. He hadn't come up to Bilyja for her. She had wasted her energy even thinking that. Her bubble filled with hope burst, and her body and spirit were shaken.

What did you expect? Dimitri's life has opened up in an amazing way. The last thing he needs is a sick—maybe even dying—girlfriend to mess it up!

Leah focussed on her breathing until eventually the buzz of the night crickets penetrated her senses. A niggling background thought crept to the forefront of her mind. Not once had Dimitri asked her about her health.

Her left side ached from the biopsy. The persistent stab of fear of malignancy grew unbearable. The memory of Matt's foul alcohol-ridden breath and his violent grip triggered a wave of nausea. Tiredness and loneliness seeped through every part of her. How easy it would be to get up and walk away and leave Dimitri in there all alone.

As he did to me!

Grabbing a tissue from her bag, she wiped away her tears.

I can't do that to him. Not to the man I'll always love.

Leah shoved the tissue back into her bag and stood up.

That was my decision. I've worn the consequence of it before, and I'll do it again.

Beloved: He has taken me to the banquet hall — SS [2:4]

Brushing off the grass from her good trousers she returned to the restaurant.

'Leah!' He stood and held out her chair. 'You look so upset; can we please talk about this?'

Shaking her head, she remained standing. 'I'm just tired; do you think we could call it a day?' *A day, a night, a year. A relationship. Over. All completely over.*

'Sure, of course. I'll go up and pay the bill.' He turned the chair slightly. 'But, please sit down until I come back.'

Leah's legs still felt like jelly and she sat down without hesitation. She couldn't be bothered quibbling about the bill. *It's been so wonderful to see him one last time.*

After he finalised the account, they left. Night had settled in. Dimitri proceeded to walk her back towards the nurses' home. If he spoke, she heard nothing. When they reached the gravel driveway, she unzipped her bag, retrieved her keys and picked up her pace.

Before she reached the front door, Dimitri reached out and grasped her elbow. Gently. 'Will you come with me tomorrow?'

She licked her lips. Her tongue stuck to the roof of her mouth. *Where? To what?* She couldn't remember.

'Lucy and I are meeting with an Aboriginal Elder. At nine.'

She couldn't meet his eyes. Why would he torture her like this? She shook her head and managed to retrieve some words. 'It's private; something between you and Lucy. Not to be shared with a stranger.'

'You're not a stranger!'

Her blood rushed to her face and she stared at him. What *was* she to him? Within a moment, her fire had died. What was the use?

She shrugged. Better to pacify him than argue.

'I'll see.'

She unlocked her front door. Without waiting for any response, she stepped inside.

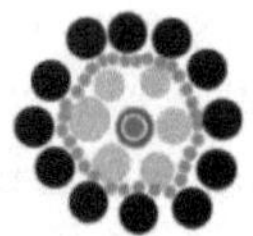

39: Leah

The phone rang right next to Leah's ear, penetrating her sleep. She almost knocked over the digital clock to answer it. She glanced at the time and groaned. Any inclination she had to meet with Dimitri at nine had been killed. It was already quarter past. A sleepless night had meant a long lie-in.

'Hello?'

'Leah McEwen?'

Her mind snapped to attention and her heart picked up speed. *Dr Campbell's nurse!* She recognised the nurse's flat, sullen tone. *What does she want? The results couldn't be back! Not already!*

'Dr Campbell's office?'

'That's right; it's Karen Lewis here, and I'm calling on doctor's behalf.'

Leah gulped. Struggling to find her voice, she croaked, 'What's the matter?'

'There was a major traffic accident yesterday on the highway and one of the admitted casualties has deteriorated ...'

'A road accident!' Leah broke in, a perverse hope replacing her panic. 'You need more nursing staff?'

'Thanks for offering.'

That was loud and clear. Thanks, but no thanks. Leah's hope dwindled.

'We do need you to come in, but not as a nurse. This is about your test ...'

'What do you mean?' Leah interrupted Karen again. 'What about my test?'

The nurse sighed, her exasperation reaching Leah down through the phone. 'Yesterday afternoon one of the accident victims required retrieval

Beloved: and his banner over me is love. — SS [2:4]

170

down to the city. We managed to send off your pathology along with him. We marked it *'urgent'* and the lab faxed through a report not long ago. Doctor asked me to call you in straight away.'

Leah lay back on the pillow and zoned out from the nurse's drone. She stared up at the ceiling, its flaking cracks bearing witness to the insidious deterioration of the building. *Dying is for the old and decayed, not for the young*, it told her.

You don't know anything yet, she argued back. *Well, why did they call me to rush in right away? Why didn't they just make an appointment for a day or two?*

Her mind tossed around possibilities and she began to slide into a pit of panic. *Why do I have to go through this again?* After a moment she realised the nurse was still speaking.

'Doctor's flying out with the other accident victim in about an hour and he'll be out of town for a while. If you don't come in immediately, you may have to wait over a week.'

It would have been better if they hadn't called her. She had been prepared to wait a week. But how could she now, knowing the results were sitting right there on a piece of paper in the next building?

'Okay,' she sighed. 'I'll be in soon.'

'Don't leave it too long.'

The nurse hung up and Leah sat cradling the phone. *Don't leave it too long.* It wasn't that easy. She couldn't bear to go to the appointment on her own. *What if the results were … what if this was it …?*

Her hand shook and the handset slipped and crashed to the floor. *Stop getting lost in all the 'what-ifs'. Get a move on, before the doctor leaves town.*

Images from the previous evening weaved in amongst her present thoughts. Dimitri's story lay like an unfinished book she longed to pick up. More than anything else she yearned to be with him again.

Where are you when I need you? Who am I kidding? This was the cause of their break-up in the first place.

Grabbing her hairbrush she ran it through her wayward hair. She paused, her brush in mid-air as she remembered Aunty Paula's promise: *You don't ever have to do this alone, kid.*

Beloved: and his banner over me is love. — SS [2:4]

171

Call her!

No!

She came into town for an important meeting. She doesn't need to be burdened with my problems.

You're just stubborn and proud!

Stop!

Thoughts somersaulted through her mind and she grabbed her mobile. She had to stop thinking and *do* something.

She typed in a SMS to Aunty and pressed *Send*.

Within thirty minutes, Leah entered the empty waiting room tucked away in the original wing of the hospital. She shivered. The room was cold. And she was scared. Very scared. She picked up a tattered copy of *Women's Weekly* and flicked aimlessly through it. Movie stars with flirtatious smiles and curvaceous physiques teased her. 'Stupid women.' She tossed the magazine back onto the coffee table.

Reaching into her bag she pulled out her mobile, yet again. No response from Aunty. She closed her eyes and focussed on her breathing. Never had she felt so abandoned.

Beloved: and his banner over me is love. — SS [2:4]

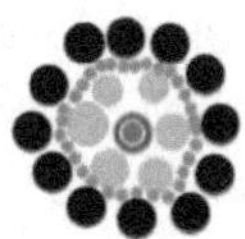

40: Dimitri

Lucy cupped her hand over Dimitri's. 'You nervous?'

He grinned. *Is it that obvious?* 'It's heaps worse for you. You've been searching for information about Pearl for your whole life. What if it's all for nothing?'

Lucy sat back in her chair, her usual smile spreading across her face. 'Nothing ever comes to nothing. There are hundreds of tiny pieces that make up the puzzle of our identity. Even if the Elder can tell us nothing about Maria-Pearl, we will both learn a little bit more about our culture.'

Our culture! He liked the sound of that. It wasn't such a strange concept anymore. But they still had a fair way to go. There was still a big chance they'd never know the truth about his mother's culture.

He stretched and relaxed his fingers, then wrapped them around his coffee mug. The café door bell tinkled and his stomach tightened. A busload of tourists trickled in. They gathered around the counter, discussing the breakfast menu on the blackboard. He looked away. Staring won't turn one of them into Leah.

He couldn't help thinking about her. He was definitely looking forward to meeting the Elder. But it was Leah he really couldn't get out of his mind. He mulled over their last conversation for the hundredth time. She hadn't said she would come. But she hadn't said *no* either.

His eyes lingered on the table in the far corner. The atmosphere of an elegant restaurant had disappeared. But her presence remained. He rested

Lover: with one glance of your eyes — SS ⁷⁹

his hand on his stomach. But the pain wasn't there. Corny it may be, but it was his heart that was bursting. How could he love her so much, yet not be able to reach her? He had planned to say so many things, to sort everything out. But he couldn't. She was blocking him out.

What was it Aunty Paula said about love? It started on a high. Absolutely! Then there was conflict. Err, yes! But then there was reconciliation. This was what he wanted. But that took two …

Mel bustled over to the customers on the table next to them. She balanced a plate of giant pancakes in either hand. They dripped with maple syrup, cream and gelato. It was a breakfast he would ordinarily kill for. But his stomach was so tight. Even the sizzling smell of fried eggs and bacon from the kitchen couldn't entice him to eat. Lucy hadn't ordered food either. He glanced at her. Definitely doing better than him, but the tension was there. They sipped their coffees.

Over the background chatter, talkback radio played comfortably. He watched Mel through the kitchen servery. She emptied the dishwasher, stacking plates on top of each other as if her life depended on it. He knew how that felt. That had been one of his jobs growing up in his grandparents' restaurant. He grimaced. Except that they didn't have a dishwasher. He had to dry and stack piles of dishes before riding off to school.

The bell tinkled again, and a young couple wearing backpacks manoeuvred their way through the doorway. A short, elderly Aboriginal woman trailed in behind them. As she skirted around them he frowned. *Aunty Paula.* Had Leah sent her?

She looked straight over to their table and grinned. 'Mornin'.'

He followed Lucy as she scraped back her chair and stood up.

'I'm Aunty Paula.' Winking at Dimitri, Aunty reached for Lucy's hand.

'I'm Lucy. It's such an honour to meet you. Thank you for taking the time to chat with me and Dimitri …' She looked from Aunty Paula to Dimitri. 'You two know each other?'

Aunty gripped Dimitri's hand. 'A very nice young man.'

Dimitri recovered his speech. 'You knew it was me you were meeting with? Why didn't Mullaya let me know?'

Lover: with one glance of your eyes — SS [2:9]

Aunty pulled back one of the chairs and seated herself. 'I didn't tell him. It's your business, not his. I don't know what's got into you and Leah, but I didn't want that to influence your decision to come up to Bilyja.'

Heat rose to Dimitri's face. *What had Leah told Aunty about him?*

Aunty Paula's eyes sparkled at him.

How does she do that? It's like she's reading my mind.

'Your parents would be proud of you. You came back to continue your search. It's not been easy for you.'

My parents? How would *she* know what his parents would think? No one knew anything about his parents. His heart thumped hard. This search to know his parents was as personal as it gets. He didn't appreciate someone making throwaway comments.

'I meant it,' Aunty Paula's voice softened. 'When Mullaya told me about Lucy's quest, that was one thing. His Department has contacted me many times in my role as Elder.' She paused and grinned at Lucy. 'Sorry, Sis, I would have helped you either way, but Dimitri here, well, he's special to me.'

Dimitri stiffened. *Is she mocking me?*

'Dimitri came up here as a young whitefulla photographer. But I could see how much he respects the land, and the life that fills it. His photos reflect that.' She leaned in towards Dimitri. 'When Mullaya told me there may be a relationship between your mother and our community, I was determined to find that link if there was one. It was tough. Aboriginal people don't like talkin' about the dead.' She paused but her eyes remained fixed on his. 'I have a cousin who's helped me a lot. After lots of questions, she's tracked down this elderly blackfulla. He remembers a light plane crash that killed a young couple and left a small child orphaned.'

Dimitri froze. He held his breath.

She continued to read him. Waited until he was ready, before she went on. 'This man, Marook, apparently knew Maria-Pearl before she married Dimitrios.'

There is someone who knew my mother? Someone who can tell me what she was like?

He hadn't expected this. Not one bit. What had he expected? An answer to the cultural question? Maybe. But what he really wanted was to know *something—anything*—about his mother. As a person, not as an Aboriginal or non-Aboriginal. He stared hard at Aunty Paula. *Is she for real?* Had she found someone who could give him that information?

He swallowed back a lump and cleared his throat. 'Where is this man?'

'Unfortunately he lives over a thousand kilometres from here.' She leaned back. 'You'll have to fly inland then drive for a number of hours. He lives in traditional country and you'll need a guide to take you both there.'

Aunty directed her attention first to him, then Lucy. 'There is one more thing. My cousin seems to think it was Marook who organised to have Maria-Pearl and Dimitrios buried on a traditional burial site.'

Dimitri gasped. Instinctively, he knew what that meant. He glanced over to Lucy who sat stock still.

'When you go to meet him—and I know you will do that—he will arrange to have you taken there.'

Lucy took a deep breath. 'If an indigenous person organised a burial on traditional land, there's no question …' Tears spilled down her cheeks and her voice faltered. '… about Pearl's identity.'

'Please, Lucy, go easy on your conclusions.' Aunty Paula rested her hand over Lucy's. 'I really don't want to see you disappointed. Maria-Pearl and Dimitrios might have just felt a real bond with Aboriginal people.'

Dimitri had never seen Lucy so vulnerable. Her eyes pleaded with Aunty Paula for it to be true.

A jingle from a mobile phone emanated from Aunty Paula's handbag.

'So sorry, guys, I really hate these things.' She reached into her bag. 'But I'm expecting a message.'

As her fingers fiddled with the buttons, Dimitri tapped on the table. *This is nuts. A mobile phone interrupting a life-changing moment.* A crazy thought crept into his mind. *Aunty's paying me back for interrupting her Song of Songs presentation. She remembers Zorba.*

'My … *friend* is over in the hospital.' Dimitri glanced up, noting Aunty's hesitation and emphasis. Why did he get the feeling there was something she wanted to tell him?

'… and I told her I'd only be a call away if she needs me.' She snapped the phone shut. 'Look, I'm real sorry but I'm going to have to go.'

Lover: with one glance of your eyes — SS ²:⁹

'That's fine. If you have to leave, we can reschedule.'

Dimitri stared at Lucy. *Are you kidding me? Both of us have waited our whole life for answers and you're happy to let her get up and walk out?*

'There is one way for you to find your story,' Aunty Paula went on. 'I will try to organise a trip up there as soon as possible.'

Dimitri's mind spun. There were hundreds of questions. But there was one bothering him. He needed that one answered before he took off on any journey. 'If we have to travel so far to meet this man and to visit my parents' burial site …' He clamped his jaw and focussed hard on keeping his voice straight. He had never imagined that maybe one day he would visit the place where his mum and dad had been buried. He couldn't bear it if it was all a hoax. 'Then why have I been told my whole life that they died somewhere near Bilyja?'

Aunty Paula sighed. 'In that case, something has gone wrong in the translation. The word "Bilyja" translated from local Aboriginal language into English simply means *red ochre*—after the desert dust. Red Ochre was the name of a mining town which is now abandoned. This is near Marook's home country. And it is where your parents lived and worked. And, tragically, were killed. Whoever passed this information on to your family, passed on the meaning of the word, but not the correct name of the town.'

Dimitri stared out the window, beyond the town to the red horizon. Someone out there—maybe even more than one person—knew his parents. The horizon blurred and he didn't bother to hold back the pool of tears. It was laughter he tried to hold back. His head felt light as if someone had come along and removed years of darkness. How had this totally amazing event happened? He was going to see where his parents had lived, and were buried. He would see something real, some proof they had even existed.

He looked back at Aunty Paula and Lucy. They had continued the discussion without him. *What is it about older people?* He didn't want to talk about it. He wanted to get up and go there. Like *now*!

Aunty Paula glanced up at the clock over the counter. 'Hey, I really do have to get goin'. Leah needs me.'

Dimitri's head jerked up. 'Leah? What do you mean?'

'Leah. She just messaged me …'

Lover: with one glance of your eyes — SS [219]

177

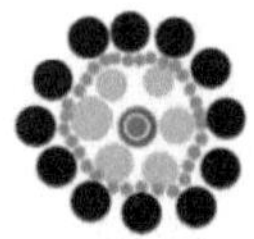

41: Dimitri

A shiver passed through Dimitri's body. He caught Aunty Paula's arm as she stood up. 'Leah? You're going to see Leah?'

'Of course. She's doin' it tough—again.' Her eyes seemed to burn into his. 'I told her she would never have to go through that all over again on her own. So I'd better head off.' She picked up her bag.

'Whoa! Hang on a minute. Go through *what* again?'

Aunty snapped her bag shut. 'The same as last time, but I reckon this is somethin' you need to go and sort out for yourself, young fulla.'

'What do you mean?' Dimitri wasn't sure he liked the way Aunty Paula was challenging him. Leah had *chosen* to have plastic surgery. So why did he get the feeling he was somehow to blame for … for what exactly?

Aunty sighed. 'They've called her in for the results of yesterday's tests and she wants me to be with her.'

'What tests? We met yesterday and she didn't say anything about tests.'

'I'm not surprised, after what happened between you after the last lot.'

The last lot? 'You mean that operation?'

'That operation! Being sick is awful, but this kind of thing is the absolute pits for women.'

'But the surgery was her choice …' His protest trailed off as Aunty Paula glared at him.

He knew it just had to be said. 'I know she had cosmetic surgery …'

'*Cosmetic* surgery?' Aunty Paula's voice positively thundered.

A sick feeling raced through Dimitri's body. He froze as the truth finally dawned on him. *Tell me I'm wrong! Please tell me I'm wrong*

He ran his tongue around his mouth trying to build up some moisture. He cleared his throat enough to produce a whisper. 'I thought it was a boob job. Is it breast cancer?'

'You really didn't know?' Aunty Paula shook her head and flicked her eyes toward Lucy, as if in apology. 'Leah had a mastectomy followed by weeks of chemotherapy.'

Dimitri looked past the two women and over the sea of customers in the now full café. The busy chatter, the echo of dishes and chairs scraping on the wooden floor, helped to crowd out the scream he felt building up inside. Customers' faces became a blur. All he could see was that same image he had carried for months. Leah, pale, weak, and so sick.

'How could I have left her to face all that on her own?' he murmured. 'How could I have not known?' He hung his head. 'She told me to go away. So I did. I was offended at her rejection of me.' He looked over to the corner where they had sat the previous night ad swallowed back a lump. 'It's always been about me. Not about her. Her own mum died of breast cancer. I should have known she was at risk.' He rested his elbows on the table and ran his fingers though his hair, digging into his scalp. 'Even when she got tired last night, I thought she was bored with me. I'm a self-obsessed jerk.'

'Dimitri!' Aunty Paula's sharp tone halted him and he stared at her. 'It's not too late.'

Yes, it is. Leah deserves someone better than me. He looked at Aunty Paula, and he wondered if she saw the torment he felt. He could barely keep his voice steady. 'What can I possibly offer her?'

'Leah needs *you*. Why don't we go see her together?"

Lucy broke into the conversation with her deep, soothing voice. 'Don't be so hard on yourself, Dimitri. Both of your lives have been turned upside down, but it's clear to me you love her.' She winked at Aunty Paula. 'What I wouldn't give for the main man in my life to admit he's a self-obsessed jerk!' She smiled. 'To me, it's pretty obvious that their paths were designed to cross again. I consider myself a bit of an expert now on following leads and I have every faith it is our living, loving God Who draws up the plans. I know that He can, and does, bring healing and reconciliation back into the most devastated relationships.'

Dimitri thought about her words, but then his shoulders sagged. 'It's far too late.'

Aunty Paula folded her arms. 'Why?'

'She's got a new boyfriend!' He thumped his hand on the table.

'What gives you that idea?'

'I saw her snuggling up, all cosy, to Matt yesterday. I decided …'

'Matt!' It was clear Aunty Paula couldn't be more astonished. 'You've gotta be kiddin'. That man's done nothin' but hassle her since she's come here.' She shook her head. 'In fact if it happened one more time we were goin' to get together with the male elders and send him packin'. We got our own law, and he's stretched it to breakin' point.'

Dimitri's fury rose as he reflected on the scene at the river bank. 'Matt was trying to take advantage of her yesterday? Why didn't she tell me? I'd have sorted him out.'

'Maybe *because* you'd have sorted him out?' Aunty Paula looked him over. 'Let's get ourselves to the hospital.'

Dimitri held the café door open for her and Lucy and let them move on ahead. The morning air had already thickened with the pending heat of the day. *Heavy*; exactly how he felt. Barely able to drag himself along.

His thoughts drifted between Aunty Paula and Lucy's conversation and thinking about what he could possibly say to Leah.

'Sorry, sister,' Aunty Paula said to Lucy. 'I wish we could have spent a bit more time goin' over the details.'

'It's okay; Dimitri has to face this first. If Leah is as important to him as I'm guessing, then she's part of this journey too.'

'You're pretty sure that Maria-Pearl and your sister Pearl are the same person, aren't you?'

'Sure as anything.'

Dimitri knew what he had to do. He caught up to the others. 'Lucy, this news about Marook is a huge breakthrough. For both of us. But I can't

Lover: with one jewel of your necklace — SS [2:9]

leave Leah. I want you to go on ahead and meet him. I can go on my own at another time.'

He knew that would be pretty impractical. But there was no other way. 'Whether Leah wants me back or not, I can't go and leave her.' His eyes burned from pushing his tears back. 'She just means too much to me.'

Lucy shook her head. 'I've waited this long and I can wait a bit longer. You go and do what you have to do.' Her voice contained so much warmth and kindness, he had no doubt her offer was genuine.

'Why don't we find out how Leah's doin'?' Aunty Paula suggested. 'A trip up north might be a good thing for her too.'

Leah, come with me? That's just too much to hope for!

'How about I go and make some calls to Red Ochre?' Lucy offered. 'We'll need accommodation and a permit, as well as a local Aboriginal guide to help us find this place where Marook is.'

'Sounds great,' Aunty Paula replied. 'I'll give you a buzz a bit later and let you know how things go.'

'No worries.' Lucy reached out and gripped Dimitri's hand. 'Hold on to her, son. There are few people in our lives we're given to love, so don't rob yourself of her.' After a quick embrace, she walked back down the main street and disappeared into the Information Centre.

As he turned towards the hospital, Dimitri watched Aunty Paula flick open her phone to check the time. 'Leah's appointment is in five minutes, so let's move it.'

He tried to rehearse what to say. Everything sounded pathetic. And what if all he caused was more pain? Leah didn't need that right now. To think what she had been through... *is still going through.*

The old two-storey hospital appeared in the distance between tall pines. Rows of glass doors opened out onto the balcony. Leah is behind one of those doors. He visualised her sitting in a dull waiting room, all alone, terrified of what might unfold. His heart ached for her.

Could she ever forgive him for walking out on her?

Could he forgive himself?

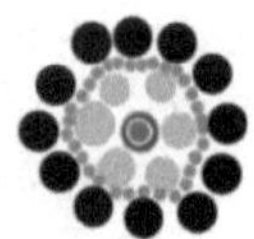

42: Leah

Footsteps echoed along the corridor and Leah stirred. She must have dozed off for a few seconds. Voices murmured as they drew closer. The last thing she wanted was to chat to another waiting patient. She kept her eyes closed.

From the other side of the room, the door to Dr Campbell's office opened. She had no choice but to surface. *This is it.*

Leah looked over to the office. An unsmiling Karen stood in the doorway. *Why send the nurse out to get your patient? Odd? Lazy?*

'I'm sorry Leah,' the nurse said, 'but I'm afraid that Dr Campbell has …'

'Leah!'

Leah spun around. For the second time in two days, she stared at Dimitri as if he were an apparition.

'It's a long story, hon.' Aunty Paula came up behind him. She looked over to the waiting nurse. 'Give us a sec, lovey?' Without waiting for a reply, she settled herself on the seat next to Leah. 'I know it's gonna be hard to take in after all these months, but you're gonna have to believe what Dimitri here has to tell you.'

'Can't this wait?' Karen called impatiently. 'I've got a busy schedule to keep.'

At the back of Leah's mind she cringed for her profession. The waiting room was empty; she doubted Karen's busy schedule.

'Have some compassion, nurse,' Aunty Paula snapped. 'You know full well what kind of illness this patient is dealin' with.'

Leah looked uncertainly from Aunty Paula to Dimitri.

Beloved: 1 am my lover's — SS ^{6:3}

'Do you reckon you could just hear him out?'

Dimitri crouched down in front of her.

'I'm so sorry, Leah!' he began.

Leah tensed. *This is so wrong! I pushed him away. I broke it off.*

'How could I have left you when you were so sick?' His eyes looked so sad. *I don't know!*

'I asked you to go.' Leah tightened her jaw and focussed on keeping her voice steady. 'And as it's worked out, it's for the best.'

He seemed to think it over for a second. 'I would have believed you once. But that's not you talking. It's the pain of the past.'

'All I can offer you is trouble and sadness.' She had to stop looking at him. He was undermining her capacity to stay strong. 'We were looking at getting engaged. That should be a time of fun, and planning for the future. I gave you a way out.' She fought back the tears. *And you took it.*

Dimitri shook his head. 'I thought you were taking the chance to be rid of me.'

'Of course I *wasn't!*' Snippets of the previous evening's conversation passed through her mind. A cold feeling spread through her body. She glanced aside at Aunty Paula and then back at Dimitri. He was serious. *He thinks I broke it off because he might be Aboriginal!*

She pushed her fist to her mouth to stifle the sob bursting to get out. But she couldn't stop its slow moan. Her voice cracked but she pushed the words out. 'I could never do such a thing.'

Dimitri reached out and lifted both his hands into hers. They rested so easily on her lap. She had missed him so much.

But the rejection hadn't been one-sided. 'What about you? I wasn't too devastated when you left me because I was sick. I can get that. But if it was because I had a mastectomy …?' Her voice faltered at that word, but she was determined to look him in the eye. *If he was like her father …*

'Leah, you have to believe me. I would never… *ever*… do that. I just didn't know. I thought you were having a cosmetic enhancement. I was just so caught up in my own issues. And …' His voice dropped to a whisper. 'And I am so sorry. So terribly sorry.'

Beloved: I am my lover's — SS 6:3

183

Relief replaced the coldness that had filled Leah. Tears tumbled out and ran down her cheeks. She wiped them with her hands but they kept coming. 'Here you go, hon.' Aunty Paula placed a tissue into her hand. 'Looks like you two have a lot of talkin' to do. '

Leah wiped her eyes and smiled at Dimitri.

'Leah!' Karen's command drew her back to the present and she looked around the stark waiting room. How could she have zoned out of the antiseptic environment? The whole reason she was here flooded back to her. She stood up.

'Sorry,' she murmured, not sure who she was apologising to. The nurse, for keeping her waiting? Dimitri, for the disruption that may lie ahead?

It's not my fault!

'Please come through.' The nurse's tone clearly expressed her impatience. 'If he's family, or someone special to you, then if you want him to come in with you, he can. Otherwise you two can sort it out later. Follow me.' She spun around and disappeared into the Doctor's office.

What could she say? He was her almost ex-fiancé?

I can't do this on my own. She searched Dimitri's face. Not a trace of distaste, just compassion and hope. Leah wiped her face dry. They may as well start at the beginning. 'Do you want to come in with me?'

He stood up. 'I'd really like that.'

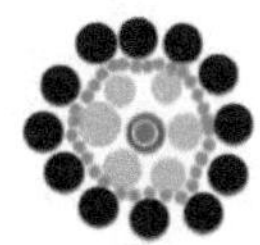

43: Leah

Ready with an apology to Doctor Campbell, Leah was confused to find him absent. Karen sat in his chair. 'Please. Take a seat.'

Dimitri closed the door and they sat on the chairs next to the doctor's desk. 'Where is he?' Leah blurted out. Why had Karen called her in when he wasn't even here?

'I'm sorry. I didn't want to discuss this with you in the waiting room, but Dr Campbell has gone.'

'Gone? Gone where?'

'The retrieval team were all set to go and since the patient's condition was so critical, he had to leave immediately.' Karen looked down at Leah's file. 'There's no mobile phone number on your form, so I couldn't get hold of you. I did try the nurses' home but you must have already left.'

Already left? Couldn't he have waited five minutes? That's all it took to cross the path from there to the hospital.

'So now what? You've obviously got the results there. Can't you just show me? We're both nurses; it's not as if there will be anything on there we don't understand.'

Karen pursed her lips. 'Leah! That would be quite unacceptable, you know that. Anyway, the doctor has filed the report with specific instructions to get you to come back as soon as he returns.'

'Which is?'

'No more than a week.'

A week! Why had they bothered calling her? Like dangling a carrot then taking it away.

The nurse picked up a pen. 'We'll need your mobile so we can call you as soon as he returns.' She looked at Dimitri. 'And a second contact in case we can't reach you.'

Leah wasn't too sure if she was ready to put Dimitri down as a contact yet. As Aunty had said, they had a lot to discuss. She kept her gaze away from him. 'Let's go and check with Aunty Paula; she might be happy for you to take hers.'

Aunty Paula stood up as they exited the doctor's room. Leah blurted out. 'He's not there. I won't know anything for at least a week.'

'Aw, hon, I'm sorry. That's so frustratin'.'

'Sure is. Karen will call me when he gets back. She wants another number in case they can't reach me. Are you happy to give yours?'

'Of course.' Aunty Paula stepped forward and conversed with the nurse.

'I hope you don't mind.' Leah turned to Dimitri. She felt awkward she had obviously bypassed him.

He rested his hand on her shoulder. 'It's okay. I get that.' His face stretched into the smile that sent shivers down her spine. How awesome to have him back again. *Well, maybe not back as in going out, but they were together. That was a start.* 'Anyway,' he continued, 'maybe if they can't reach you, they can't reach me.'

'What do you mean?'

'I'm heading inland to meet someone who knew my parents. It's definitely going to be out of mobile phone range. Maybe you want to come with me? It will fill your week in, while you wait.'

'Great idea!' Aunty Paula came up behind them. 'I'm sure Leah would love to get away from town. Won't you, hon?'

'Well, it sounds like you two have it all sorted.' Leah turned from one to the other. 'Maybe you should tell me what it's all about first?'

It didn't really matter what it was all about. Being together was what mattered. And Dimitri obviously wanted that. So did she!

Aunty Paula grinned. 'I reckon I'll leave you young ones to talk it all over while I go back and have a yarn with Lucy.'

'Wait! Tell me what you've found out. I've figured you're the Aboriginal Elder who met with Dimitri and Lucy? Did you know Dimitri's mum?' She caught Dimitri's eye. '… and do you know if she was Aboriginal?'

'No, hon, I'm sad to say I never met Dimitri's folks. But my cousin knows someone who did. He lives in the region where Dimitri's family lived and worked.'

'And where the plane crashed,' Dimitri added.

'That's both sad and exciting,' Leah said. 'At least you'll be able to go back to that part of your life that's been blank for you.'

'That's true,' Aunty agreed. 'As for being Aboriginal, it's still very unclear. Lucy's gone off to make a few calls to Red Ochre. You'll have to fly up to Alice Springs, then take a four wheel drive past the ranges and out to the desert. We're hopin' and prayin' that once you meet Marook, you'll have that question answered.'

'That's so exciting.' The air almost vibrated with hope and adventure. Leah looked around the sterile room. This wasn't the place to celebrate. 'Let's get some fresh air.'

'Agreed.' Dimitri grasped her hand.

She smiled, betraying the thrill of his skin against hers as he steered her towards the exit. A massive gum tree outside was abuzz with galahs. Funny how she hadn't noticed them on the way in.

'It's going to be a warm one,' Aunty Paula declared. 'And I'm heading for some shade. You two keep cool, and I'll talk to you later in the day.'

'Thanks, Aunty … for everything.' Leah wrapped her arms around Aunty Paula in a light hug.

'You're worth it, kid, and don't ever think otherwise.' She reached into her bag and retrieved her sunglasses. 'Catch you later.'

Left on their own, Leah fell quiet. So much had happened between her and Dimitri it was impossible to know where to begin.

'What about we get out of town?' Dimitri broke through the silence. 'Do you remember that picnic we had in the national park? We could do a repeat?'

'Sounds like a plan.'

Beloved: and my lover is mine — SS 6:3

'Okay, I'll put some food together and pick you up in about an hour.'

Leah nodded. She would love to have a proper shower. Her biopsy dressing had been on for almost twenty-four hours and she would be able to take it off now.

They separated at the gate of the nurses' home. Leah grinned as she watched him retreat with a definite spring in his step.

Once inside, she opened up the curtains in the stuffy lounge, slid back the windows and enjoyed the air circulating through the room. While the kettle boiled, she looked out the window and gazed upon the vast expanse of desert surrounding the tiny town.

She replayed some of the conversation they had just had. So fixated on his response to her mastectomy, she hadn't even considered he might think it was elective surgery. She poured the hot water into her cup and dangled the tea bag. *Plastic surgery! Breast implants!*

It was such a ridiculous thought that she threw her head back and laughed. *Guys!* A mastectomy clearly hadn't even occurred to him. Obviously they had been in completely different zones!

Leah stirred in the milk and sipped her drink slowly, allowing the warmth to calm her. 'We've been such fools.' Her eyes fell upon her bible on the kitchen table. Aunty Paula had encouraged her to develop a habit of not leaving home without morning prayer. This morning she had been too rushed. She pulled out a chair and opened it. One of her bookmarks had stayed in the same place since their anniversary dinner.

She ran her fingers down the page. *'For love is as strong as death, its passion as relentless as the grave. It burns like a blazing fire, like a mighty flame.'*

It was true. What else but love could have brought them through this past year? And Aunty Paula would say that it was God's love that had made it possible.

Her finger tips touched her breast. The biopsy site remained tender. There was still a major upheaval to conquer. If tested—truly tested this time—would their love be stronger than death?

Beloved: and my lover is mine — SS [6:3]

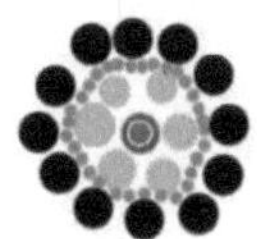

44: Dimitri

As Dimitri turned the car around, Leah took one last look at their picnic spot. The final glow of sunlight produced a slideshow of russet colours over the canyon. The desert wildflowers encircled the base of the rock, expressing the new life she felt inside. She couldn't remember ever spending an afternoon so enjoyable, yet so thoroughly draining. So much had separated them, yet they seemed to slip comfortably back into each other's lives. She had no illusions there was still much to repair, but she believed they could do it.

As the town lights came into view, Leah sensed they were heading back into the world, not with the naiveté of first love, but with a love tested and strengthened.

Dimitri's SMS tone beeped and she reached for his phone. 'Should I read it for you?'

'Of course. It's probably Lucy. She might have news of some travel plans.'

Leah tapped the screen. 'You're right; it's from Lucy.' She scrolled down. 'Flight booked, three people, ten a.m. tomorrow.'

Dimitri slowed his speed as he prepared to enter the town. 'She's pretty good!' He threw Leah a side glance. 'You know I really want you with me, but your health comes first. Are you sure you're up to this? It's going to be a rough road trip. And emotionally it's going to be huge.'

'I thought we just agreed that we're in it together; your life and mine.'

He smiled. 'I'll take that as a *yes*.'

Lover: How delightful is your love, my sister, my bride! — SS [4:10]

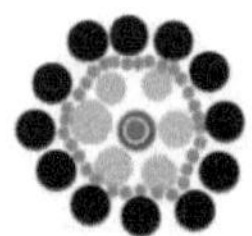

45: Dimitri

What's with my hand? Dimitri released Leah's fingers before they slid from his. Perspiration that had commenced in his brow now dripped down the side of his face, along his neck and broke out in his palms. He couldn't take his eyes off the single engine Cessna filling the tin hangar.

He must have been mad to agree to take a flight in such a tiny aircraft.

He wasn't afraid of flying. The trip to New Zealand had been great. But this was different. *He was going to be inside his dream.* The tail of the plane was in one piece, but for how long?

He blinked to force his eyes open. He wanted to shut them, to block out the plane, standing cold, waiting to lead him into danger. Yet if he shut them he knew what he would see. He had seen it too many times in his dream. Flames licked the back of the plane.

His eyes wandered to the door. His mother's feet had kicked it open. He felt her hand push hard against his spine. *'Run! Remember the wombat!'*

What wombat? Always the wombat. What had she been talking about?

The staff bustled around them, inspecting and loading the light aircraft. He could almost drown out his thoughts with the roar of engines and fans, and beeping trucks. 'Hey, if it's not Geek the Greek.'

Dimitri snapped out of his trance. His heart pounded as he recognised the arrogant voice booming above all the noise.

'That missus of yours; she's a nice piece of work, ain't she, mate?'

He spun around and only just managed to stop himself bringing his fist up. One of Matt's arms was restrained by the grip of a khaki-clad police officer. Matt threw back his head and laughed. 'Don't forget, she's a damaged one!'

In two quick strides, Dimitri stood centimetres from the face of the smirking troublemaker. 'Keep away from her!' His whole body trembled with the effort of keeping his fist under control. He'd never punched anyone but there had never been this level of provocation before.

The officer grabbed Matt in a firmer grip while raising his free hand in a warning to Dimitri. 'Step away, mate,' he commanded. 'He's got a big mouth and he ain't worth the trouble you'll find yourself in, if you don't back off.'

Dimitri clenched his fist, trying desperately to restrain himself.

'Let it go, Dimitri.' Leah's plea reached him from behind.

Aunty Paula ambled up to the scene. 'What's goin' on, Officer? You've arrested him by the looks. But what's happened?'

Matt's coarse laughter echoed above the noise. 'You always was a nosey biddy. Well, there's one thing you never knew about me, and that's my missus is after me.'

'You're *married?*' Leah gasped, clearly dumbfounded.

'He's married, all right,' confirmed the officer, 'with a warrant out for his arrest. Robbed her blind; gambled away their home, left her and the kids homeless, he did.'

'*Children?*' Leah continued to stare at Matt.

'Yip,' the officer responded. 'Two kids and a wife in a family shelter back in Queensland. All he left them with was an old wreck of a family car which they lived in until welfare got wind of it.'

Dimitri felt sick at the thought of how Matt had treated Leah. The sleaze continued to wear a smile that appeared hard and cold.

'Yeh, check it out, Lady Leah, what does your fancy fella think of you now? Flirtin' with a married man, eh?' He stared into Dimitri's face. 'She's not the innocent woman you all thought she was.'

Aunty Paula reached out and supported Leah by the elbow. Her voice projected above the chaos. 'Dimitri, you know he's talkin' rubbish. There's not one bit of evidence Leah ever led him on.' She faced him with a look he had come to recognise as one of authority. 'You got one fine lady here.'

Lover: How much more pleasing is your love than wine — SS 4:10

Dimitri turned away from Matt, and wrapped his arm over Leah's shoulders. 'No one ever has to tell me that.'

'Let's go.' The officer hitched up his trousers over a slight middle-aged bulge and pulled Matt's arm. 'Co-operate or it'll be the cuffs for you.'

Matt scowled at the group before being steered away.

'He won't be botherin' you any more, hon.'

They watched him disappear into the plane on the other runway.

'Guess all we can do is pray for his wife and them kiddies.' Aunty Paula sighed. 'Alcohol and gambling are not a good mix.' After a moment she pressed her lips together in thought. 'I wonder if he was tryin' to come good. Every now and then he showed he wasn't a bad bloke, and he *did* find an alcohol-free zone to work in. Maybe he was tryin' to put his past behind him. It does happen out here.'

'I guess so,' Leah agreed. 'Maybe it's a good thing they tracked him down. At least he can get some professional help now to recover properly.'

An announcement through a crackly speaker caused Dimitri's heart rate to increase again. It was time to board.

He stared at the door. How could he possibly step through it?

Aunty Paula embraced Leah, then shook Dimitri's hand. 'Both of you are goin' to be okay. I'll be prayin' for you every day you're away, don't you forget that. The good Lord knows what's best in everythin'.'

He had a decision to make. Aunty Paula had offered him a source of strength to take that step.

'Thanks so much, Aunty Paula, you've been a rock for me.' Leah was smiling.

This trip wasn't going to be easy for her. She'd had a huge shock. And the not-knowing hung over head. If she could step out of her comfort zone, so could he.

'Now get into that plane and get yourselves seated.' Aunty Paula smiled at him. A smile that said *you can do this.*

Leah stepped in front of him and, lowering her head, cleared the doorway and disappeared inside. His heart continued to pound and he gritted his teeth. It was dark in there. How hot was it? He wiped his hands

Lover: How much more pleasing is your love than wine — SS 4:10

on his jeans and with a deep breath crossed the threshold.

It was surprisingly dull. What had he expected? *To be ablaze with flames that licked everything in its path … including his father?* He looked into the open cockpit at the pilot. *Could this man fly them to safety?*

He followed Leah as she settled into a window seat. A sudden roar outside announced the departure of Matt's plane. He looked over Leah's shoulder to see it race along the runway. What a relief to watch it ascend into the rosy purple morning sky and disappear between scattered clouds.

'Are you okay?' Leah looked up at him. 'I took the window seat … I just wasn't sure if you were happy to look out …' Her voice trailed off.

Dimitri reached for her hand. 'It's pretty scary, but it's in the past. I have to look forward. I'm pretty sure that's what my parents would have wanted.'

The plane taxied along the soggy runway, turned, picked up speed and climbed into the air. Dimitri looked out the window at the land quickly shrinking below.

'It's hard to believe this is usually bone dry desert,' he yelled at her above the aircraft noise. Leah didn't answer. Having a conversation was useless. He needed to spend the time getting himself to relax.

The spectacular view down below helped a lot. Ancient gums extended their fingers from intermittent patches of water like twigs in swamps. Red ochre peeped between huge expanses of multi-coloured wild flowers. The plane ascended higher and the clouds gradually obscured their view. Dimitri rested his head against the seat and tried to focus on what lay ahead.

Lucy had spoken briefly to him the previous evening about their plans. It hadn't taken her long to locate the name of the settlement where Marook lived. Apparently it was around five hours' travel by rugged road from the nearest town, and she was trying to arrange for a local to drive them out there as soon as possible. The enormity of this meeting was unarguable, but Dimitri couldn't face the emotional implications just yet. *One step at a time.* What a difference it was to have Leah with him on this critical leg of the journey.

Before too long, the plane descended and, as the clouds cleared, a sprawling township appeared, surrounded by nothing except barren desert. He knew many people disliked the harsh changes in climate this country afforded, but he loved it. *Floods or drought*, he thought, *each bring their own challenge and beauty.*

Lover: How much more pleasing is your love than wine — SS ^{4:10}

As they prepared to land, Dimitri clasped Leah's hand. Once again, he ached for their lost opportunities. *Never again!* No matter what lay ahead, they would face it together. The plane turned and lined up over the runway and he watched Leah close her eyes tightly. It wasn't until the wheels jolted to a stop that she opened her eyes and relaxed.

'Wow!' she cried as she looked out the window at the massive aircraft alongside their tiny Cessna. 'I can't believe this little plane actually did it!'

The heat hit them as soon as they stepped onto the bitumen. 'The ground feels odd after months of squished earth!' Leah yelled above the noise of the aircraft.

'Go inside!' Dimitri yelled. 'Lucy and I'll find your bags.'

She hung onto her flapping skirt and walked briskly to the entrance. Dimitri knew the combination of heat rising from the ground, deafening engines and propellers, and putrid fumes would have been enough to make her feel sick. It had been only forty-eight hours since her biopsy, and on top of that was the impact of Matt's recent harassment.

Whenever he thought about the scene at the river, his fury grew. *That man should have been charged with assault!* He had told Leah to make a police report, but she was adamant she had been through enough. *Anyway, some justice has been done*, he thought, recalling this morning's encounter.

He waited with Lucy for the trolley to arrive with their bags. As soon as he caught sight of it, he grabbed them so he and Lucy could hurry into the terminal. Leah waved them over to a seat under an air-conditioner vent.

'Here, have a drink.' She passed each of them a bottle of spring water she had purchased from the vending machine.

'Thanks.' Lucy smiled gratefully as she twisted the lid open.

'I think I've been living the life of a hermit.' Leah looked around. 'What are all these people doing scurrying around?'

Dimitri laughed. 'You've become a real bushie, haven't you? Believe me, this place isn't busy, not when you've come up from the city.'

'I know what you mean,' Lucy said. 'The first time I stepped into a regional airport after only ever knowing Pearling Bay, I couldn't believe the chaos. And that's tiny in comparison to most places.' She replaced the cap on her bottle and slung her pack over her shoulder. 'Let's get ourselves over to the car rental desk and we'll be set to go.'

Lover: How much more pleasing is your love than wine — SS 4:10

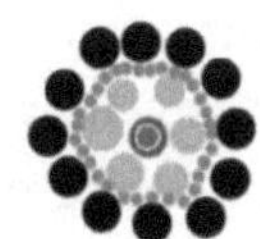

46: Leah

Lucy and Dimitri fell into step together as they discussed their itinerary. Leah was happy to lag behind. She found herself staring at useless merchandise; the airport stalls that sold souvenirs no one needed, takeaway foods, overpriced clothing and magazines filled with gossip. *How much of this stuff do people really need?*

Months of restrictions due to the floods had taught her how much more simply life could be lived. Or was it the possibility of a shortened life that had changed her perception of true value? Having no desire to examine the latter possibility, she shrugged off her reflections and hurried to catch up to the others.

When they approached the rental car bay, Leah grinned. What was it with guys and cars? Dimitri ran his fingers over the silver bonnet of the brand new Santé Fe. 'She's a beauty!'

'Mmm, pretty slick.' *What am I supposed to say?* 'It's a pity it's about to be driven over hundreds of kilometres of red dust! Who's doing the car wash?'

'Are you happy for me to drive?' Dimitri pretended to ignore her.

'Let's put it this way,' Leah said. 'I'd have a hard time getting those keys out of your hands.'

Dimitri looked down at his hand clutching the keys and laughed. 'Well, it *is* in my name. I was trying to be polite.'

'Yeah, yeah! Go for it, Dimitri. I'm happy to sit back and be chauffeured.'

'Come on, you two.' Lucy interrupted their teasing. 'Let's get our bags

Beloved: his desire is for me — SS 7:10

in the back and be on our way.' She smiled. 'And how about I let the two of you sit up front and I'll be the one that's getting chauffeured?'

'Sounds great to me.' Dimitri clicked the remote and unlocked the vehicle.

'From what I've heard,' Lucy remarked as they cruised through the town, 'most people here are either tourists or business travellers on their way up to the Top End. Most of the locals stay away from the town and live out on traditional Aboriginal land or are working on large cattle properties. I think there are also some mining companies still scattered across the desert.'

Leah glanced at Dimitri. It could have been a company plane that went down, taking Dimitri and his family with it. He didn't flinch; he was concentrating on entering an address into the GPS. The cultured voice of an English woman began to announce directions and they set off.

It wasn't a long trip. They almost reached the highway when the motel sign rose up ahead.

As they climbed out of the car Leah grimaced at the shabby accommodation. 'Do we need a motel? I thought we were meeting up with a guide as soon as we got here.'

Leah frowned as she noticed Dimitri and Lucy exchange glances. *What was that look for?* She jumped as the ground shook beneath her feet. 'What's that?'

A road train thundered past, its weight rippling across either side of the road. *This is horrible. Not to mention the fumes!*

'Sorry!' Lucy called above the engine. 'I knew we were going to be close to the main highway, but I didn't think we'd be just about on it …'

'Look at that!' Leah cut her off. Parallel to the road, a mob of emus chased after the long vehicle. 'No turning back now!' she called to them.

Emus can't walk backwards; that's what she suddenly remembered from school. On the Australian coat of arms the emu held his neck straight and face forward. With one foot in front of the other he only looked ahead. All that was behind propelled him closer to his goal.

She didn't know what Dimitri and Lucy were scheming, but it didn't matter. This trip was about them putting in place another piece of their puzzle.

'Come on; let's get out of this dust!' Dimitri said.

Beloved: his desire is for me — SS [7:10]

Leah wiped grit from her lips. 'Good idea.'

'Velcome!' the young woman behind the desk greeted them, 'I am Gudrun.'

She positively sparkles!

Bright beaded loops jangled from her ears, multiple strings of coloured beads hung around her neck; bangles jingled up to her elbows and rings decorated every finger. 'You came on the flight from Bilyja, ya?'

'We did,' Lucy replied.

'Here for long?' Gudrun leaned back on her stool, clearly readying herself to learn whatever she could about them.

Leah had no energy to embark on an explanation. She stepped back from the counter. Let the others tell their tale.

'Not sure,' Lucy replied politely. 'We've booked two nights for now.'

After a moment of awkward silence, Gudrun sighed, clearly giving up her quest. It must be pretty boring working, and maybe even living, in the outskirts of this isolated town. Leah felt a bit sorry for the woman, but no way was she going to be the one to provide that distraction.

'Sign here for your keys.' Gudrun's acrylic pink fingernails tapped a blank space on the register. 'Make sure you give me plenty of notice, if you're staying for longer.' She handed Dimitri one set of keys and Lucy the other. 'Ve don't always have rooms for let.'

Leah looked up at the row of keys still dangling on the hooks and wondered if it ever got busy here.

'Thanks, we will.' Lucy maintained a straight face but Leah was pretty sure there was a smile in her eyes. She looked away, frightened they would both collapse into a hopeless giggle.

'Your rooms are next to each other. They open onto the car park.'

'Thanks.' Dimitri smiled. 'This looks like the perfect place for us to stay.'

Ever the charmer! Leah watched a slow warm smile light up Gudrun's face. 'Anything you vant, just ask.' She clearly ignored the women and focussed on Dimitri.

Leah caught his eye, and with a cheeky grin, he reached for her hand. 'Come on; let me help you with your bags.'

Lucy unlocked the motel room door and pushed it open for Leah to step in first.

Beloved: his desire is for me — SS 7:10

'Nice and cool in here.' Leah sighed and spread out on one of the single beds.

Lucy dropped her bag on the other and opened the door again. 'I'll be back in a minute.'

Before Leah could question her, she had left. She could hear Dimitri and Lucy having a conversation outside. Something was definitely brewing between the two of them. And it excluded her. Her good intentions dissolved and she went into a spin of self-doubt.

What do you expect? I invited myself along, didn't I? What if they were just being polite? I mean, it's their trip, isn't it? Who's to say that Dimitri trusts me enough to even be there when he meets Marook? He didn't trust me before. Why would he now?

The murmur of conversation continued outside and sadness welled up inside. She got up and switched on the fan. She didn't really need it as well as the air-conditioner. But it would drown out the voices outside. And clearly she wasn't meant to be listening.

Leah rolled over and allowed her aching wound to be supported by the mattress. 'No!' Her thoughts took a new direction. *Maybe he doesn't want to be around in case my results are bad.*

That's crazy! He said he would never have left me if he had known last time. Well, maybe that's what you wanted to hear. It's possible he didn't really mean it.

Not these dratted tears again. But she couldn't help it. They were silent, but her sobs shook her whole body. What was she thinking, coming out to the desert on a venture that had nothing to do with her? She couldn't languish in a dump of a motel while they careered across the desert. She would catch the next flight back to Bilyja.

Exhausted by her own sobs, Leah's eyes became heavy and the voices outside receded into the background. The click of the overhead fan lulled her into a light slumber.

A gentle shake on her arm drew her back into consciousness.

'Come on, kiddo, Jack's waiting outside for us.'

Leah remained curled up on her side. 'You go ahead. I … don't feel up to it.'

Beloved: his desire is for me — SS [7:10]

Lucy didn't move. 'Is your side hurting?'

Everything's hurting.

'Could you let Dimitri know I wish him well? I'll meet you back in Bilyja … if he still wants to.'

'You don't have to go back to Bilyja, Leah. That's why we booked a motel in town. At least you can stay close by while we're gone.'

So I can look after everyone's things?

A lump blocked her throat and she couldn't reply. She remained on her side, staring at the grey wall.

After a moment Lucy said, 'You don't look too good. What can I do for you? I hope you didn't mind, but between Aunty Paula and Dimitri, they asked me to look out for you.'

So they were *talking behind my back.*

Leah swallowed hard to push away the lump in her throat. 'The best you can do is to leave me alone. I'll get back to Bilyja and be out of everyone's way.'

'Leah! What are you talking about? If you think you're up to coming out with us, we'd love to have you. And if you're not, being close by to share our news would be the next best thing.'

Leah rolled over and searched Lucy's face. Perhaps she was just being kind. 'You're just saying that. I don't think Dimitri really wants me to be with him.'

Lucy stared at her. 'Dimitri loves you. Anyone can see that. He's just worried about you. It's a long trip. That's all it is.'

'Then why the motel?' She wasn't ready to let go of her anxiety just yet. 'I got the feeling you booked it for me. There's no real reason to stay in town when the location is a ten-hour round trip.'

'Not everything's about you.' Lucy got up off the bed and went to the fridge. Neither said anything while she grabbed a jug of water. 'Drink?'

'Thanks.'

They sipped the iced water in silence, the air tight between them.

'Look, there are a lot of factors,' Lucy said after a while. 'You're partially right. We wanted a motel in case you didn't feel up to the trip. We also needed access to a landline in case Aunty Paula had any news from the doctor for you. Mobiles are hopeless out here.'

Beloved: his desire is for me — SS [7:10]

They really do care about me. Leah's self-pity turned to embarrassment. *How could I have been so self-absorbed!*

'But the other thing is, we did it for Dimitri and me. We don't know what we'll find when we get out there. There's always the chance there's nowhere for us to stay.'

Leah doubted that. From her community health experience she had always found rural people more than hospitable to visitors. Even if it were a swag under a tree, there would be a place. There was definitely something else.

'All right, you got me! Neither of us seems to be very good at keeping our thoughts hidden. The truth is, I'm concerned about how Dimitri will cope with the news. I've been doing this search for a long time and I've had lots of disappointments. If Maria-Pearl doesn't turn out to be my sister, I'll be disappointed.' She looked away for a moment before taking another sip. 'Hugely disappointed. But I'll cope. I've done it many times. But for Dimitri, this is new. If Marook's information isn't about his mother, I'm not sure he'll be up to staying around. We don't want to arrive back to town in the early hours of the morning and have nowhere to stay.'

'I can't believe that I even doubted Dimitri's commitment to me. This trip is all about him, not me. I had already decided I would try to forget my own issues while I'm up here. That didn't last long.'

'Hey! Don't be too hard on yourself. You've been through a lot and it's understandable. We all need each other.'

Lucy rested her arm over Leah's shoulders. 'So you're ready to come with us?'

'Absolutely!'

Beloved: his desire is for me — SS [7:10]

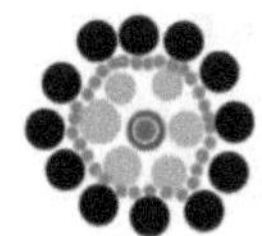

47: Dimitri

'Hey, Leah!'

Dimitri knew the smile stretching across his face made him look over-eager, but he couldn't help it. There was still a part of him that found it hard to believe they were back together again. He had all but convinced himself his Aboriginal journey was a big cause of their breakup. To have this theory completely busted took a bit of getting used to. But, yes, it was real, she was here, and ready to come on the trip with them.

'This is Jack.' He introduced a slightly-built Aboriginal youth, sporting an akubra hat.

'Akubra Jack.' The youth tipped the brim of his hat. He didn't smile or make eye contact with any of them. His few words were so softly spoken Dimitri had to strain to hear him.

'Hi Jack, I'm Leah. We're so lucky to have you come on this trip with us.'

'It's true.' Lucy was smiling. 'Good thing Jack was in town. He lives in the same community as Marook, so it works out well that he gets a lift back home.' She turned to Dimitri. 'Make sure you take note of his directions because we'll be relying on your navigation to get us back here again.'

'Too easy! Okay, everyone ready?'

This is it! When they returned, would he be bringing home anything new about his mother? Would he like what he found? His stomach tightened and he forced his thoughts to the immediate task.

Akubra Jack sat up front with him, and Lucy and Leah settled in the back. He smiled in the rear vision mirror at Leah. *She is so beautiful! How could I have ever let her go? I must have been mad.*

Not long into the journey, conversation between the back and front of the vehicle became difficult to keep up. They all lapsed into a comfortable quiet. Dimitri turned to focus his full attention on the journey ahead.

He had become used to long road trips. And the inevitable reflection they allowed. *It's okay to run with your thoughts.*

He couldn't keep forcing aside all his questions and fears. This was huge. There was a lot at stake.

Meeting someone who had known his mum felt awesome. *If Marook had met her,* he corrected himself. *Big if.* Aunty Paula had done her best, but there was no guarantee the information that travelled back and forth across the communities was completely accurate.

Akubra Jack indicated left with his hand and Dimitri steered the car off the main road onto an unmarked track.

Okay, now I've got to look out for some landmarks to get us back again. At least he had the GPS. *Except they've been known to lead people into dead ends as well.*

The track stretched towards the horizon with minimal twists and he settled back to enjoy the drive. The sunlight played with the vast plain, at times it shimmered in silver before switching into a crimson red. He imagined generations of Aboriginal people inhabiting the seemingly inhospitable desert with confidence and pride. Could this land possibly hold any identity for him?

He felt Lucy's presence behind him. He could learn a lot from her about patience and trust. She had more to lose than him if this came to nothing. She had spent so much of her life tracing her Pearl. *What would she do if she was wrong?*

A group of rock wallabies feeding on the sporadic scrub looked up and hopped away as they sped by. In the cloudless sky solitary black dots hovered. They could have been kites, crows or even wedge-tailed eagles circling, sweeping and feasting on wildlife who had met with their death.

He drove past hundreds of elongated termite mound sculptures dotting the land. An occasional unmarked track veered away from the road, evidence of private homesteads, pastoral land or even unused mining tracks. Dimitri sighed. He loved the land. He got why Aboriginal people felt so connected to it. It was more than a place to carve out a living. *Much more.*

The rugged track softened and merged into a sandy trail. The sun gradually lowered, turning the dull rusty land into a fiery copper. Dry scrub captured the transforming light, its grey foliage turning to gold.

Dimitri threw Akubra Jack a look. If they didn't reach their destination soon, it would be pitch dark. He wasn't confident he could stick to the trail at night. Not to mention navigating the nocturnal creatures that would soon emerge. Akubra Jack's expression didn't change. He didn't seem worried in any way. Dimitri had to learn to trust.

Almost exactly five hours after leaving town, a cluster of giant red rocks appeared. They lurked overhead, casting long shadows across the track. Every photographer's dream! Dimitri fought back the temptation to stop and take some shots. It wasn't the time or place; they were racing against complete darkness.

As the spectacular light show almost came to its conclusion, the last shimmer of light glistened on a cluster of tin roofs. Stately river ghost gums stood guard over a creek, the life source of the people who had settled there. As Jack gestured a halt sign, Dimitri felt his heart rate pick up speed.

Lover: Your head crowns you like Mount Carmel — SS 7:5

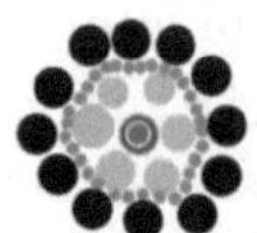

48: Dimitri

Dimitri cruised into the clearing, manoeuvring his way between a crowd of children and barking dogs. The children raced each other to touch the car, laughing and chatting. He pulled to a stop. 'They're not shy!'

Some of them pounded on the windscreen or pressed their faces against the passenger windows. Dimitri smiled back and stepped out of the car. Leah and Lucy clambered out as well and were immediately surrounded.

Jack opened his door, straightened his hat and nodded to a group of older boys. They ceased their chatter as he spoke a couple of words in their own language.

They ran off. Dimitri guessed they had gone to find some adults. A knot of apprehension tightened in his stomach. What had the community been told about him? And Lucy?

To distract himself he turned to Leah, already crouching down at eye level and chatting comfortably with the children. In less than five minutes she held a toddler in her arms and another two were playing peekaboo behind her flowing skirt. *How could I ever have suspected she might be racist? Vlakas!*

A small group of women came out, their smiles wide and engaging. As they extended their hands to each of them, Dimitri's reservations about being welcomed disappeared.

The boys returned and Jack gestured for the visitors to follow him. He led them to a grass clearing, a bit like a town square. Dimitri looked over the homes. A mixture of weatherboard and brick veneer, many were dilapidated.

Aunty Paula had explained the houses had been established by the government. Unlike the town, remote rural properties received virtually no maintenance.

A group of men sat under the shadow of a huge red gum in the clearing.

'We might have to find out the rest of this story via Dimitri later on.' Lucy turned to Leah. 'In some Aboriginal groups, men and women mixing freely is taboo.'

Dimitri issued Leah a sympathetic look, imagining her disappointment. He was confident Lucy would manage this without question. Accepting indigenous cultural norms was part of her upbringing.

'Don't forget,' Lucy cautioned him, 'it's taboo to say the name of the person who has died, unless the Elder takes the lead and does so.'

'I know.' Dimitri nodded. 'I hope I don't say it without thinking, as I really don't want to cause offence. It's so generous for them to have us here and give us the chance to talk about the past.'

'You'll be fine.' Lucy smiled. 'I think they'll be pretty forgiving; just show that you're respectful, that's all.'

Jack gestured for them to stop. 'Wait.' Approaching the men, he spoke to them in the local language. It was the most he'd said all day.

A strong, fit-looking man in his middle years stood up and left the group. He extended his hand first to Dimitri then the others. 'Hi, I'm Mick and you fullas are all very welcome here.' He smiled and turned to the older men. 'These are our community Elders and we look forward to hearing your story. Grandfather Marook will come, but it's late. First we eat.'

He instructed the other men to make room for the visitors to join the group. Dimitri and Leah looked to Lucy for direction and, after she nodded, they both settled down next to Dimitri and Mick.

The men conversed with each other in their own language and Dimitri found himself relaxing. Leah looked around the group and asked Mick: 'Where are the women? They followed us to the circle, then disappeared.'

Mick laughed. 'They've gone to make sure there's plenty of food to share.' As the last of the grey sky darkened into charcoal, he stretched out his arm. 'The Elders said to sit and have a yarn while we wait for the food.' He looked at Lucy. 'They invite you to tell your story.'

Lover: Your hair is like royal tapestry — SS ^{7:5}

As she began, everyone fell silent. Occasionally she stopped for Mick to interpret for the older men. No one interrupted; every now and then they nodded to acknowledge they were listening.

You can feel the sadness in the group. Dimitri reached for Leah's hand. It made such a difference to have her here. When Lucy finished, the silence continued. It was like they were paying their respects at a funeral. Dimitri looked at Lucy who sat stock still, her eyes lowered to the ground. Had anyone really listened to her like this before?

Mick got up and fetched a bundle of branches and twigs from a stockpile a few metres away and placed them in the centre of the group. He struck a match and blew the tiny flame until it travelled across a pile of twigs, the fire growing in size.

The men spoke amongst themselves, then Mick turned to Dimitri. 'The Elders invite you to tell your story.'

He swallowed hard. He had never told his story from the beginning before. He looked around the circle at the dark faces of the Aboriginal men. They were warm and kind, and he … he just … belonged. It should have felt strange, but it didn't. He had been in this circle before.

No way! Where? When?

That's right. But that was just a dream.

The wombat dream and he wasn't in the circle at all. The wombat was. He was just an onlooker.

He shrugged off the lonely feeling that always followed the dream. He had been asked to speak.

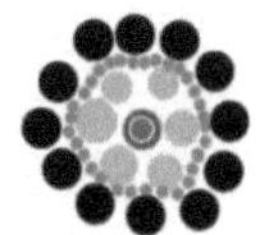

49: Dimitri

He began with the plane crash. How he ran from the flames and how at every explosion he wanted to turn around but he remembered his mother's words. 'Run! Don't stop for anything!'

He took a breath. *I've just remembered something new!*

'I ran until someone stopped me. It was a man. He scooped me up in his arms. His arms were strong and dark and safe … and familiar.'

He stopped talking. He couldn't share his story. He didn't even know it. There were new memories stirring, mixed with the old. He looked closer at the faces in the circle. How could he have felt he belonged? He didn't. He had no idea where he belonged before coming to live with Yaya and Papou.

'It's okay, mate,' Mick said. 'You don't have to say anything. Only if you want to.'

Dimitri leaned back and rotated his shoulders until his tension eased. Sitting here, it was as if a series of fireworks exploded from his past. A past his grandparents said didn't exist. He let go of Leah's hand and stretched his fingers.

Dimitri's earliest clear memory had always been meeting Yaya. She had reached out for him but he clung to a woman. He had always presumed the woman was a social worker. Yaya smelt funny. She spoke funny. The social worker told him Yaya would take him home.

He leaned forward, and stared into the fire. 'I want to speak. I think I need to speak. I can see a train now. I was curled up with my face against the window but we weren't going home. The land changed from red, to brown, to yellow with patches of green. Finally it disappeared. Buildings, roads and traffic filled the space instead. When the train finally stopped, Yaya took me to my new home. They had rooms above their restaurant and a tiny herb and vegetable garden. I lay on my new bed, curled up again in a tight ball wanting to go home.'

He took a deep breath. 'I remember once telling Yaya about the plane. I told her my dream but she told me it was my imagination. I had been too young, she said, and couldn't possibly have remembered.'

He rotated his ankles. The scars on his feet were his reminder. It had been real.

Then there was the wombat. Was he ready to tell anyone about the wombat? Why were his grandparents so determined to wipe out his past? He sighed.

What's the use of holding a grudge? I'm here to find out more, not to blame my grandparents.

'Yum! That smells great.' Leah broke through his musings.

Women and older children carried pots and plates of food over and settled them on a table nearby.

'Can I give you a hand?' she asked.

'No, just enjoy,' one of the women said. 'You are our guests. We got roasted kangaroo and steamed bush vegies especially for you.'

'Eat.' Mick handed out plates to the guests.

The charcoal-cooked meat smelt like Uncle Spiros' restaurant. He pushed the thought of his family aside. If there hadn't been so much secrecy around his parents, it wouldn't have taken him until he was *twenty-one* to reach this place. *How on earth did Yaya think she was going to keep my age a secret forever?* What excuse had she planned on using when he inevitably found out? *Clerical error?*

He heaped his plate with meat and bush tucker. It had been hours since he last had a meal and he was starving. This was an amazing feast.

Mick turned around and called out to a woman around his age. She came over and joined him. 'This is Kate, my wife.'

Lover: The king is held captive by its tresses. — SS [75]

'Hi Kate, I'm Leah and this is Dimitri and Lucy.'

Kate smiled as Mick continued, 'You can stay with Kate and me tonight, so whenever you're ready to settle let her know.'

'Thanks Kate, that's generous of you,' Leah said.

'I'd love to have you; we don't get many visitors out here. How about we sit down near the fire and eat? Grandfather won't be too long now.'

Dimitri was confused. 'Is Marook your grandfather?'

Kate threw her head back and laughed. 'Not in the way you mob say. It's different, like the way we understand aunty and uncle. Grandfather is a term of respect, and it doesn't have to be a blood relationship.' She turned away. 'Come,' she instructed, leading them to a small clearing on the other side of the fire.

Men and women sat freely together, so Dimitri and Leah seated themselves next to each other. Lucy settled herself between two women around her age, clearly comfortable. Between the flames, Dimitri watched Lucy's eyes dance, her face aglow. She might not understand the language or share the culture, but she definitely looked at ease.

'You look totally at home here,' Dimitri said quietly to her.

Leah nodded. 'I am, but it's also something I know never to take for granted.'

Dimitri ate in silence for a time, happy to observe the large group gathered to enjoy the evening meal with them. The festive atmosphere of the meal gradually died down. As the women collected the plates many of them grabbed reluctant children, trying to convince them it was bed time. Dimitri didn't blame the children for wanting to find out a bit more about their visitors.

A hush fell over the group as an elderly man shuffled towards them, aided by two sticks, and assisted on either side by two young men. When he drew close, Dimitri felt his own heart race in a mixture of anxiety and excitement. The expression on the weather-beaten face framed with wild grey hair was hard to read. The whites of his eyes glowed against the darkness and Dimitri prayed that the wisdom and knowledge that must surely reside in him would lead to a revelation of the truth.

The two young men assisted as he lowered himself onto a chair. After recovering his breath, he passed one of his sticks to one of them. With the

Lover: The king is held captive by its tresses. — SS [7:5]

other he stirred the embers. The crackling of the twigs was the only sound coming from the huge group. Beyond the circle, hundreds of night crickets whistled to each other over their own din.

'When I was a young fulla,' the old man began after a moment, his words slow and careful, 'I remember stories from my grandfather.' He looked up and pointed with his stick to the surrounding plain, now completely hidden in darkness. 'He told us about our country and about our mob who belong to this land.' He looked back to the fire and, as if he was reliving the memory, his voice became heavy. 'Then my father reached an old age and he took his turn to tell stories. They were new stories. Stories about Aboriginal people who came here because they had no country anymore. Whitefulla mob had come and moved onto their land.' Grandfather looked up at his visitors. 'My father said the land could have been shared, but it wasn't.' He shook his head. 'They lost their country. The land their fathers and grandfathers and their kin had belonged to for a long, long time had disappeared.'

Dimitri drew Leah closer to him. He kept his eyes fixed on the ancient face, straining to hear his ageing voice, barely more than a whisper.

'But then came more stories no one liked to hear.' He shook his head and stared into the fire for a few moments. 'It was the women who told us their stories. They wailed as they told us about their children being taken away.'

Dimitri looked over at Lucy and a hard knot formed at the back of his throat. Her knees were drawn up, her head buried against her chest and she cradled her body with her arms.

The women next to her wrapped their arms around her and all three rocked gently back and forth.

A tragic, gentle moan rose up from all the women in the circle. His own anguish throbbed against his throat as he replayed the scene of Pearl being ripped from her mother's arms. *That couldn't be his mother! What on earth was he doing here?*

He ached to fill the empty space where the invisible link to her existed. But was this the right link? He swallowed back the lump in his throat and allowed himself to receive the comfort Leah's grip offered him.

Marook leaned back into the shadows; clearly exhausted. Mick spoke to him in his own language and Marook nodded.

Lover: The king is held captive by its tresses. — SS [75]

'Grandfather will talk in our language and I'll interpret. I'll speak for him.'

That sounded like a great idea. Dimitri didn't want the evening to wear out the old man. He was pretty generous to even be there; especially since it was getting so late.

Marook looked up at Dimitri and spoke a few words. Mick interpreted. 'You've come here to ask about your mother?'

Dimitri held his breath, too afraid to respond unless the moment disappeared. He cast his eye over Lucy.

Mick glanced at her. 'And Lucy, your sister?'

Lucy nodded and, like Dimitri, made no reply.

Grandfather nodded his head. He continued to speak and Mick interpreted. 'My wife—she's dead now—was a cook with Maria-Pearl at the mine. She wasn't married then. She would ask to come and stay with us when she wasn't working.' Marook leaned forward and spoke quietly into the fire. 'She was different to the other white girls.' Mick was swift with his translation. 'Her skin was a bit darker, but it was her ways; she was like us. When we danced our stories, she wanted to know what they were. Then in the day, she told the kids again. "Don't forget your stories," she would tell them, "so you can tell your own children."'

Dimitri blinked hard against his tears. He pictured his mum listening to the Elders and watching their dances as they relayed tales dating back generations.

'She told us she had no stories,' Marook went on.

No stories! To have no stories in an Aboriginal culture was to have no identity.

Of course she had a story! I am part of her story! But she was robbed of that too! This was so unfair. What did his mother ever do to have such a rough deal?

'She said her folks had brought her here from the West but they told her she had no place and no mob.'

Marook stopped to catch his breath and Lucy spoke. 'Do you mind if I explain a bit to Dimitri and Leah?'

She directed her question at Marook and Mick. When they both nodded, she went on: 'When Maria-Pearl was young, most people in the

Lover: The king is held captive by its tresses. — SS [75]

cities never knew about Aboriginal kids being stolen from their families. It only really started to get out as those kids grew up. Maria-Pearl's foster family always lived in rural Australia and had close contact with our people. If Maria-Pearl was interested in Aboriginal ways, she would have heard the stories much earlier than city folk.'

'It sounds like she knew she was fostered,' Leah remarked. 'It wouldn't have taken much figuring out for her to question her own background.'

'That's right,' Lucy replied. 'What I'm hoping is that being with Aboriginal people triggered early memories for her. I think her problem may have been trying to figure out if they were real or imagined.'

Dimitri knew that feeling. 'It doesn't sound like her parents, or foster-parents, told her anything about her background, yet they let her spend time with Aboriginal people. That doesn't make sense.'

'It's just the way it was in rural areas,' Lucy explained. 'There were lots of "new Australians" working, so no one could afford to be racist against anyone, including Aboriginal people. Even so, on the one hand people all mixed in; while on the other hand it was accepted there was one set of rules for the blacks, and one for whites. I reckon the Alvarez's were protecting their daughter from being excluded by the white majority. If she was Aboriginal, they would have seen it as doing her a favour.'

Marook looked up at Lucy for a moment and nodded as if he agreed. He spoke a little and Mick interpreted once more. 'Maria-Pearl told us one day she felt like she was Aboriginal. She left the mine at Red Ochre and said she was going home to ask the truth. Her parents had moved down South. If she found out she was Aboriginal, she said there was one thing she wanted to pass on to her kids. That was a totem.'

'A totem?' Dimitri remembered the term. It's what Aunty was going to discuss at the talk. The one he never showed up for.

Marook had become quite breathless again and indicated for Lucy to speak instead.

'A totem is like a name we give to our children when they are young. It shows them the close connection they have with the land and it can be taken from a creature or a plant. My family's totem is a dingo. And I think that's so true!' She managed a quiet laugh. 'For haven't I spent my time roving this land, hunting the truth? And if Maria-Pearl is my sister, it's clear she did the same.' She looked thoughtfully at Dimitri. 'Perhaps you can see those characteristics in yourself?'

'Well, I guess we can all draw parallels to aspects of nature. Couldn't totems just be superstitions?'

'No.' Lucy responded. 'Not superstitions. Like the land, they are our identity. Too many Aboriginal people are disconnected from their culture and family and either don't know their totems, or, sadly, don't have one.'

'If your sister was Aboriginal, she would have been too young to know her totem.'

'Sadly that's true,' Lucy agreed, 'but I hope she knew how special her birth name was. For over a hundred years our dad's family were pearl divers. My father would say thousands of oysters can be caught but only one may contain a pearl, and less than one percent of these have the quality of a gem. My mother would tell Pearl she was that one in a thousand and that she was our family gem ...'

Her voice trailed off and Dimitri couldn't trust himself to lift his gaze from the fire. Tiny embers glowed, sparking fire from twig to twig. A fire was the place where Lucy had witnessed Pearl's abduction.

'I only hope the people who raised her knew her for the treasure she was,' Lucy whispered.

Marook muttered a few words and Mick listened carefully. 'After about a year she came back to Red Ochre with a husband. My wife helped her when she gave birth to her baby son. Someone had gone to get help but got there when it was all over. Maria-Pearl scribbled a message and told my wife to give it to me.'

Marook's tired mutter became almost inaudible and Mick leaned closer. 'I still got that paper.' Grandfather passed his stick to Mick and reached into the kangaroo pouch dangling over his hip. He removed a worn folded sheet and his voice rose again. Mick passed it to Dimitri. 'I knew one day you would come for it.'

Dimitri's hands shook. His mum's fingers had touched this piece of

Lover: The king is held captive by its tresses. — SS [75]

paper. It was the closest connection he had made with her. Leah's palm rested over his back.

Dimitri unfolded the note and, moving it slightly out of the shadow, he read the text out loud. 'We have a son and he is Dimitrios Wareen Kostos.'

That was his mum announcing his birth. She must have been proud of her new baby, just like any mother was. She wanted to tell the world about the best baby ever. He had been born out in the bush, not in a hospital. There had been no telephones to call her family and friends. It's possible this community were her family and friends. Yaya had claimed she knew nothing about the way he was born. He had never heard from his other grandparents. Maybe they didn't know either.

He should be happy, over the top, thrilled at having this missing piece of information returned to him. Instead he only felt numb.

The numbness wore off and a heavy layer of disappointment settled over him. He looked away from the fire out into the darkness. Knowing the story of his birth was great. Awesome, in fact. But it didn't tell him whether he was Aboriginal or not. At least if he was in hospital a nurse might have ticked a box. But there was nothing like that.

He read the paper again then looked up at Marook. 'You've kept this note all this time. And you said you knew I would come back for it. I really appreciate you holding onto it.'

He didn't feel like being polite anymore. He wanted to yell, throw a tantrum. All this energy in coming out here. And what did he come away with? A note with his name on it. 'But I already know my full name. I already know that Maria-Pearl was my mother. I'm really happy to know someone who has met her, but I need something more. I need to know an answer to my final question. This doesn't tell me anything.'

Dimitri couldn't believe the anger that gripped him. It was like all the months of frustration bubbled up from deep inside and spilled out.

No, not months, years! The lies to explain his dreams. Changing his age by three years! *Refusing to welcome, or even meet his mother. Why? Why? Why?*

Marook held his hand up to stop Dimitri's babble. He spoke in English, slowly and clearly. 'The paper. That's how I know she was Aboriginal. She gave you a totem.'

Lover: The king is held captive by its tresses. — SS [75]

214

Dimitri looked at the paper again. 'What do you mean? Dimitrios is Greek, and I'm named after my dad. And Wareen, it's a common name, and not even spelt correctly. They've put double e instead of double r.'

The Aboriginal elder pointed to his stick and Mick picked it up and passed it to him. He poked the fire but said nothing. Dimitri's agitation increased. He looked over at Lucy who sat still, patiently waiting for Marook to continue. Leah held him closer. At least he had her, willing to stay with him no matter what they discovered—or didn't discover.

Finally the old man looked from Dimitri to Lucy and back again. He nodded, as if in silent agreement with them both. 'Aboriginal people from many places in Australia would come here. I asked people from many languages to read this paper. Eventually I found an Aboriginal man who translated for me.' Dimitri felt Marook's eyes burn through him. They were filled with kindness. 'Wareen is an Aboriginal name. It means *wombat*.'

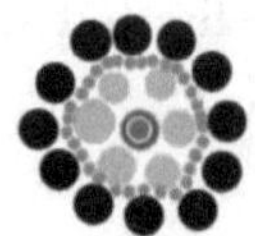

50: Dimitri

This was another dream. Only it couldn't be; the smoke filled air, the noisy crickets, the background chatter from people's homes, the ghost of a wind; you don't get these details in dreams.

Dimitri stared at Marook's dark, papery face wrinkled into a tight smile. A tingling sensation crept up his spine, spread across his shoulders, down his legs. His hands shook and his mouth dried up. He ran his tongue around his gums and managed a whisper. 'Wareen means *wombat*?'

Marook continued to smile.

'I have a totem?' Dimitri pushed his words through his voice box. 'Wombat is my totem?'

'You bet Dimitri.' Lucy penetrated his daze. 'Your mother gave you *wombat* as your totem!'

Dimitri stared from Lucy to Marook. The tingling evolved into excitement. 'My mother was Aboriginal?'

'She was.' Marook nodded.

Dimitri stared at Lucy. The smile across her face said it all. 'You've found your sister!'

Lucy stood up and settled herself next to Dimitri. 'Unfortunately it's too late to have found my sister.' Her voice broke for a moment. 'But I've found her son.' She picked up his hand. Her tears streamed down her face, glistening in the dancing flames. 'In our culture, since my sister cannot be your mother, then I take her place. Lucy clasped his hand. 'You are my son.'

Lover: O love, with your delights! — SS [7:6]

He looked down at Lucy's hand, her fingers connected with his. *I am now your son?*

'I'm Aboriginal!' He squeezed Lucy's hand, let go and reached for Leah's.

'What are you feeling?' she asked.

He reached past the outer layer of shock, the interior voices clamouring for his attention. 'I've come home.' He broke off.

Tears poured down Leah's face. 'Yes, you've come home.'

People around the fire began to chat and laugh. Lucy stood up and many of the women came over, taking turns to embrace her. Dimitri pulled on Leah's hand and they stood up as well. His homecoming belonged to everyone. After lots of hugs and slaps on the back, Dimitri turned back to Marook and Mick. 'Grandfather, how do you think my mother knew the Aboriginal word for *wombat*?'

Marook shook his head, his smile still covering his face. 'That's what she was like, she asked lots of questions. Maybe she asked Aboriginal people from many language groups about their totem.'

'But why choose wombat as a totem? She came from the West and I don't think wombats are very common there.'

'Did your father grow up in wombat territory?'

'I guess so. Wombats do live in the south where my dad grew up. In fact it's one of the places I love to photograph. My uncle told me my dad loved to go there as well.'

He imagined his mum choosing his name. Clearly she had honoured his dad, but also brought the two cultural worlds together. There was no way she would have hidden his background from him.

'Run! Don't forget the wombat.' It was his Aboriginal heritage she wanted him to hang onto.

After the laughter had settled down, he looked over at Marook. He was fading fast and Dimitri still had questions. He had better hurry. 'Grandfather, in my dream when my mum pushes me off the plane, she tells me to run and don't forget the wombat. I get what she means now about the wombat. She wanted me to run towards the wombat; to find my Aboriginal background. But what about my other dream? In that one, the wombat has become a

Lover: O love, with your delights! — SS [7:6]

217

monster and he is chasing me.' Even thinking about that dream was horrible. 'Why would I have nightmares about a wombat? If a totem is a protective symbol, it doesn't make sense that it tries to attack me.'

'Tell me your dream,' Marook said.

Dimitri sat back down and described the nightmare. Marook poked the fire and said nothing. Dimitri shifted uncomfortably. He hadn't shared this before. It was a childish fear, and he should have grown out of it by now. Who was to say it had any meaning anyhow?

Marook turned to him. 'The wombat chased you but didn't attack you.'

'What's the difference? I felt just as terrified as if it did.'

Marook was really struggling to breath now. As the night air had drawn cold, Dimitri imagined its fingers tightening around the old man's throat and he knew that Marook should leave soon.

Lucy intervened. 'Do you mind if I try to explain?' she asked Marook. He nodded and she looked over to Dimitri. 'It sounds to me that you had an awful lot to be terrified of while growing up. You lost your parents and your home and were sent down to the city to live. Then you were surrounded by family who held a secret. You were frightened to ask them about your mum; every time you did they were angry with you, so you kept your questions to yourself. You felt rejected, maybe even felt it was your fault your parents died.'

She paused, picking her words with care. 'When we are chased into a corner like that, there comes a time when we have no choice but to turn around and face what we have run away from. It's my guess your mum told you your totem when you were very young and that, deep inside, the wombat in the dream connected you to your past.'

Dimitri looked over to Marook who nodded in agreement.

Lucy nodded at him. 'You've turned around, Dimitri, that's what this journey has been about for you. I doubt whether you'll have any more of those dreams.'

He stared at her. She had described things pretty well. *Too well*. 'Is this how things have been for you?'

Lucy shrugged. 'Exactly like that.' She smiled. 'Minus the dream.'

Dimitri ran his fingers through his hair. 'I guess only time will tell if

Lover: O love, with your delights! — SS [7:6]

the dream stops.' Hundreds of questions still tumbled through his mind. But there was one that he wanted to know above everything else.

He turned to Marook once again. 'My grandparents said my parents were buried up here somewhere. We have checked records in all the churches and cemeteries in the region but there is no record. Do you have any idea at all?'

Marook spoke to Mick. He continued for a long time before leaning back in his chair. Mick turned to Dimitri. 'Grandfather is very tired and wants to go now. I will tell you what he said, but he has much more to tell you. He said to stay and tomorrow you can talk again.'

Mick picked up the other stick and passed it to Marook. The two young men came to his side straight away.

Dimitri and Lucy stood up. 'Thank you, Grandfather.' Dimitri stretched out his hand. 'This has just been the best.' Marook smiled and gave a half wave.

'Yes,' Lucy agreed. 'I can't tell you how much this means to me.'

The old man turned his face to Leah and held up his stick. 'Wareen's wife will be welcomed into the community.'

Dimitri's heart raced and he grinned as Leah's face flushed.

'They're not married. Yet.' Lucy looked from Leah to Dimitri. 'But maybe one day.' She smiled. 'Leah is well respected in Bilyja and has been given an Aboriginal name, Marrawi, *Peaceful Dove.*'

'Marrawi and Wareen.' Marook nodded reverently. 'Stay and celebrate.'

He turned away and shuffled off into the darkness, supported by his two assistants.

'Grandfather said there is so much more to tell,' Mick said. 'I can only give you the summary of what he told me.' He nodded. 'Marook said that Maria-Pearl came out with her husband and son to visit regularly.'

Dimitri looked around the group. He *had* been here before. He may only have been very young, but his dreams were definitely based on memories.

'Marook had gone deep into the bush, about half way between here and Red Ochre, when he heard the plane crash.'

So it was Marook who came for me?

'Grandfather said he caught you running away from the plane. The ground was so hot and your feet were burnt. He could do nothing for your

Lover: O love, with your delights! — SS [7:6]

parents; fire had already engulfed the plane. But he picked you up and ran with you to protect you from the explosion.'

That filled in another gap. 'What about their … bodies?' Dimitri had worked hard to keep his final image—the only image—of his parents away from what had happened *after* the plane had gone. Instead he recalled his mum kicking the plane open for him, and his dad disappearing in a haze of smoke. These images were hard enough to handle. But he couldn't keep avoiding the reality. He had to know what had happened to them after. 'Why wouldn't my dad's parents have taken his body and buried it back in Adelaide? Or Maria-Pearl's foster parents buried her somewhere near them?'

'Grandfather said they had an Elders' meeting. They agreed it was important Maria-Pearl not only have a Christian burial, but a traditional Aboriginal burial as well. They knew she had lost her real Aboriginal family, so the Elders became that for her.'

'Wouldn't her foster parents have objected to that?'

'No, they apparently moved around a lot and so they gave their permission. Her husband's family—your family—wasn't happy but they agreed because it was better than separating them as husband and wife.' Mick took a deep breath. 'They are buried in a very old cemetery in an unused church not far from where the plane crashed.' Looking over to Jack sitting in the outer circle, Mick nodded. 'Akubra Jack can take you there.'

'Wow! Thank you. I could never have asked for such an amazing blessing.'

Dimitri looked down at the paper Marook had saved for him over the years, and traced the words with his fingers. His mother had written this with her own hands! If only she had known how significant her action would turn out to be. He caught Lucy watching him and passed her the paper. 'I have something else for you too.'

Lucy watched him as he retrieved the passport-sized photo of his mum from his shirt pocket. 'I hope you'll forgive me, but I just couldn't bring myself to show you this until we knew for sure that Maria-Pearl was your sister. I thought it would bring even more pain if it all came to nothing for you.'

Clearly Lucy wasn't taking much notice of his words. All her attention was given to scrutinising the only photo she had ever seen of her sister.

Lover: O love, with your delights! — SS [7:6]

220

'This is amazing! I'll send a copy to my mum so she has something to hold while she's waiting for me to come home and complete the story.'

A group of women gathered around Lucy to look at the photo and to congratulate her on the news. Dimitri turned to Leah.

'Marook thought you were my wife! Is it possible my life could be made perfect all in one go?' He drew her into the shadows, their backs to the fire, and he lifted her chin gently. Her lips were warm on his. He had missed her so much! But *marriage*? Weren't they a bit young? *Hold on … I keep forgetting my age.*

He shrugged as his thoughts spun around, on top of the other ones racing around in his mind. They had been through more in one year than many couples would experience in their whole life. Maybe marriage wasn't too crazy. He stood back and searched Leah's eyes. He definitely had her total support. Just as she had his, no matter what happened. 'Maybe we can get up early before there's too much going on and talk about us?'

Dimitri wasn't sure if a look of panic leapt into Leah's eyes. It vanished and she gave him a small smile.

'Hey, you two, are you going to stay and celebrate?' One of the young guys called out on his way back from Marook's.

Dimitri grabbed Leah's hand and they rejoined the group. It wasn't long before modern and traditional musical instruments were retrieved and the celebrations began.

Lover: O love, with your delights! — SS [7:6]

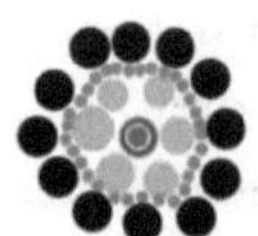

51: Leah

Leah loved the thump of dancing feet, rhythm of clap sticks and the haunting echoes from didgeridoos as they rang out across the desert. As the news spread, more and more people joined the group. *Where have they come from?* In no time the gathering had developed into a party.

As she sat observing people, it wasn't long before she realised the dry-zone rule was being followed. Like Bilyja, this community was clearly still managed by Elders. The celebrations felt more real somehow and definitely more relaxed without the fear of alcohol-related violence.

Leah's energy was waning and she caught herself bracing her left side against a dull ache. She didn't want to be a party pooper but just wanted to lie down. Lucy and Kate stood nearby and she caught Lucy's eye.

'No worries.' Lucy picked up her signal easily enough.

'I think we'll get you settled for the night.' Lucy tapped Dimitri's shoulder. 'You've got one very tired girlfriend here, Kate's here to take her home.'

'Leah! I'm so sorry; I'm just trying to find out as much as I can …'

'That's okay.' She stood up and kissed his lips lightly. 'I want you to, but the last couple of days have caught up with me and I need to get some sleep.'

'Of course you do; I'm sorry. We'll meet early in the morning, okay?'

'That sounds great.' Leah kept her voice casual and kissed him goodnight again. His lips touched hers, sending a wave of pleasure through her. *If only …* she pulled herself away. It was just all too complicated. 'Goodnight,' she said softly, 'I love you.'

Beloved: like a seal on your arm — SS [8:6]

'I love you too, Leah.' His arms were warm and strong around her waist. 'It's meant so much to have you here. I want us to be together always …'

Leah extricated herself from his embrace. 'Shh! We'll talk in the morning, remember?'

He clapped his hands over hers, before letting her go. 'Good night,' he murmured.

'See you in the morning.' She turned to follow Kate into the darkness.

As Leah navigated the track, she felt his eyes watching her retreat. *Oh Dimitri! How can I talk about our future when I don't even know if I have one?*

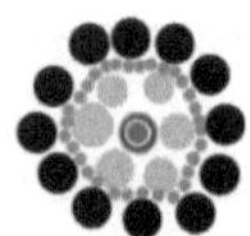

52: Leah

Despite the persistent thump of the music outside, Leah fell easily into sleep. It took her almost a minute to reorient herself when she awoke to her room flooded with light. The full throttle of birds from the trees growing along the river bed informed her morning had definitely arrived.

She got up and looked out the window across the sunburnt landscape. Dimitri was born out here. This was part of him. His mum might have come from a different part of the country, but their family were traditional custodians of the land.

Leah remained motionless. God was present in the land. Just as He was present inside her. Whatever happened, she just had to invite Him to be part of it. Both of their lives had been far from perfect, yet they both knew that love, God's love, was greater than everything.

The house was still quiet and Leah decided to skip her shower. She would need another one by the time they arrived back at the motel anyway. She pulled on the previous day's clothing and grimaced. This definitely wasn't the best she had ever looked.

There was a bite to the air when she stepped outside and she pulled her jacket around her. It was hard to believe that, within a couple of hours, they would be sweltering. She approached the campfire where they had sat the previous night. Dimitri was already up and had prepared a billy of water over a low fire. He looked up and greeted her with a smile as exuberant as the previous evening's. 'Mornin', sleepy head. I thought you'd changed your mind.'

'You must have got up early. I didn't hear you. Did you get any sleep at all last night?'

'Just enough.'

'You've done well to get a billy going.'

'There was a bag of supplies in the back of the four wheel drive.' He tipped water into a tin mug and added a tea bag. 'Here you go. It'll have to be black, though.' He passed her the cup and his hand lingered on hers. 'Sorry about last night.'

'Sorry?'

'I got so caught up in my own excitement I forgot how exhausted you must have been.'

'I was fine, don't worry.' Where had that snap come from? *He's treating me like an invalid! I was tough enough to cope before he came back, so what makes him think I'm not able to now?*

'What is it, Leah? Is something wrong?'

Mortified at the thoughts she was having, Leah shook her head. *I'm just terrified about this talk!*

They sat together staring into the ashes and the warm red and grey glow of the small fire he had managed to rekindle into life. 'I meant what I said last night, Leah. I love you so much.' His fingers grazed her forehead as he pushed away her hair, but she couldn't look at him. 'There's nothing more I want than for us to be together.'

Her eyes remained fixed on the fire. After a moment she looked up at him. 'How is our love stronger than anyone else's? Look at us, Dimitri. Our love didn't even stand its first test!'

'Maybe not. But we're back together and we've learnt a lot of lessons.' He lifted her face and looked straight into her eyes. 'We know that love has the power to forgive and to heal.'

'What about death?' She turned away.

He reached for her hands and held them. 'Look at me, Leah.' His eyes were steady, intense. The lightheartedness she loved about him had gone. She had never seen him so serious. But there was softness there, a determination to make her believe what he believed.

'Your test results could go either way. And even if they are all clear now, we still don't know what the future holds.'

Leah's heart thumped hard against her chest. She had been the one to say the word. But she didn't want someone else to talk about her life being cut short. She wanted to get up and run, but Dimitri held her hands even tighter.

'Are we going to allow this to stop us from sharing our life, for whatever time there may be left?' His eyes were looking into her soul. 'Yes,' he continued, 'love does have power over death. Maybe not our love, but we both know God's love. God broke the power of death the day Jesus rose from the grave. That's power. That power means we can live forever.'

Leah was surprised. Where had Dimitri's faith suddenly blossomed from? He'd been, by his own admission, a token Christian. But she relaxed, now she was on familiar ground. Faith had become as familiar to her as her breath. At critical moments in her life when a crisis erupted, there it had been, latent but available. Grace had somehow exposed it as an immovable bedrock. It had been thin at times but it had sustained her when her father had walked out on them; and when her mum had died; and when she found out she had cancer and underwent surgery; and when Dimitri had gone; and when she had faced chemo without his support.

What about now? Here she was again, facing the awful merry-go-round of the medical world. Underlying everything there was always the cold fear of the word 'secondaries'. Did she believe Love had conquered Death so that she could cross from this life straight into His embrace? 'I have no doubt about living our life with Jesus after death,' she finally replied. 'My doubt is our ability to love each other in the face of this huge trial that could lie immediately ahead. What if it's just too much for us?'

'The only way our love can be sustained is inviting Jesus to be central to our relationship.' He looked steadily at her anxious face. 'I think you've probably already done this as an individual, but we haven't done it as a couple.'

Rick! Was it Rick who was responsible for Dimitri's sudden plunge into the depths of faith? Not entirely certain where he was going with his statement about the centrality of Jesus, she narrowed her gaze.

'This doesn't sound like the Dimitri I know.'

Beloved: for love is as strong as death — SS [8:6]

'Of course it does!' The brilliant smile was back. 'It started with the *Song of Songs*. I kept reading it, so I could quote it at the woman I love. Remember?'

'I remember.' *How could I forget?*

'And then, at Easter, I was at church with my aunt and uncle. And the reading was about Jesus meeting Mary Magdalene in the garden. What they say is from the *Song of Songs*, you know. That made me interested in reading about Jesus, then … I guess you'd say my heart was open.' His eyes seemed to hold a twinkle. 'Anyway, as I was saying, we haven't got Jesus as the centre of our relationship as a couple.' He paused. 'To do that, we need to declare our love publicly before our friends, our church family, and most importantly, before God.'

Leah struggled to keep her voice steady. 'You're proposing!'

'What did you think I wanted to talk to you about this morning?'

'Not marriage.'

'You don't think I'm serious, do you? Leah, I'm talking about marriage vows in a church before God's people of faith. There's power in that. It's this power that enables us to sustain our marriage, no matter what lies ahead.' He pulled her up by both arms and smiled lightly. 'Come on. So, what do you think? Give it another try?'

'*Marriage?* Isn't it a bit soon? Aren't we a bit young?'

'We're both over twenty-one. In some places around the world we're almost past it! Anyway, it doesn't have to be right away. But a promise is a promise.'

What could she say? Neither of them could possibly know how high their next hurdle would be. Yet saying no to marriage wouldn't make that any easier to get over. In fact, the opposite was true. They loved each other; of that she was certain. *So what am I waiting for?*

'But you haven't actually asked me yet, have you?' she responded.

'Asked you what?'

'Well, you know, this wasn't exactly a romantic proposal, was it? It was more like an explanation.'

He gave a whoop and in an instant was down on one knee. 'I love you, Leah, more than you could ever imagine and I want to share my life with you. Will you "*set me like a seal on you heart*"?' He took her hand.

Beloved: for love is as strong as death — SS [8:6]

She was terrified. 'Ye …'

It was hardly out when she was in his arms. A crowd of children clapped as they kissed.

'Rent a crowd!' Dimitri stepped back. 'Come on; let's go for a walk near the river.'

He held her hand as he filled her in on some of the previous night's conversations she'd missed. 'Jack said the old church where my parents are buried isn't too far off the track on the way back. So if it's okay with you we can do that later today?'

I have a fiancé. 'Of course!'

He stopped and took both her hands again. 'The other thing I really want is for both of us to meet Grandmother.'

'I think that would be great, but … it might have to wait … in case …'

'That's fine. Lucy said she's frail but her spirit is strong.'

They walked in silence, the birds quietly warbling in the background. Leah tried to ignore the scratchy spinifex at her ankles. The heat of the day had already prompted her to remove her jacket.

'When I meet my grandmother,' Dimitri said, 'I want to introduce you as my wife. She can pass on her blessing for our family.'

Leah kicked away loose stones in her path, her mouth suddenly dry. There was still so much they hadn't talked about. What had she said *yes* to? After a long silence she murmured, 'We may never have a child.'

He stopped and tilted her face between his hands. 'I know that and it's going to be tough but, with or without children, you and I are family. Besides …' He gestured with his head back towards the children at the settlement. '… somehow I think we're not just marrying each other, but marrying into a community where there are plenty of children.'

They returned to Mick and Kate's home where breakfast was waiting for them.

'If you want to reach town before it gets dark, you had better get going soon,' Mick told them. 'I know you wanted to speak with Grandfather Marook again, but it's a bit early for him. Now that you know where to find him, you'll get other chances. And we'll get whatever information we can from him.'

Beloved: for love is as strong as death — SS [8:6]

Leah looked over at Dimitri and knew that he too heard the silent *just in case.*

'That's all good.' He looked over at Lucy. 'But please let him know how thankful we are for everything he told us.'

'I'll do that. Keep in mind there will be a formal process between yourself, the Department that has linked you together, our mob and Lucy's people to confirm your Aboriginal identity. After that there will be formal welcoming ceremonies, one here and one in the West. So it won't be long and we'll be seeing you again.'

'Awesome!' Dimitri's smile was radiant.

Within a short time, Leah found herself in the passenger seat, being waved off by an even bigger group than on arrival. As Dimitri turned the car around, she knew his life direction had completely altered. Now they needed to know what lay ahead for her.

Beloved: for love is as strong as death — SS [8:6]

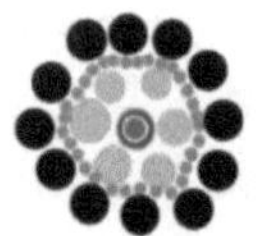

53: Leah

After the hot dusty drive back to town, Leah could have killed for a shower. Not to mention a bottle of iced spring water. They entered the motel reception and were greeted by Gudrun.

'Ah! Back so soon? Did you find vat you vere looking for?' Without waiting for an answer, she shook her head. 'I don't know vy people vant to go driving around in all that heat for.' She sighed. 'Give me a car with snow chains, and vite roads any day.'

Honestly, why do tourists come to Australia and then wish they were back home again? 'There's a beauty in the Australian Outback that grows on you.'

Dimitri threw her a cheeky look and turned to Gudrun with his charming smile. 'Thanks, we had a great time.'

Gudrun looked at him, clearly waiting for more information. Leah knew there was no way they could provide an explanation through a light conversation.

'Any messages for us?' Lucy redirected the discussion.

'Ya, someone called for Leah.'

Leah felt her pulse throb against her neck and she swallowed. 'Who was it?'

'A voman.' From a pile of papers on the counter, she retrieved a scribbled note. 'Ah ya. She said she vas your Aunt. Paula?'

'Did she say why?' Her voice quivered.

Gudrun sighed and shook her head. 'I did ask, but no, she told me nothing.' She handed over the note. 'Here's the number. No long distance calls from the rooms. Guests make calls all over the vorld and they leave vithout paying. There's a pay phone over in the corner.'

'Thanks.' *A pay phone? How old was this motel? No use arguing.* Leah turned to the others. 'How many coins can we dig out between us? We can't rely on our mobiles out here and I don't want to be cut off. It's got to be important or she wouldn't have called.' Her words stumbled into each other, as fast as her heart was beating. While Lucy and Dimitri sifted through their change, she fiddled with the zip of her handbag but it didn't budge.

'Let me help.' Lucy took it from her.

'Aunty Paula must have had contact with the doctor or why else would she call?' Leah looked wildly from one to the other. Neither of them answered. Clearly they were thinking the same thing.

Dimitri counted out the pool of loose money. 'There should be enough here for a couple of minutes. How about you read out the number and I'll press the buttons for you?'

As Aunty Paula's greeting emanated from the other end of the receiver Dimitri passed the handset to Leah and stepped back.

'Hi Aunty Paula, it's …'

'Leah! How ya goin', hon? I tried to get hold of you last night, but the woman said all you mob disappeared, and she had no idea when you were comin' back. I'm glad I got hold of you.'

There was so much to tell Aunty Paula but she was far too nervous. 'What is it Aunty Paula? Did the doctor call for me again?'

'He's passin' through the General Hospital up there in the town tomorrow. He says he's happy to see you there, if you want.'

'Is everything okay? Why would he want to see me before I get back to Bilyja?'

'He just said he felt bad about bein' called away and all that. He's givin' you the chance to see him, if you don't want to wait.'

Leah's thoughts whirled around as she tried to think about this new possibility. She had primed herself to forget the results while she was away, but what benefit was it really to put it off again?

Beloved: its jealousy unyielding as the grave — SS [8:6]

'Sorry, kiddo, I just thought you'd like me to tell you so you can make your own choice, you know? Maybe you won't have to rush back here.'

Leah really didn't know what to feel. Having bad news would destroy the new hope and joy of the past twenty-four hours. However, it would also put an end to the agony of waiting.

'You got Dimitri with you now, kiddo, whatever happens. He's a good young man.'

'We're engaged!'

'Hon! That's fantastic! Congratulations.'

'And we found out last night that Grandfather Marook did know Maria-Pearl when she was young. It's a long story but he's confident she was Aboriginal.'

'Hey, that's great!'

The final coin dropped into the chute and the line went dead.

'So what's happening?' Dimitri stepped forward.

'Dimitri, it's happening too quickly!'

He reached out and rested his arms across her shoulders. 'It's okay; we're in this together now.'

'I know, and how blessed am I!' She looked over to find Gudrun leaning over the counter, clearly trying to piece together details.

'Let's go out and get some air.' Leah kept close to Dimitri as they all made their exit. 'Dr Campbell is in town and he's given me the chance to see him here instead of waiting until we get back home. Aunty Paula said he feels bad he had to cancel the appointment.'

'What do you think?' he asked.

Leah shrugged. 'I really don't know.'

Lucy rested her hand gently on Leah's shoulder. 'If there's anything I can do to support you, I'll do whatever I can.'

'And of course you know I'll be with you,' Dimitri stated firmly.

'Thanks.' Leah grinned and turned to Lucy. 'I do know what you can do! Let me be first in the shower!'

'Easy done!'

'How about we meet for dinner in about an hour? There must be a

Beloved: its jealousy unyielding as the grave — SS ^{8:6}

take-away in the town, or something,' Dimitri suggested.

'You two go ahead,' said Lucy. 'I've had enough movement for now; lying flat and still on that bed is looking very tempting.'

Leah smiled her appreciation; clearly Lucy was giving her and Dimitri some space. 'We'll bring you back some take-away.'

'You're on. Now, to the shower.'

Beloved: its jealousy unyielding as the grave — SS 8:6

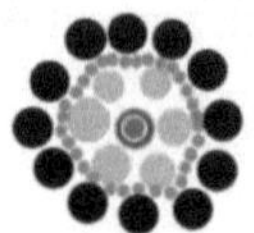

54: Leah

Leah and Dimitri sat hand in hand in the outpatient department of the General Hospital. They had spent time the previous evening discussing the advantages and disadvantages of visiting the doctor. Despite the overwhelming desire to get up and run, Leah knew she had made the right decision. She had held herself together for long enough and now it was time to face the inevitable.

Each time the doctor entered the busy waiting room with his patient list, she jumped, only half hoping she would be next. Trying to focus her thoughts away from herself, she watched the activities of the others in the overcrowded room. 'It looks as if everyone has come prepared to spend the day here.' Almost all the seats were taken up with families and young children; many others were sitting on the floor. Despite worn signs banning food and drink, the majority of the children sat with packets of snacks and plastic drink bottles. A lot of indigenous families contributed to a vibrant atmosphere. It seemed people were happily using the time to catch up with family or friends.

But she didn't have the concentration to think about other people's lives for long. 'I'm so glad you're with me.'

'There's just no question now of me not being around.'

'Leah McEwen.'

The doctor stood at the reception desk scanning the room for his next patient.

Leah and Dimitri both stood up. His hand gripped hers and they walked into the doctor's office together.

'Please, take a seat.' Dr Campbell smiled and indicated two chairs. He settled himself on his office chair and leaned forward looking carefully from Leah to Dimitri. 'I'm sorry about your cancelled appointment but I had a medical retrieval that couldn't wait. That's the way of rural emergencies, as I'm sure you understand.'

Leah nodded but her jaw felt too tense to attempt a reply.

The doctor pressed a few keys on his laptop and briefly scanned the words on the screen before turning his attention to her. 'There are a couple of factors to discuss.'

Leah's heart sank. *Surely the result was either okay or not okay?*

'Fortunately,' he went on, 'the biopsy showed no signs of malignancy.'

She remained silent, waiting for him to go on, only partially conscious of her tightening grip on Dimitri's hand.

'But I've discussed the report with your oncologist in Adelaide and he agreed with my thoughts. You've had to go through the trauma of waiting for these results and to be honest with you, Leah, the chances of another episode like this remain high. It's probable that throughout your life you will continue to find cysts and dismissing any of them is not an option.'

'What are you saying?' She finally managed to speak, despite her parched mouth.

'We don't suggest this very often but with the type of cancer you had, followed by your recent scare, we think you will have a much better chance of no recurrence if we do a prophylactic mastectomy.'

Leah looked from the doctor to Dimitri and back again as if to assure herself this was really happening. 'The lump is benign,' her voice began as a whisper then escalated, 'and you want to remove the breast?' This was a proposal she had not even considered. A terrible, horrible proposal. Why would she *volunteer* to have her breast removed?

'We can do reconstructive surgery at the same time, or if you prefer, can wait and discuss doing it later down the track.'

A wall of dread pressed in around her and she took gulps of air to help with her sudden erratic breathing. She looked over her shoulder to the door. She needed air, but she couldn't move. Her legs were like jelly and her body was weighted to the chair. Dr Campbell continued his speech with Dimitri, but Leah heard nothing more. Their voices could have been talking about another person.

Breathe! Gradually her chest loosened and she re-entered the conversation.

'I guess this means we'll have to go back to Adelaide to have it done?' Dimitri asked the doctor.

We? Tears slipped down her cheeks. What a world of difference that word meant.

'This is unbelievable.' She shook her head. Her hand felt like lead in Dimitri's warm supportive grip.

Dr Campbell spoke kindly. 'You'll be much better off down in the city, my dear. We just don't have the facilities in these rural centres, and you'll need specialist care.'

'Of course.' It was sensible to go back to Adelaide. If her oncologist was recommending surgery, then she wouldn't want anyone else to be co-ordinating her care.

They left his suite with Leah clutching a letter of referral in one hand and a bunch of tissues in the other. Dimitri rested his hand on her back and guided her past curious patients. They followed the corridor around towards the exit. As they passed the hospital cafeteria, the scent of freshly brewed coffee wafted into the corridor. Leah cleared her throat and tried her hardest to keep her voice steady. 'I think we should stop and celebrate.'

'Oh?'

'Despite everything, the results *were* negative.'

His eyes filled with pride, and he held the café door open for her. 'Your resilience is amazing. For all your losses, it's the gain that you focus on. I know we're going to get through this, whatever it takes.'

Beloved: It burns like blazing fire — SS ^{8:6}

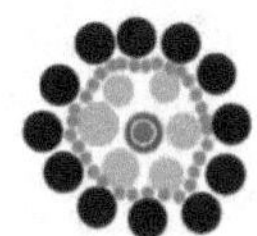

55: Dimitri

Dimitri stood alone in the graveyard behind the old stone church. At his feet two wooden crosses marked the burial site of Dimitrios and Maria-Pearl Kostos. Almost one year had passed since Akubra Jack had first driven them through a rough track to this old church. Dimitri had knelt there, hand in hand with Leah.

Lucy's fingers had traced the letters of her little sister's name. 'You were our pearl of great price,' she had whispered. 'Rest in peace.'

He now crouched, careful not to stain his hired suit. Kissing his fingers he touched each of the crosses and murmured reverently. 'Goodbye, Mum and Dad, I pray we will meet at the Great Banquet.'

He straightened himself, thankful for these few moments before entering the church. Taking out his starched white handkerchief he wiped his eyes as well as sweat trickling down the back of his neck.

'Ready, mate?' Dimitri turned around just in time for the flash of Rick's camera.

'Thanks!'

'That's a hopeless pose; you'll have to do better than that if you want a few decent shots for that *Reconnections* magazine.'

'I still can't believe I let you talk me into having our wedding photos published for everyone to look at.'

'It was Mullaya behind it; I'm just the photographer. Anyway, you'd have to agree, it's the least you could do after the way everything's worked out for you.'

Beloved: Like a mighty flame — SS [8:6]

'You're right. There's no way I could ever pay back what's been given to me.'

Like, a whole new family, community and culture!

Rick grinned and closed the camera shutter. 'Come on; let's get everyone out of this scorching heat.'

Dimitri looked over to the dirt car park where an array of vehicles covered in red dust had transported the wedding guests. It had been a huge effort for most of his family and friends to get there. But they had made it, and he really appreciated that. They had come not only for the wedding, but to celebrate Leah's smooth recovery. They had decided it was simpler to hold a family dinner with Leah's father and step-family once they returned to Adelaide.

Best of all was being allowed to marry in this disused church. Reverend Conner from the local Diocesan Office had listened to their story and had agreed without any hesitation at all. 'It's all part of the Red Ochre parish,' he had said.

Uncle Spiros and Aunt Elpida looked uncomfortable in their formal clothes and dragging them away from the restaurant had taken a lot of convincing. As Aunt caught his eye, she sent him a huge smile and his heart swelled with love for his guardians. She had got over her irritation at his meddling into his past as soon as she knew about his engagement to Leah. 'Sensible girl!' she had told him.

Cousin Kossie had flown back from a working holiday. Over his parents' protests, he'd secured an extension and now everyone knew the reason why. A gorgeous blonde Canadian girl clung to his elbow, shooing flies with her other hand. He wondered how much she missed her snow-covered landscape.

Unfortunately, Grandfather Marook was too frail to attend but he knew Akubra Jack and Mick and Kate were here to pass on his blessing.

Dimitri watched Lucy proudly as she chatted with city folk, ensuring they felt welcome while waiting for Aunty Paula to appear with Leah. In the shade beneath the eaves, a woman stood frantically cooling herself with a fan. Her jewellery glistened in the sunlight and Gudrun lifted her fan in a wave as she caught Dimitri smiling at her. He and Leah had given in to her curiosity and welcomed her into their celebrations. It had been a challenge to convince her that a wedding could be enjoyed amidst the heat and dust of the Australian Outback. He had to admit, though, how grateful they were for Gudrun's offer to hold the reception in the air-conditioned comfort of the motel function room.

He looked beyond the humble gathering to the great land of his ancestors. He would soon meet his grandmother and Uncle Kev and the circle of reunion would be closed. The midday sun shimmered over the dry plain creating the familiar illusion of pools of water. He smiled. They held no illusions for a perfect marriage. But the *Song of Songs* held a secret that would help their relationship succeed.

Dimitri lifted his eyes to the cloudless blue sky. *Spiritually speaking, You are the real Lover, and we are Your Bride.*

He turned to face the church. *But if it's all good with You, I'm still going to be Leah's Lover today and she is my Beloved.'*

Beloved: Like a mighty flame — SS [8:6]

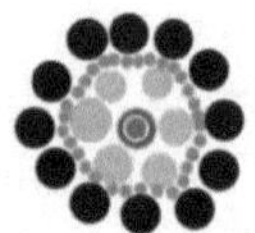

56: Leah

Leah stood in front of the mirror and smoothed her hands along her magnificent silk gown. Trust Gudrun to think of putting a full length mirror in the trunk of the car.

'I don't know vat you vant to go and get married in a broken down old building for!' she had complained. 'But don't get dressed until you get there. All that red dust in the car and the heat on the vay! There must be some back room or something the vicar or priest or vatever you call them, gets his gown or collar on. You vill need a mirror, the men von't have that.'

Leah turned slightly to view her profile. She loved the way the skirt gradually draped from her slim waist and fishtailed to the ground. Pearl buttons lined the entire back and delicate beads covered the bodice. Yet hidden beneath the perfect gown were the scars on her flesh.

Her breasts were gone. She looked into her own eyes and refused to flinch. The surgeon had done an amazing job with reconstructive surgery. Besides that, her beauty was so much more than her physical body.

Her face broke into the best smile. Above everything else, she was alive! And her life included Dimitri.

Leah fingered the tiny gold cross and chain he had given her. They were about to promise to love each other until separated by death. But they wouldn't be separated by death. For they were both loved by the Divine Lover, whose love was stronger than death.

Leah slipped the veil over her face ready to meet her Lover.

Beloved: Many waters cannot quench love — SS [8:7]

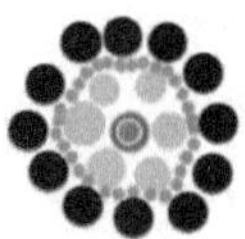

Epilogue: Leah

'Four generations of your family in the one place!' A year to the day later, Leah looked at her husband, his face aglow. His idea of the perfect wedding anniversary was hard to top.

'My mother's side of the family was just a blank to me and now look at us.'

'It's taken a lot to get us all here,' Lucy agreed. 'But it's been worth every step.'

Dimitri's grandmother looked up from the smouldering embers. She was hard of hearing but clearly knew when they were talking about her. Her skin creased into a dozen wrinkles as she smiled at her family.

Leah wondered what she was thinking as she sat in the same place her baby Pearl was stolen. This was the first time Grandmother had returned since that tragic day.

'It's been critical that we return,' Lucy told them. 'Culturally we needed to complete Sorry Business.'

'We are so blessed she is still alive to see this day.' Dimitri looked over at Grandmother and returned her smile. 'It took us longer than we thought to get over here.'

'It did.' Leah shook her head, still spun out by the events of the past year following their wedding. 'And look at what we brought with us.'

Grandmother held a newborn to her chest, jiggling it up and down and soothing it until it quietened.

Dimitri reached out and took Leah's hand. 'God is good. What was

Beloved: rivers cannot wash it away — SS [8:7]

241

stolen has been returned. Twice over. I have a family with you and a family with Lucy. As well as Uncle Spiros and Aunt Elpida.'

Leah smiled. She looked beyond their family gathering. In the distance the sea rolled up against the sand, an eagle perched on a leafless tree above them, a group of kangaroos looked on from a safe distance, ready to bolt if approached, and from across the desert a pair of dingoes howled to each other.

Yes, what was stolen has been returned. For me as well.

Twice over.